Flamingos

ALSO BY MARC SAVAGE:

Scratch

Flamingos

Marc Savage

A PERFECT CRIME BOOK

DOUBLEDAY

NEW YORK LONDON TORONTO SYDNEY AUCKLAND

A PERFECT CRIME BOOK

PUBLISHED BY DOUBLEDAY
a division of Bantam Doubleday Dell Publishing Group, Inc.
666 Fifth Avenue, New York, New York 10103

DOUBLEDAY is a trademark of Doubleday, a division of
Bantam Doubleday Dell Publishing Group, Inc.

Book design by Tasha Hall

Library of Congress Cataloging-in-Publication Data
Savage, Marc.
Flamingos / by Marc Savage.
p.   cm.
"A Perfect Crime book."
I. Title.
PS3569.A827F57   1992
813'.54—dc20   92-5021
CIP

ISBN 0-385-29738-4

1   3   5   7   9   10   8   6   4   2

First edition in the United States of America

For the ladies:
Valerie, Lisa, Wendy
Laura & Sugar too

ACKNOWLEDGMENT

I would like to thank David Padow, who
took the time to give me a shot.

Flamingos

Chapter 1

When Elvis Mahoney left the lush, river-cleft town of Durango, Colorado, the air had a meat-locker snap to it. It was early May. Fresh from a two-year, three-month tour at Lompoc, and a week's rest in San Diego, he had flown to Durango to pick up his car and chat up his half brother, Bobby Muhammed, a Las Vegas pit boss who might know something about his friend Del Rebus. It did not hurt to know as much as possible about a potential business partner. He exercised one other precaution, making sure his seven-year-old Dodge Charger got a jolt of Freon.

Lompoc is a prison in southern California. Elvis wound

up there, due to a slight miscalculation, on a conviction of aggravated assault. In the dispassionate logic of the law, a person emerging from his car to discuss a stoplight rear-ending with a party of the second part who did the rear-ending, who happened to be gigantic and inflamed by alcohol, and who approached with the clearly articulated intent of ripping specific organs from the body of the first part, that this person of the first part has no defensible argument, under the law, for breaking *both* arms of the party of the second part with a tire iron as a means of restoring a spirit of civil discourse. Elvis Mahoney still had a vivid memory of the big blue tattoo on the guy's right forearm, a spider, where he laid the tire iron the first time the guy lunged. And the guy so juiced and stupid he just looked a little surprised, then brayed, his lips flung wide so that the pink of the roof of his mouth was visible. "Gotdamn sumbitch," he said. "But shoot, I don't need but one hand anyways, whip a little spear-chucker like you." Well, that was *his* miscalculation. . . .

Elvis Mahoney drove with the Triple-A map spread open on the seat next to him, his route clarified by a felt-tip pen. He seldom exceeded the speed limit, even through the Canyon de Chelly, a stretch of forlorn and fugitive beauty in northeastern Arizona that is punctuated by gas stops with ugly drunks in them. He thought about using the jail stare, challenge them, but every one of the drunks was an Indian full of shame and rage, having breathed the air of hopelessness too long; each man with the energy to approach him and slur his request got a dollar. The descent into Phoenix took him through ranks of saguaros as eloquent in the dying violet light as pre-Columbian sculpture. Stunted mountains poked out in black relief, a dotty geologic crown around the valley the city inhabited. It was nearly eight o'clock in the evening when Elvis Mahoney entered the city limits, and the mercury was still flirting with 114 degrees Fahrenheit. Even with the fresh boost of Freon, he could feel the heat penetrating, the relentless, primitive presence of the desert.

He checked into the Hoyt Park on Adams under the name embossed on his Gold MasterCard: Leslie Murdock. The original Mr. Murdock, through no fault of Elvis, resided in a Pasadena cemetery, but his credit lived on, at a new residence.

A young man processed the card through the electronic validating device. His name, Whitney Wills, was visible on a plastic bar pinned to his shirt pocket. He had blond hair, airy gestures, had just completed a mission for his church, promoting the gospel in a besotted district of Munich, Germany. Watching the black man, Mr. Murdock, sign for his room, he was struck by the delicate features of the man's face, the thin nose and narrow lips, the brown eyes with long, almost feminine lashes. It was a magazine model's face, which contrasted sharply with what appeared to be a sturdy physique and large, hard hands. Mr. Murdock was smooth shaven and wore his hair cropped close, with a part shaved back from his left temple. Whitney Wills noted with approval the white shirt, the subtle silk tie (a dusky blue with jacaranda accents, faint teardrops), a milk-colored linen suit. He recognized the Italian tailoring and assumed the gentleman must be a professional athlete he hadn't heard about.

"If you would, please," Mr. Murdock was saying, "see I get all the morning papers."

"There's just the one, sir, *The Republic*."

"One paper for a city almost a million folks?"

"They put out an afternoon edition, *The Gazette.*"

"Ain't that sweet. Keep it all in the family, huh?" Mr. Murdock tugged on his left earlobe and smiled. "Family's the backbone of the nation, Mr. Wills, my daddy preached that till the day he died."

"A minister, sir?"

"Attorney. Specialized in divorce. Do you suppose, Mr. Wills, you could prevail upon room service to deliver a digestible repast in one half hour, say?"

"I sure can," responded Whitney Wills, feverishly punching up the menu and blushing.

This was five days later. Mr. Irwin Field and wife had reserved a bridal suite for a long weekend, and Mr. Irwin Field leaned affably on the marble countertop, smelling of a sweet cologne that Whitney Wills identified as Canoe, and of something else he suspected of being whiskey. Mr. Field wore a Hawaiian shirt with trumpet blasts of color in it that hung out over faded jeans. He danced his fingers on the countertop, his manicured nails catching the light in little pinkish gleams. He was humming, and his eyes, not really focused on any one thing, twinkled. He was a tall—about six foot—and solid man with a high widow's peak and a long nose, and a red one too, and when he smiled, his mouth lifted at the corners, suggesting to Whitney Wills the aspect of a jolly devil. Brown hair was brushed straight back and flush to the skull with streaks in it the color of dust. His skin was creased, colored by the sun enough to suggest a man of leisure. Forty-plus was Whitney Wills's evaluation. When the man turned to address his wife, Whitney Wills saw that the sun-bleached hair was pulled tight at the nape of his neck, from which a short ponytail sprouted.

Mrs. Field was something else. Distant and elegant in a sleeveless white dress, wide-brim straw hat tilted on her dark head, dark glasses, and luminous red lips. Tanned arms that were slim, but looked sinewy, as if she might swim a good deal or play tennis. A supple body. Onyx beads hung loose around a strong throat. She was ten to fifteen years younger than her husband, or Whitney Wills was wasting his tuition money at Lureen LaVelle's Licensed Academy of Cosmetological Science.

Upon presenting themselves, Mrs. Field had inquired of the proximity and hours of the Phoenix Zoo, and then retreated, to stand with her arms folded beneath her breasts, the angle of her lovely head implying complete lack of interest in her surroundings. She looked gorgeous and bored, a quintessential California lady.

Mr. Irwin Field said, with an air of imparting a confidence, "The wife's got a thing for zoos. You know what an elephant is, Mr. Willis? It's a mouse built to government specifications."

Whitney Wills smiled and blushed. "It's Wills, sir," he said deferentially, glancing at the screen of his monitor, almost wishing he could disappear into it. Mr. Field did not look like a man who easily tolerated correction. But the moment passed. The man's face softened, and soon he was grinning his roguish grin, spinning jokes, smutty ones too, until the paperwork was done.

And now Whitney Wills handed Mr. Field his Visa

Gold card and signaled to a bellhop. "I sure do hope you enjoy your stay, sir. And if there's anything I can do, please don't hesitate to ask."

"There is one thing." Mr. Field appeared to roll his eyes, contemplating the chandeliers. "Stop putting so much starch in your shorts, Mr. Willis. Live a little. Who knows, you might learn to like it."

Mr. Field winked mischievously. Whitney Wills blushed clear into his hairline.

He watched the couple stroll toward the elevators, her arm beneath his, her hand resting above his elbow, the elevator doors parting, and Mr. Murdock stepping out, his feet in white socks inside of white Reeboks, white satin shorts and white mesh tank top, ready for his nightly jog around some of the city's seedier citizens. Mr. Murdock was not tall, not as tall as Mr. Field, but his chest and biceps bespoke a man capable of negotiating with the rougher elements.

Whitney Wills saw him step out from the elevator and stop, tug on his earlobe, then spread his arms. Into them plunged Mr. Irwin Field's elegant wife. They hugged, and while the brim of her hat hid whether they kissed, Whitney Wills could see the hand extended to shake Mr. Field's, and the other one possessively gripping the lady's waist.

Together, the three of them and the hop boarded the elevator, the three of them laughing.

Whitney Wills heard Mr. Field saying, "See, there's this priest, this rabbi, this spade on a plane. Pilot comes back, he goes . . ."

Chapter 2

The small man with black metallic eyes and queerly bent fingers sat beneath a pay phone next to an archway at the rear of the bakery, a newspaper opened on the Formica table, an index finger that bowed up from the second knuckle moving slowly line by line through the obituaries. His jet hair, which owed its color to a cheap mail-order ointment, was crowned with a shapeless gray fedora. The brim rippled with pinched curves and the silk band above it showed fraying and the soft, stained felt hadn't been new when Jack Kennedy became president, ushering in the hatless look. Somebody forgot to mention it to the small man.

His name was Joseph Vincent Scorcese. He was known by other names. In New York City law-enforcement circles, the names charted the course of his career, becoming progressively less flamboyant, so that now he was identified in every precinct and station house simply as the Baker.

At this hour of the morning all of the customers in the bakery were women, and after snatching a ticket from the spool of them next to the cash register, each fell to gabbling about the weather that had descended from the Catskills. Four clerks behind tiered glass cases chirped out numbers, and each woman, when her number was called, cried with delight, only to confess to a species of guilt, a kind of umbrella for her appetite. The pastries were famous. People came from as far as Brooklyn on Sundays to get the taste of religion out of their systems.

Through the plate-glass door Joe Scorcese watched it spit and hiss on Metropolitan Avenue. Across the street the red-and-green-striped awning of Vacanza's Market flapped and shifted, and Luigi Vacanza stood a little in from the sidewalk with his large rough hands balled on his hips, counting the leaks. Joe Scorcese could see the bins of produce rolled out for display—the Bosc pears, tangerines from Florida, green grapes (a weakness of his), melons, hothouse tomatoes with flesh like wet sand, and pale strawberries. It was too early for strawberries, but try telling Vacanza that. The man had no soul, no poetry. He was a man who counted the leaks in his awning in order to complain about it to his ugly, unwed mountain of a daughter before retiring to his office, where, as everyone knew, he slept off his hangovers and occasionally dialed a service that provided obscene conversation. His daughter Magda paid the phone bills with the

900 area code billings, and she wasn't shy about whom she told. Joe Scorcese recalled that his youngest son, Paul, who lived most of the year now in Phoenix, had shown his stuff early, financing that business. A good boy, Pauli. Time he should be married, start a family.

From habit Joe Scorcese glanced at the windows immediately above Vacanza's, but they were washed an impenetrable slate color. The fire escape that slanted between them and dripped onto the awning zigzagged for three more stories. It looked stark and brand new in the rain. Inclemency was kind to Middle Village. Metropolitan Avenue swam in it looking smooth enough to drape around the bare shoulders of a debutante.

Into the bakery now backed the widow Fratennella shaking down her umbrella before she dragged in her two-wheeled laundry cart, its wire sides bent and dripping. She wore a black scarf, this Fratennella, and a black raincoat strained almost purple across her broad shoulders, and black cotton socks inside black laced shoes with short heels, and she bore herself with an air of restrained mourning, although if it was grief for her deceased husband, Jimmy "The Creep" Fratennella, she had masked it beautifully for more than three decades. Joe Scorcese could still trace in his memory the curve of her spine between those magnificent peasant shoulders, the slope and swell of her breasts when the only black she wore was reserved for expensive and perfumed underthings. He brushed one of his crooked fingers along the rose-colored tile on the wall beneath the pay phone and thought of smooth flesh, youth, heat.

The scent of rain reached him through the mingling sweet air of the bakery. It smelled like nothing at all.

As she stepped near him to take a ticket, she was careful to avert her eyes, and her salutation—correct, respectful—was close to a whisper. Such modesty, he observed, murmuring his greeting, had only taken her sixty-one years to acquire; what age robbed from the flesh it returned in the coinage of virtue.

There were exceptions, of course, and one of them was the woman married to his oldest son, Angelo. The little chink with airs: the French accent, French magazines and designer clothing, teaching the children—*his* grandchildren—to talk through their noses in a language he couldn't speak. And him virtually helpless, because of his son's stupidity, to stop it. Until now. She had finally rewarded his patience, his vigil over the years, by taking to bed a young stockbroker from Forest Hills who drove a sapphire Jaguar XJ, license number WINNER. Joe Scorcese did not believe after his meet this afternoon at four with Angelo that the guy would feel like a winner much longer. And the marriage would be kaput.

Joe Scorcese saw through the plate-glass door a gleaming black Saab growl up to the curb, the wire wheel of the front tire wink and disappear behind a fire hydrant, saw the driver, and then saw the two passengers scrambling, almost brawling to get out the back door and onto the curb.

He thought: three spics in a Saab. It cost him.

The two had crossed the sidewalk pulling sawed-off, double-barrel twelve-gauges from their raincoats. An instant after Joseph Vincent Scorcese, age seventy-two, dived and rolled through the archway behind him, the plate-glass door was kicked open, and two crazed men leaped into the aperture, got momentarily stuck there shoulder to shoulder, wrestled their way into the bakery, and unloaded their cargo. Pink tile and glass exploded, women shrieked, and Joe Scorcese, bleeding profusely, lay very still and thought about three spics in a Saab.

The windows immediately above Vacanza's Market went up.

Chapter 3

Luis Cortez tried to explain it the day before to the monster with one eyebrow. "Man, look, a thin' like this, man, you don't wanna fuck aroun' widda stars. We gonna do it, man. Soon as Tia Juanita say is good for me, the signs is right."

They were sitting in a booth toward the rear of a dimly lit Cantonese restaurant in the Bronx, about midway between the courthouse on Grand and Yankee Stadium down by the El, and Luis Cortez watched the monster consume his fourth egg roll and with his mouth full of brownish yellow mush point toward the front and say, "Look out there. Go ahead. Tell me what you see."

Well, it was better than looking in the monster's mouth. Squirreling himself around on the plastic seat that was red with strings of black running through it, Luis Cortez squinted, lightly touching his moussed and jet-colored ringlets, but did not understand. "The street, man, tha's what I see. Fulla nothin' and nobody 'cept the usual junkies there by Rico's candy stand too junked up to notice it's rainin' prob'ly."

"Yeah," said the monster. He stuck a thumb and forefinger into his mouth and worked them around in there, then wiped them on his pants. "Rain. That's right, Luis, rain. How in a fuck you see the stars in weather like this?"

Luis Cortez, practicing self-control, cut his lips into a grin. It was hard, because everything in his life was like this, full of frustration and idiocy. He had to remember that the man across the table with the small pig's eyes and pig-bristle eyebrow was going to pay him five thousand dollars cash money (*cinco mil!*) to take out this bookie that didn't honor his debt. Still, it was hard: not only had the monster been breathing all over him, but Tiger and Little Cedric, they been on his case, even hinting he, Luis Cortez, was hiding behind a woman's skirts.

"I esplain to you," Luis Cortez began, wearily, "my chart say is—"

"No, Luis, I'm payin' the freight, I'll do the explainin'. You get your act together by tomorrow, or there's guys in your old gang—fuck's the name—Scarlet Rapers?"

"Is Raiders, not rapers."

"Yeah, whatever. There's guys in there gonna go, hey, what is this guy, some kinda pansy?"

Something stabbed at the back of his eyes. "This is no

true." His right hand flicked from sight, and an instant later emerged from his scarlet jacket with six inches of blade visible, the cleanest, brightest surface in the restaurant. He moved catlike from the booth and stood, coiled. "No man calls Luis Cortez a pantsy."

"Siddown," said the monster amiably. "You're made a good stuff, Luis. Tomorrow then?"

Luis Cortez did not sit down; before he spun on his heel, sticking the monster with the price of lunch, the twenty-year-old, unemployed, ten-year veteran of turf wars issued a warning: "Tomorrow. You don't show for lunch with the cash, you don't got no laundromat no more. Tha's all I'm sayin'."

The monster began laughing.

Luis Cortez smiled maliciously and called him a son of a whore and strode away.

The monster laughed harder. "*Hijo de puta* to you too, Luis," he roared. Spics. They were a hoot.

His black hightops squeaked on the tracked-up linoleum of the laundromat next door, the very one he would torch if the monster tried to run a game on him. Luis Cortez was almost five ten, with large dark feminine eyes, long black lashes, a face without a blemish: beneath a radiant black mane, it was a face that had watched two boys and three men die without showing any emotion stronger than impatience. Tia Juanita, who had powers beyond description, had confronted him once (this was right after the night he had clubbed a black man to death with a baseball bat for $250 plus tickets to see the Moonwalker himself) and she asked him why. Only that one word. But he had understood immediately, such were her powers and the intensity of her eyes, one blue, one green.

A man, he said, *he goes to war to keep his way of living. He kills for it. Me, tha's what I do too.*

Do you know what becomes of the ones you kill?

Tia Juanita, everybody knows that.

Their souls are unprepared. They cannot die, Luis. They wander among us unseen, unheard, alone, suffering the torment of dying but never the peace of death. We will have a séance. For seven days we will pray. It will be your penance.

Tia Juanita, he said, *it was him or me. Tha's all I got to say.*

There was an office to the rear of the laundromat, off to the left beyond the wash machines. A window of bullet-proof glass left just enough space beneath it to exchange bills for coins, and through it Luis Cortez could see Little Cedric in a chair with his feet up on the desk talking on the phone. Little Cedric with his muscled pectorals that he was forever fondling beneath his navy blue mesh shirt, popping his biceps. Four women were doing laundry, and Lila, an old toothless Anglo wino who made infrequent, feeble passes with a broom, calling it sweeping, snored now on a bench beyond the driers, an orange kitten tucked beneath her colorless cardigan, its little head bobbing on the heaving swell of breasts. Luis Cortez loved cats for their grace and because they were loyal only to themselves. They understood life.

He kicked a steel door and was admitted to the office.

Little Cedric went back to the phone, settled into the chair, continued his conversation. In the minifridge behind him Luis Cortez found a cold can of Budweiser and sneered at it, because he knew it belonged to the guy that worked nights, Otto Cruz, who aspired to become a cop. Luis Cortez puckered his lips and made as if to spit over his shoulder, then cracked the can of Budweiser. He took a sip, then rolled the chilly can across his forehead. He needed to think. He could hear Little Cedric making indecent promises to his wife of three weeks. They weren't married in the Anglo way with all the papers and signatures and people in your face, but they were moved in together and happy, joking a lot about the kid they were going to have in five six months. Little Cedric managed the laundromat days and was the one responsible for introducing Luis Cortez to the monster, who owned the place, although Little Cedric had no idea who had given him the contract, or for how much. Little Cedric was in for a century, same as Tiger, only now, as Luis Cortez thought deeper into the situation with the stars, he saw an opportunity to mitigate their influence.

Instead of using Tiger to scout and give the high sign, they'd both be armed. Hit the man together, *wham*, and get outta there. Tiger was a Pisces and he was a Leo: no way could they have anything like similar charts. That way, if the stars didn't look so good for him, there's Tiger, man, to counterbalance things. Yeah . . . Then he thought: of course, I gotta sweeten the pot.

Little Cedric had to put the phone down to answer the banging on the door, and when it was opened, Luis Cortez saw a thick-shouldered, paunchy figure in a sharp black double-breasted raincoat, shades, water dripping off his pale Outback hat, one side of the wide brim pinned flush to the crown, the other side drooping over his tiny ear. He looked short because of his fire-hydrant physique, but he was in fact the same height as Luis Cortez. With a handkerchief he mopped his cordovan-colored face, then split it with a smile that revealed a completely silver incisor. When he removed his Aussie hat, his trademark black-and-yellow-striped bandanna was visible tied pirate fashion over his thinning, but still nappy hair.

Luis Cortez locked right thumbs, knocked right elbows with the man in the double-breasted raincoat. "I been thinkin'," he said. "Tiger man, how you like to take home two centuries?"

Tiger huffed on the lenses of his shades, squinting through bloodshot eyes at Luis Cortez like maybe this was a joke or something. Little Cedric told his wife of three weeks to stop crying, he wouldn't never stop loving her even if she did get big as her momma with puffy rag-doll ankles.

Luis Cortez grinned suddenly, a trick he had learned long ago was the perfect camouflage for deceit. "Two centuries, man, no shit. Same as me." And turning, snapped, "Hey, Cedric man, give it a rest. We gotta talk."

Little Cedric took his hand out of his shirt and told his wife of three weeks he'd love her till the day he died.

The next morning Luis Cortez crept from his mother's apartment early and passed up the elevator, taking the back stairs four flights to the main floor so that he wouldn't risk bumping into Tia Juanita, who lived next to the shaft. He could not believe the luck of his mother in finding an apartment in such a building as this with good security and no writing on the walls. It overlooked a small greenbelt and a playing field, where after supper when the weather was good, the brothers would play football—the real football, the way it was played all over the world except in the United States. Luis Cortez, before he became a small-time dealer and contract killer, had entertained the notion of returning to Puerto Rico to hone his skills, maybe get a shot at turning pro, tour Latin America, man. Who knows, Europe, try some of that Swedish ass.

This was a great part of the building, the main floor. Two wings converged at an oblique angle onto the lobby. The walls of the wings to a height of five feet were covered in a pale marble, a dusty white threaded with yellow veins, and above the marble the plaster beamed from a recent coat of yellow that Luis Cortez associated with the Orient. There were brass mail slots, and they were polished, unvandalized. The walls of the wings rose ten feet above the scrubbed black-and-white tile floor, and when he wore his high-heel boots, as he was this morning, he loved to listen to the solemn racket of his heels echoing in the high spaces.

Down four steps to an octagonal lobby, also tiled, also in the exotic shade of yellow, and by virtue of its depth even more impressive to Luis Cortez. If it hadn't been for Little Cedric, he would have had no way to describe his awe. Several weeks ago Little Cedric had acquired a VCR off Tiger in exchange for a gram of blow. Little Cedric ran out and rented a bunch of tapes, one of them under the impression it was some kind of dope movie, because the title was *Reds*, but what it was, this was a true story about some old Anglos that went off to Russia during a revolution they were pretty hipped on, and there were a lot of speeches, and Warren Beatty gave this chick some looks and Jack with the name like that golfer's made the moves on her, but like every swinging dick in the movie he talked too much, and Little Cedric, stoned, fell asleep snoring, which allowed Luis Cortez, bored as Little Cedric's wife-to-be, to put the moves on her in the kitchen. Of course, she cried afterward. It must be something the nuns teach them, he thought.

But now, entering the lobby of the apartment building on Jerome Avenue, he experienced the sensation of entering a palace in St. Petersburg. It was like walking into history. No, better than that. It was like he was *somebody*.

And that's how he felt emerging from the lobby through the two security doors and into the dripping, splattering morning. He snugged his London Fog to his rib cage, raised his collar. Yeah. He'd like to see Warren Beatty be in control the way he was, knowing in an hour or so he was going to walk up and do a guy, for real. No fucking second takes or catsup or stunt men. The real thing.

Down the steps he saw Tiger's pale blue '71 Pinto with oversized rear tires burping and farting at the curb, but the sight of it did not take its usual toll on his self-esteem. This morning nothing could stop him.

Little Cedric flung open the door and climbed in back. The air in the car was ripe with the scent of cannabis. Both Tiger and Cedric were drinking from cans of Miller High Life. There was a sack full of six-packs behind the driver's seat, and also a heap of blankets. Everybody was smiling.

Tiger said, "Tia Juanita, she say the signs is good?"

Luis Cortez said, "Fuck Tia Juanita."

"Tha's what I hear," said Tiger, "somebody already doin'."

Little Cedric gurgled like an idiot and said, "Tiger man, hey, turn up the radio. Less have some sounds!"

* * *

They crawled along the Major Deegan, inched into the traffic crossing the Triborough Bridge. Tiger bitched continuously, but Luis Cortez took advantage of the lousy weather, the fogged windows, to inspect the shotguns, break them and check their loads. The shells, Tiger told him, were Express Magnums, double-aught motherfuckers that'd make a mess good as frags. The guns were on loan from a junkie up on Tremont Avenue, who was holding them for a boyfriend, but owed Tiger. Luis Cortez, getting the feel of them and liking their weight and authority, said, "What's frags?"

Tiger was doing a line off the back of his hand. "Fragmentation bombs, man. Like we used in the Nam."

"Oh," said Luis Cortez. He handed the weapons to Little Cedric to put back beneath the blankets. Then he glanced at the cordovan face beneath the Aussie hat. "I forget sometime what a old fucker you are."

Tiger's silver incisor showed. "I was prob'ly killin' guys before your daddy got off the round that was you. An' you with all that serious shit yesterday, how it's him or us. You fuckin' think I'd be here I din't know that? Goddamn fuckin' rain."

"Hey Tiger?" said Luis Cortez. "I bet prob'ly you could see better you took off them shades."

Once over the bridge, gaining some speed as they entered Queens, Tiger got himself caught in a passing lane, missing the BQE turnoff, and before they knew it, they were on the Grand Central Parkway farting along past LaGuardia Airport, lost as only Bronx boys could be who regarded the borough of Queens as something on the order of a foreign country.

However, a half hour later found them trundling south

on Dry Harbor Road, Little Cedric into his third beer, Tiger mopping up his fifth, and Luis Cortez remembering some of the landmarks now from his visit last week, after he'd agreed to do the job. That nice park there on the right, then the strip of little shops, then beyond them that big cemetery with a cathedral like right in the middle of it practically. The rain was coming down hard, stomping across the roof of the Pinto, so that even with the radio turned off, Luis Cortez had to raise his voice. He guided them along Metropolitan Avenue past the bakery, explained once more how it was to be done, then they circled back to park the Pinto on a street he had selected off Furmanville, across from the cemetery. It was a quiet block of redbrick one-family homes that Little Cedric couldn't believe just one family lived in there.

Tiger and Luis Cortez stuck the Remingtons beneath their raincoats. Little Cedric chugged the rest of his beer and got out, pissed against a big black tree for what seemed like forever. Then they bent against the blowing, wet morning to trudge back to Dry Harbor and along it past another Catholic church and on toward the several outdoor flower shops that did such a business having a cemetery right across the street.

And there one was, it wasn't luck, he had studied the habits of the people who stopped to purchase flowers. The boxy car droned up to the curb, the guy jumped out holding his khaki hat with the little holes above the brim, wipers going, tail pipe blatting exhaust. Little Cedric moved around to the driver's door and Tiger stayed behind to watch the shop the guy had gone into. Luis Cortez rapped on the window, saw it glide down, saw the young Anglo lady with pale blue eyes. The eyes very cool, haughty, then very scared seeing the six inches of blade in the rain. Luis Cortez grinned: "Escuse me, but you inna wrong car."

Man, but she got out fast, didn't she?

Luis Cortez climbed onto the backseat with Tiger and closed the door and savored the torque of this classy automobile and had a flash of himself and Tia Juanita alone in such a vehicle, just the two of them.

Tiger said, "So who is this guy we gonna do?"

"Jus' some ol' guy is a baker," said Luis Cortez, dreamily. He leaned forward and caught a scent off the woman's headrest, the same perfume as Tia Juanita used. Man, talk about signs.

Chapter 4

Homicide lieutenant Tom McClanahan had just gone end of watch, the midnight-to-eight haul, and had stopped with his partner, Ken Takimoto, for a morning brew in Punch's Place. McClanahan had promised the wife he'd tackle the Plymouth this morning—it needed a new distributor—but the rain nixed that, because he couldn't work in the garage due to a short he had planned to repair last Sunday, until Ken phoned with tickets to the playoffs, Knicks versus the Celtics in the Garden. So when Takimoto, who was prone to bolt drinks the way he did his meals, slammed down his empty schooner, said he had to shake his chopstick, how

25

about another, McClanahan didn't even consult his watch, just jerked the knot of his stained tie looser, struck a match for his Marlboro, and woke up the barkeep: "Yo, Artie! Do us again, whaddaya say."

Scratching his chin, the stubble there, McClanahan paused over a photograph in the sports section of the *News* showing Larry Bird tagging a fadeaway jumper. As the sleepy barkeep shuffled up to gather the empty schooners, McClanahan muttered, "Next game, Birdman, you beautiful—" and heard all hell break loose a block away.

Outside of Punch's he witnessed a black foreign car careening east on Metropolitan, saw it swerve into the opposite lane, narrowly missing a westbound bus, strike the curb with sickening force, its velocity plunging it bouncing furiously into a yard full of marble monuments, where it came to a battered rest, its hood sprung, the radiator fuming. McClanahan bulled his way into the bakery in less than thirty seconds, stepping over a figure in a double-breasted and belted raincoat lying flat on his back, one of the lenses in his dark glasses shot out along with an eye. McClanahan saw terrified women and girls hugging, smelled cordite thickened by the moisture and the unmistakable scent of wetted pants. Shaking open his wallet with the gold shield, he announced that it was all right, he was a police officer, it was all right now, it was all right. . . . The women and girls continued to scream and weep. An old woman with a black scarf on her head he mistook for a nun at first was inching her way blindly on hands and knees through an archway. He touched her shoulder, and she cried out in a broken whisper, "Joey, Joey, Joey . . ."

Then he recognized the small, still shape beyond her,

and the huge man kneeling over him with the abbreviated Hitler mustache. It was Cato Dellacroce, the Baker's number-one insurance policy.

Somebody had found a loophole.

McClanahan restored a semblance of order by shouting at the women and girls to shut the fuck up, then fed coins into the pay phone above an undisturbed table with a newspaper opened on it. He waited, yawned, issued code numbers to the police dispatcher, repeated them, and hung up. He watched the woman on her hands and knees sway, unable to continue, and he bent next to her once more, fumbling the words of comfort, and damning himself as he did so, but she was resolute and would not lie down. She voided her bowels and died like that, on her knees, his clumsy words still washing over her.

Takimoto came through what was left of the plate-glass door, surveyed the mayhem, made his way gingerly through the women and girls. "Mac," he whispered, "you believe this? The hitters had to be complete fuckups."

"Hey," snarled McClanahan, "there's a lady present, huh?"

Standing beneath the awning of the bakery, but getting wet anyway, McClanahan and Takimoto watched the blues on the scene in their yellow rainslicks diverting traffic past the shape in the street ringed with flares. An Emergency Medical Service unit was at work inside the bakery, and the sound of another unit approaching wailed out of the north. Takimoto scratched away in his notebook, the stump of his cigarette smoldering in a corner of his mouth. To save money he had taken up rolling his own, which, together with his ratty raincoat and lousy haircut, sealed his credibility as a doper, a cover he had worked with great success for close to three years, earning his gold shield in the trenches. Eight months a dick, seven of them with McClanahan, but he was still the same chain-smoking sleazoid. Over the months of partnering, McClanahan's candid hostility toward Takimoto and his rumpled appearance had evolved into something closer to a concern that was almost motherly. It was McClanahan who had received a reprimand from Chief Inspector Moriarity for punching out a fellow officer (and Mick) over an idle racial slur. Takimoto, without a word having ever been exchanged on the subject, ceased to wear the gold stud in his earlobe and occasionally remembered to have his shirts sent to the cleaners. Contrary to his private habits, in his professional conduct Takimoto was fastidious in the extreme, a quality McClanahan was veteran enough to appreciate. Though fifteen years separated them, they were Kenny and Mac to one another, regular Queens guys.

McClanahan peered through the window into the bakery. Joe Scorcese, with a profusion of tubes attached to his sticklike shape, was being wheeled slowly toward the door on a gurney under the supervision of two medics and Cato Dellacroce. As the entourage came out onto the sidewalk to load the Baker into the EMS van, the old man briefly opened his eyes, and McClanahan saw, or thought he did, that cloudy, milky look that means only one thing.

Takimoto said, butting his cigarette in the rain, then sending it spinning into the gutter, "The old woman dead?"

"Dead," said McClanahan. The anger that had stolen through him was just a wisp now, a few ashes of emotion.

"Know something, Kenny? What I think, the old lady saw it coming down a split second before they hit the door, and she took some of the stuff intended for the Baker. Her goddamn face is practically shot off."

"Makes four fatals then, so far. Guy in the Saab, bullets didn't do the job, taking a header through the windshield guaranteed it. People, when're they gonna learn to use seat belts?"

They watched as several more blue-and-whites converged on the scene, sirens blaring, effectively shutting down the flow of traffic on Metropolitan. In five minutes they'd be screaming bloody murder in Forest Hills. McClanahan scowled, and muttered under his breath.

"Mac, where you goin'?"

McClanahan strode into the rain, flipped his shield at the blue nearest the body in the avenue, then crouched next to it, rolled it over. It was probably a handsome face when its owner was alive. Long ringlets of hair, smooth skin, teeth bright and straight: a street-corner charmer. And a dope. Most likely a dope *on* dope, a cowboy with a load of artificial courage. McClanahan didn't bother to count the entrance wounds (that would be documented in the coroner's report), but after rolling the body back over, he glanced at the windows above Vacanza's Market, certain that behind them was a vacant room with a distinctive metallic scent in the air. The scent of recently discharged automatic weapons. Who knows, if they were lucky, they might even discover a casing the shooters neglected to pick up, in their haste to be gone. Still crouching, he said to Takimoto, who was hunched over, trying to protect his scribbling from the rain, "You think we move the guy, Ballistics could possibly miss it?"

"Victim took some clean through-and-throughs. Exit wounds much lower than entry. Probably from those windows right there, just above the fruit market. Some of Joe's squish."

Behind a motorcycle escort a black Chevrolet with a detachable gumball on its roof prowled in the wrong lane up to the perimeter of the crime scene, the bright orange plastic pennants drooping mournfully from a rope stretched across the avenue. The gumball was snatched off the roof, and from the shotgun side of the black automobile emerged a stout gentleman dressed in a double-breasted cocoa brown suit with a matching homburg sheltering his pate in style. A snub nose was set in a coarse face, something so blunt and gritty that a wag on the force had suggested you could strike a match off his reflection in a mirror. His partner with the Wild West mustache hastened to open an umbrella over the stout man's hat. The latter approached as if his feet hurt or were too small to properly transport his opera tenor's torso. "Detective Takimoto," he said, slipping something into his mouth, "McClanahan, what've we got besides gridlock?"

McClanahan's knees creaked as he rose to greet the officer in charge. He nodded at Lieutenant D. James Cox and his partner, something Fitzsimmons. "Kenny," he said, "I see you know Coxy. This is Detective Fitzsimmons. Fitz, my partner, Kenny Takimoto."

The young cops acknowledged each other with shrugs.

McClanahan went on, "Coxy, how about we get this stiff outta the street, let the citizens through."

Cox held out his hand for the umbrella. "Wall, have 'em move the body next to the market there. Vacanza's, isn't it?"

"Yeah, I think it is. Kenny?"

"Luigi Vacanza. Age sixty-two. In his youth, the Baker's ace enforcer, until the position was taken over by the Baker's oldest, Angelo. Now he fronts some businesses and is a bagman for the family. Got a daughter he's looking to marry off."

Lieutenant D. James Cox pulled on his bottom lip, absorbing the recital of street news. He thanked Takimoto and said to McClanahan, "You guys witness it?"

"Heard it," said McClanahan. "Saw the tail end, the wheel guy losing it. Kenny was in the can. But shit, lookit it: you didn't have to be there to see this was the work of possibly the three dumbest guys on the planet. Figures, right? All the smart weight looking to move on the Baker and along come the Stooge brothers."

Lieutenant Cox's eyes, which were a murky green, flicked from McClanahan to Takimoto, probing the young detective's face. "You wanna toss anything more in the hopper, son?"

"Like Mac says, it looks like they came straight from stupid town. Jacked themselves up with drugs and did it. But . . ."

Takimoto was trying to get one of his hand-rolleds lit, stalling for time, because he did not want it to appear that he was out in front of McClanahan on this. He would sooner bite off his tongue than show up Mac. Cox's eyes went away for a moment, then came back. Takimoto would have sworn the old bastard winked.

"What say," Cox said, "let's dry out at Punch's, see if we can't get a handle on this."

They watched the blues lug the corpse from the street and drop it face up next to Vacanza's. The flesh of Luis

Cortez, shot sixteen times, flopped like something dumped on a pier at Sheepshead Bay.

The crime-scene cordons were withdrawn from the avenue, the squad cars dispersed. Within minutes traffic was moving in both directions along Metropolitan Avenue, and McClanahan and Takimoto were bellied up to the bar in Punch's, sipping beer and staring straight ahead. Lieutenant Cox came away from the door, where he had been issuing instructions to his partner, Fitzsimmons, and straddled the stool next to Takimoto. "Coffee, black," he said to the barkeep, then leaned forward, his face cocked, his eyes combing the profile of the young detective. "*Cui bono*. You familiar with the phrase, Kenny?"

"It's Latin, isn't it, sir?"

McClanahan yawned. "Means something like 'who benefits.' "

"Right. Homicide like this, it's the first question oughta be asked. Or am I presuming? Dispatch made it sound like the Baker bought the farm."

"He's in the process," said McClanahan. "Way he looked, Coxy, he'll close the deal in a coupla hours."

This time Detective Takimoto recognized what it was that Cox popped into his mouth: a wafer of dried plum. The guy reached for them the way other men reach for cigarettes.

Lieutenant Cox tasted his coffee, dabbed at his lips with the back of a freckled hand. "Either you guys believe the shooters were acting on their own?"

McClanahan grunted, picking up the paper that was

folded to the sports section. This wasn't his watch, and the shooting wouldn't be in his caseload. The motives of the morons didn't interest him any more than the doings of lady tennis players.

Takimoto, however, itched to hear the lieutenant out. Cox was practically a legend, close to twenty-five years on the force, a Vietnam vet who went his own way, which was why he was still a lieutenant, a field stiff instead of some decorated fat ass shuffling papers behind a desk. This was one of the best working dicks in the borough, and he, Takimoto, was not going to let the opportunity elude him to spar with the man. He squirmed forward on his stool, trying to hunker over the bar, a difficult feat for someone who is only five seven. "I was down in the street a long time, Lieutenant," he confided, "and I don't recognize the guys as any players I ever knew."

Lieutenant Cox pawed his mouth, possibly to obscure a sardonic grimace. "Raises a interesting question, then. Were the shooters complete dummies or was it the guy who set them up."

Takimoto said, "I don't get it."

"The shooters didn't have a prayer. Once they made their move, they were shark bait."

"Yes. Yes." Takimoto dashed back the remainder of his beer and brought the empty schooner down smartly on the bartop, grabbing Artie's attention. "So if they weren't players, somebody was using them, knowing they wouldn't live to collect."

"What it looks like," agreed Lieutenant Cox, another wafer of dried plum disappearing into his mouth.

"Well, dead men don't talk, Lieutenant."

"No reflection on you, Kenny. But whoever set them up was just dumb enough to think that was a clever idea."

"Sir?"

"Loyalty's a two-way street. Whoever's behind this mess, if the Don was rubbed, he's gonna surface. Sooner or later, he's visible, because he's making his play. To do that, he's gotta have soldiers, right?"

Takimoto emptied half his schooner in a single go, pinched the residue of foam residing in his sparse mustache. "Muscle's what it's about," he said.

"*Loyal* muscle, Kenny," Cox said. "The genius behind this move could be taking his soldiers for granted. Dead men, like you say, don't talk, but live ones do. They see a guy dump on his people this way, it makes the troops squirrelly. The Baker would never have pulled a stunt like this. What happened here was bush league. It's the reason punks, they ain't exactly famous for their longevity."

"You got a particular genius in mind, sir?"

Lieutenant D. James Cox finished his coffee and sighed, slid another wafer of dried plum into his mouth. "If I did, Kenny, I wouldn't be sitting here listening to myself be brilliant. Right, Mac?"

McClanahan said, "Yo Artie! What's the early line on the Knicks Celtics tomorrow night?"

Chapter 5

Mai (pronounced "my") Lee Scorcese was delivered by mid-
wife in a small hamlet in the Mekong Delta in the year 1952,
the issue of a French serviceman on leave from the fighting
around Hanoi and a Saigon B-girl. The mother, who had
suffered unnamed depredations under the Japanese occupa-
tion, instilled in the child a passion for things French, Euro-
pean, Western: Mai Lee was raised on Babar books and *Le
Petit Prince*, imbibed the blood of Christ every Sunday, and
was taught to revere the Diems, a good Catholic family trying honorably to govern a country that was 85 percent Bud-
dhist. Before Mai's eleventh birthday she watched a young

man on a Honda motor scooter shoot her mother dead in the street and drop a leaflet. The leaflet accused her mother of being an enemy of the people. A criminal. A papist parasite.

Taken in by an order of French nuns, Mai Lee excelled scholastically to such an extent that by the year 1969 she had already secured a position as translator at the U.S. embassy in Saigon. In July of that year she witnessed the pomp attendant upon the arrival of a president of the United States. She was intoxicated by the palpable emanation of power. Respect, control: this was heady stuff for one so dispossessed, an outcast, a child of disparate lineage in a culture absolute about its parameters.

Within four years she was routinely escorting delegations of senators, congressmen, and entertainers on designated tours of the country, on a first-name basis with some of them, building her bridges. And then the new sentry arrived.

He was a marine assigned days to the front desk. He was a formidable presence with a thick neck, blunt nose, eyebrows conjoined above small, glittering eyes. At first he intimidated her, behaving as he did in a manner to suggest that he was an authority unto himself. He sneered at the legislators, seemed barely to tolerate the visiting entertainers, referring to them variously as the "faggots from Vegas" and the "Hollywood hoors." But oddly enough, toward her he exhibited something approaching manners, almost deference. The first time he spoke to her, he stood up and leaned over, doffed his bright white cap with the polished black beak. His voice drummed on her ear: "You are one bitchin' lady, Mai Lee. There's more'n dink blood in you, ain't there?"

She had stared at him, not certain whether she was

more appalled by his coarseness or shocked at his familiarity, given the unwritten policy discouraging fraternization between civilians and the military.

A week later they had cocktails in a bistro on the Rue de Chanson, then dined in an American haunt nearby, where ranking officers not only recognized this sentry out of uniform, but sent gratuities to their table, stopped to socialize. He introduced her. The officers nodded, they kissed her fingers. He walked her home with a jeep trolling behind them, Americans in the jeep with their helmets on and weapons in their arms. Clearly this was a man of consequence, and of some mystery too.

The night ended innocently enough with a single kiss.

But there was a war on. Within weeks they were as mutually intoxicated as lovers in legends ever were. Mai Lee gave herself passionately, sincerely, perversely to the man who had shown her the shape and dimension of answered prayer. She drew blood with her nails, cried out *Mon ange, mon ange . . .* She politicked with all of her orifices, called it love, *l'amour incroyable,* for she was campaigning for her freedom, her dignity, safe haven in a society she believed to be more civilized, where she would not be judged upon the pallor of her skin, her thin Gallic nose, the washed-out blue of her Breton eyes. And in the United States, she had read, it was permitted, even easy, for a woman to walk out of a marriage, with money, should she tire of her angel's crude affections.

Now, seventeen years later and modeling a full-length sable coat for her husband, Angelo Scorcese, in the master bedroom of their trilevel home in Howard Beach, Mai Lee continued to marvel at the irony of her fate, even as she refused to submit to it. She had fled exile from one society by marrying into a family from which there was no walking away, except dead. She luxuriated in the ebony fur. In three-inch Ferragamo heels, scallops of pearl gray on jet leather, and wearing nothing else, she was still possessed of a face and profile that arrested conversation in nightclubs, charmed traffic cops who pulled her over for speeding in her ivory 500 SL, and which utterly isolated her from the wives and mothers and sisters and girlfriends and myriad mistresses of the men who did business with her husband. It was a state of affairs that suited her fine. She despised these women as examples of perfect communists. Weak and petty and full of themselves, like all tyrants.

With his hands behind his head in a mass of pillows, and stretched out on the bed bare-chested in green fatigues, crepe-soled black leather hightops equipped with steel toes, Angelo Scorcese instructed his wife as to how he wanted her to pose. Mai Lee had never believed him handsome. There was an animal energy about him, and a kind of primitive innocence that occasionally still touched her, although she had long ago written him off as a hopeless force without her behind him. It was she who for years had had to nudge him in the direction of reality; she who had convinced him that control of the family would not be handed to him—he would have to seize it. He said to her now: "Coat there, babe, run you close to a hunnert thou, third what the house is worth, you believe Jimmy."

Jimmy Capistrano was downstairs in the rec room, knocking back shots of peach schnapps, playing a solitary game of nine ball to celebrate the successful theft of several millions in Russian sable from a TWA holding pen at JFK.

Cap had brought a compromised fairy freight handler into the deal, and Angelo, with his father's permission, provided the truck, uniforms, untraceable nine-millimeter automatics if trouble developed, and most important—a genius locksmith when he wasn't opiated over a chess board. The Scorcese family took a piece out of any airport hijacking. Jimmy the Cap, aka Gentleman Jim, was famous for dispensing gifts (something above and beyond the understanding) to the people that worked with him. Hence the marten coat inside of which Mai Lee pirouetted naked at the bidding of her husband. . . .

"Awright," he said. He waved one of his paws at her, which she saw in the mirrored closet door, her back to him. She stopped turning and looked at the faint lines radiating away from the corners of her eyes, began to assemble her arguments for a face-lift. "You look like a million bucks, babe, that Rooskie fur. Which I gotta tell ya, you ain't goin' nowhere in public in."

She raised her eyes to meet the reflection of his. "Your father. Because of the Mercedes you gave me."

"Even it's registered to one a my joints, Lorenzo says it's no sweat, but Pop don't like it. Lorenzo might be *consigliere*, but he's also just a son. It's Pop's way. He don't like to attract no attention. Long as it's Pop's show, it's the way it is."

"*Bien sur*," she murmured. She had known from the day they were introduced that Joseph Scorcese despised her for having outmanipulated him, however briefly, her passion more than a match for the years of stern, solemn, sometimes graphic education. She knew too that the Don chalked it up to his son's oafishness: the progeny of a man of his stature wedding a chink, a rice-paddy midwifed slut (oh yes, the

Don, she knew, had a file on her thicker than anything in Immigration, or the State Department). She understood almost instantly upon meeting the Don that her survival depended upon a facade of obedience (and later, upon keeping to herself the searing knowledge that the Don's own mother was a midwifed infant from a small Mediterranean island, given in matrimony at the age of fourteen in exchange for a pair of goats). So she lowered a face almost as harsh in this moment as it was beautiful, and in her hushed voice said, "Of course. As you say, *mon Ange.* We must honor the old ones. Your father is a man of many years. But someday, maybe someday soon . . ."

"You'd like that, wouldn't you, Mai?" he growled.

"I want only what it is you want."

He vaulted from the bed to stand behind her, his powerful arms locked on her, thick fingers stirring against her powdered flesh. "You blue-eyed dink bitch," he said, "I'll tell you what I want." She closed her eyes and pulled his hands to her firm, surgically enhanced breasts, let him twist her tumescent nipples. His demands upon her were infrequent and brief now, but when the pull was on him, Mai Lee gratified it, even eagerly, meting pleasure for eventual power. If she could not escape the Scorceses, then she would rule them.

The white phone on the shelf above the headrest began to ring; only it went *neet, neet, neet.*

Angelo stayed with her, the thick hunger of him coming at her steadily there on the carpet, her buttocks lifted from the cool silk lining of the coat, her spine and shoulders heating, so that she knew in the mirror afterward she would see the skin mottled, not quite abraded, but a strawberry shade somewhere between the hue of a birthmark and the flush of outrage. His chest surged above her, whorls of black hair radiating and entangling, almost as clearly defined against his skin as the weblike tattoos the flesh merchants of Saigon favored, the ones who bought and sold women for sex and men for lethal sport. She pulled him to her, licked sweat from the hollow of his throat. And then heard the voice of Luigi Vacanza on the recording machine: "Angelo? Jesus Mary and Joseph, the Padrino, they tagged him. You unnerstan' I'm sayin' here? Ange? Pick up the fuckin' phone."

She saw her husband's pale, hairy ass as he climbed onto the bed. She heard: "Yo, Luigi? It's me, Angelo. Get a fuckin' grip, awright? Now we're onna phone here. Talk to me, but remember, we're onna fuckin' phone here."

When he hung up he rolled over and put his feet on the carpet, and she could see that his member was not shrunken, but just lolling there along his thigh. Reclining in the Russian sable, she worked him with the tremor of a smile, then hiked herself up on her elbows to show her breasts to advantage. The bedroom mirrored Mai Lee's taste for stark contrasts: carpet and walls an arctic white to play up the large lithographs purchased recently in Greenwich Village. Framed in black and struck on black paper, the works were luminous bursts of color, each blur representing a season of the year. According to a friend, who was a collector and drove a sapphire Jaguar, the Japanese artist was on the verge of being taken up by the Manhattan glitterati, so Mai Lee did not hesitate, her mother's phobia notwithstanding. She was a Scorcese now. Present and future, not the past, were the measure of all things. She rose to her knees.

"Your father," she said, "can it be true?"

Angelo Scorcese was not much as an actor. He exercised the skin above his mated eyebrows. "I don't believe it. Pop. There some guys with shotguns, real rumdums, they tapped him out."

"*Mon ange,* but this is terrible," she said. "You wouldn't know who it might be . . ."

"Who, me?" Tucking his head down between his shoulders, a face full of boyish innocence.

She leaned forward then between his legs and knew for a certainty that she would not be seeing her friend with a Jaguar for a while. With a dinky income of a quarter mil? When she was holding hundreds of millions in her fingers? With an empire between her lips?

Chapter 6

There was a bar near Van Buren Avenue, a classy one for the area, that Elvis Mahoney said was a watering hole for heavy hitters—political people, attorneys, players from Greyhound Raceway. Greyhound was the premiere dog track in the Valley. Unlike the ponies, the dogs ran year-round in Phoenix, providing constant action. The name of the bar was Sport Time.

The morning after his arrival in Phoenix, Del Rebus (registered as Irwin Field) topped off a late breakfast of scrambled eggs, chorizos, and fried potatoes with a Bloody

Mary delivered by room service. He tipped the plump delivery boy an amount equal to the price of the cocktail, in cash, and asked him how many drunks it took to screw in a light bulb. The plump boy went out the door smiling, said, "Is good, is good," and repeated the punch line to himself so that he could tell it to his younger brother, who knew English better and could explain it to him. Senor Field, he thought, was a most amusing hombre.

Del Rebus strolled back across the suite nibbling on the stalk of celery that came with the drink, gratified to have made the little fat guy grin. There was a jade-colored towel wrapped around his waist, which was hard, if not exactly trim, and that was all he was wearing as he padded barefoot up to Elvis Mahoney and Franny Lott. They were sitting at a glass-topped table on a balcony filling with sunlight. Stacked to one side were plates with the rinds of muskmelons, crumbs from toast, cups glazed on the inside by the dregs of coffee. Franny, who was smoking a menthol cigarette, glanced at her wristwatch, and Elvis fiddled idly with the arm of his aviator shades, alert behind the lenses but not tense, trying to learn from the man. Del Rebus brought the glass with the drink in it away from his lips, and a pale tomato stain accentuated his grin. "It's like my daddy always told me," he said, "make a man laugh, and you've made a friend. Make enough friends, and you can retire."

Franny Lott put her eyes on Elvis, along with a cool, sardonic smile. "Did you see anybody laughing besides Del?"

"Mex kid gave it a shot. Smiled real hard. Three on a scale of ten."

Del Rebus scratched around in his chest hair as if he

were weighing their opinions. "Say the name of that bar was, Elvis?"

"Sport Time."

"Ah." He swallowed some more of his drink, then strutted out into the sunlight and leaned over to plant a kiss on the nape of Franny Lott's neck. "Elvis, why don't you and Frances the talking beauty here take in the sights, let the old rock 'n' roller make some new friends. Sport Time, you say. Ah, yes. You feel what I'm feeling, Frances?"

"What's that, Delbert?"

Standing behind her, he winked at Elvis. "Good vibes."

"What?"

Pushing back his chair, Elvis said, "Don't ask. It's too early in the morning to hear about the sixties."

With Elvis at the wheel of the Charger, they went east on Van Buren Avenue, taking in the splendor of date palms soaring sixty feet above the traffic median and the squalor of charred motel courts. Used-car lots infested the avenue, advertising instant credit and owners with names like Buffalo Willy and Serious Pete. The avenue climbed, and Franny Lott was shown the Tovrea Castle, a glimpse into the heart of an obsession. They turned north into Papago Park. Softly sculpted red buttes commanded the area. "Surprises you," he said, "middle of a city. But those rocks *belong* here. It's us that don't."

Franny Lott said, "Oh? Del said you spent a lot of time in the library, but he didn't make it sound like you were reading Edward Abbey."

"Who?"

"A guy that wore out a lot of walking shoes. Here's the turnoff."

They followed the signs to the parking area, placed a cardboard sunscreen on the dashboard, locked the car, and strolled toward the entrance to the zoo. Ducks and swans glided in the water below, and a pair of geese were visible downstream clambering up the bank, wings lifted and hissing, challenging some fool kids trying to make friends with their goslings.

Whatever edge or aura of sophistication that Franny Lott possessed vanished in the instant the turnstiles admitted them. She grasped Elvis Mahoney by the hand and tugged, drawn by the army of flamingos massed along a shady embankment. She deposited the dark glasses in her beige canvas shoulder bag and leaned over the railing, murmured endearments. She told him about their plumage, how they were classified, tossing off Latin like sports buffs use stats, called his attention to the creatures' reversed knees, the way the lower half of the leg snapped forward. She was wearing leather sandals, and her bare heels sprang free from the straps in her enthusiasm to explain. Then she grew quiet, appearing contemplative, though Elvis had not been a free citizen long enough to be lulled: they were both wary, because they both had reason to be. And he knew something else: they were each curious as hell.

"I was just thinking," said Franny Lott at last, "you and I, we're about as weird as flamingos in Phoenix, to hook up with a guy like Del. Or don't you think so?"

Elvis looked at her over the top of his dark glasses and let it go at that.

"You know how I met him?" she said.

"No."

"My husband, he's this genius with numbers, he's earning six digits creating computer games for the Japanese. Elvo, we're talking serious six digits. This is a man who picked me up when I was a senior at Berkeley sitting behind a card table selling arm bands to save the whales. David was —is—a man who walked out of an L. L. Bean catalog. So six years later we're still wearing the khaki and plaid, hiking and rappeling on the weekends, no kids, two-point-four dogs, money in triple-A munis and mutual funds, condo worth a half million, a four-wheel Jeep and a BMW. We're invited to this private party in Tahoe for a New Year's bash, and my husband the number freak is losing his ass at blackjack, mostly to this funkball with incredible charm."

"Who is prone to quoting his daddy when he can't think of a lame joke to tell."

"He let my husband write a couple checks after his cash was gone, then tried to cut David off. When David's ego protested, Del said, okay, one hand, just the two of them. If David won, he'd tear up the checks. If Del won, he kept the checks, but promised to spend them on a new wardrobe for me. With Del dealing, my husband drew a red ten and black ace. Del went bust. He tore up the checks. I left my rings with the hostess and left Tahoe with Del. He's the sort of man my mother would distrust instantly and my father would want as a business partner."

Elvis Mahoney said, "And you?"

"I think he just might be the last living romantic."

Elvis Mahoney tugged on his earlobe. "Let me tell you what, chile," he said, and planted a hand on his hip, his elbow out there for her to grasp, and they strolled leisurely away from the flamingos.

After he was stripped and every orifice was probed and he had been showered with disinfectant, Elvis was issued a pale green costume with an elasticized waist, like an intern's, and canvas shoes without laces. He was introduced to a counselor, who explained the ground rules. Then they admitted him to the yard.

This was an area of several thousand square yards, open to the sky and supervised from the watchtowers, the guards using binoculars to monitor the activity below. There were some concrete slabs and hoops for half-court basketball, and several sandy areas for volleyball enthusiasts to hurl themselves about in, and a cinder track at one end for anyone who wanted to run without getting shot for the idea.

The men not participating in sports, Elvis noted, clustered in groups or kept moving, or kept to themselves, their backsides against a hard broad surface. This was no place for idle reflection. And this was certainly no place for a twenty-two-year-old musician, aspiring to revolutionize pop by introducing it to the classical persuasions of the violin.

He wasn't in the yard five minutes before he realized he had a problem. A big, ugly one. This was a white boy about six two with long black hair and wearing a spare belly, it looked like, one of those types that would always carry a quart of grease under his fingernails and look like an amputee without a Hog between his legs. The big white guy parked his belly directly in front of him, and before he could even think about a decorous retreat, there were white boys all around him. That was scary enough, but what gave Elvis pause was the tattoo on everyone's forearm, a blue spider that he wasn't liable to forget. The guards in the towers looked about as menacing as bird-watchers. "We been expectin' you, fiddle boy. You the little shitball busted botha Dwayne's arms. My, my. With a tire iron, they say. Well, here we do it the old-fashioned way. Start with the fingers, one at a time."

Elvis never saw the fist that collided with the pit of his stomach, just found himself on his knees, the tears spilling from his eyes, his hands sprawled instinctively over his dick and balls. Then he heard the flat twang of a midwestern white man, a weird enough sound in California, let alone intruding itself into the midst of these rawboned shitkickers. "Boys, Lester, excuse me. What's this, a little exercise in Aryan superiority?"

The man crouching in front of Elvis looked older than most of those in the yard, basically the lines around his eyes and the touch of gray in his hair, but he was hard, and he had the neck of an iron pumper. He gave away an inch in height to the one called Lester, and maybe close to one hundred pounds, but if it came down to it, the smart money would go with the older guy. He helped Elvis to his feet and moved his eyes over all the tattooed tough boys, scratching the side of his long, narrow nose. "It must've escaped your attention, fellas, I'm deacon of the yard for the white guys."

Lester bunched up cabbage-sized fists. "Del," he steamed, "this fuckin' nigroid bust a brother's arms, both'm, with a tire iron."

"You read the man's jacket?"

"I don't give a rat's ass what the file says."

"That's what I thought. Why read, when it's so much easier to be stupid. Let it go, fellas. He'll do his time, you do yours. And Lester? Don't even think of messing with him, unless a career change to a max lockup in, say, Alabama, appeals to you. I've still got the juice. Up to you, Lester."

Lester sneered, staring long and hard at the older man. "You best watch your ass. There's more a me'n there is you. Send me to 'Bama, you signed yer death warnt."

A gob of ill-colored spit landed between Del Rebus's feet. The blue-spider crowd shuffled off, guffawing, making remarks.

Del Rebus watched them, a finger alongside his nose, idly brushing it. His lips curled at the end in this queer sort of smile, as if he were enjoying a truly wicked joke.

Elvis Mahoney used what little breath he had to thank the man.

Del Rebus put a hand on his shoulder and nudged him along into walking with him, flanked by men who took their cue from the older man. "You mind if I give you some fatherly advice, one or two pointers?"

"Fatherly advice. Man, I'm a nigger."

"Yeah, I noticed. You see the large gentleman third court over, guarding the basket, the shaved head? That's Isaiah. He's the man for you. Mind what he says and you'll jail okay."

"Uh-huh."

"But for insurance, it was me, I'd make it a point to work some iron. Like my daddy always told me, a guy with a ton of friends can still find himself alone some night. Name's Del Rebus."

The man's hand was there, and he shook it in spite of his instincts. "Elvis," he said, "Elvis Mahoney."

"I know. Your momma have a crush on the Hound Dog man?"

They both grinned.

"My father. He sold Mr. Presley a 1965 Cadillac convertible, tomato red with all white interior. Sold it straight off the showroom floor. Said Mr. Presley was the politest man to walk the earth. Any of us kids misbehaved, we were asked what Mr. Presley would think. Every year until I was eight or nine, on my birthday I'd be photographed next to a Gibson. Now let me ask you something."

Del Rebus nodded.

"You putting your ass on the line for me, I'd like to know what that's about."

The older man's eyes traveled skyward, as if the same question had occurred to him, and then he brought them down, leveled on Elvis. "The year your daddy sold that Caddy to the Hound Dog man, I was twenty. Those were outrageous times. Marches, demonstrations, sit-ins, be-ins, teach-ins . . . love-ins. We *believed* in things. Call me sentimental, but I think what the world needs is more musicians, and fewer Lesters. Also, if I let him mess with you, I could have a race riot on my hands, couldn't I? Make me look bad. Be a real disappointment to my daddy."

They drank Coors from tall paper cups and nibbled on footlong hot dogs that were overpriced and undercooked. They sat in the shade, but not out of the heat, among other tables overlooking water and a small grassy island with trees and shelters on stilts for the ring-tailed monkeys. There were families at the other tables with very small children, and the children shrieked with delight whenever a peacock wandered up, the peacocks calm as movie stars among autograph hounds. Out in the sun the air quivered above the asphalt walkways.

"This your thing," said Elvis, "zoos. Commune with nature, all that shit."

Franny Lott was wearing her dark glasses once more and smoking a cigarette, patting a handkerchief between her breasts. "This isn't nature. It's just a reminder that people aren't the only creatures on the planet. Me, I need that."

Elvis could feel the heat in his cheekbones.

Across the table from him Franny leaned forward, blew smoke from the corner of her mouth. "What's this about, this payback Del says we're here for?"

Elvis calculated quickly: Del Rebus had been paroled prior to Thanksgiving of last year, making it almost six months before Elvis walked out of Lompoc and was driven by Franny (their introduction) to the third-floor apartment in San Diego with a view of Mission Bay, water-skiers in wet suits dodging about in the gray mornings, executing bravado cuts across the wakes, shoulders so low they seemed to buffet the water. He remembered aching for a taste of that. They spent a week together, the three of them eating and drinking and talking and taking in the sun and Pacific surf. But he couldn't remember Franny Lott being any part of the conversation concerning payback. This was a topic that surfaced without apparent premeditation whenever she chose to visit Seaworld or Wild Animal Kingdom, or whenever Del and Elvis took it upon themselves to hit the local markets, shopping for the evening's victuals. Payback appealed, the way Del explained it, as much as flying across the water at high speed a few inches above disaster. Elvis was game.

Though he liked this lady with her high cheekbones and encouraging smile, her candor and priorities, anything about their business he wanted to run past Del first.

"Del's a gambler," he said cheerfully. "Gonna show the new boy, me, how to relieve the high rollers of their unnecessary baggage. He's giving me a leg up is all it is. See, he lost a wager back there."

Back there being the joint, Lompoc, the way they talked about the time without naming the place.

Franny Lott smiled. "You lying sack of shit," she said, rising from the table and depositing their debris in a brown plastic disposal.

Elvis followed her, his admiration growing: the lady had just shot his jive to pieces, but she didn't gloat. They walked down to the water where the grounds were daubed by the shadows of trees, cypress and eucalyptus. There was a cage there with a green parrot in it, his beak almost a pecan color, and he climbed to the top of his cage as they approached and unlimbered a sharp wolf whistle.

Franny Lott inserted a finger between the bars and stroked the bird's cheek. "This one's tame," she said, "that's why they've kept him away from the others. He couldn't cut it with the wild ones." She made kissing noises against the bars, and the green bird cocked its head. "Elvo? Del is a little on the wild side. I can walk away, but I don't know if you can."

Her eyes were invisible behind dark glasses, but then so were his.

"You notice what time it was he started with the Bloody Marys?" she said. "Not even ten in the morning."

He said, "Let's go back to the hotel, get outta this heat."

As they passed through the lobby on the way to the elevators, Elvis Mahoney heard himself addressed from a distance, shyly. That would be young Mr. Wills, with the fashionable haircut and habit of blushing when at a loss for words. Elvis Mahoney repented playing with the boy's head, pulling a Del on him his first night in Phoenix. He was too easy a target. Angels would be tempted to mischief upon meeting Whitney Wills.

He stood behind the counter shaking a folded newspaper. "It just arrived for you. *The Gazette*, sir." He moved his eyes as they approached. "Missus Field, how are you this afternoon?"

"Desiccated, totally." There was a smile for him beneath the dark glasses, a smile that in an instant caused Whitney Wills to surrender his impression of her as a California lady. "Has my husband returned to our suite, or do I need to ask for the key?"

"I just came on. Let me check your box. It looks like— no, here it is."

She put her hand out for the key. "Life with a workaholic," she said. "Thank you, Whitney."

Whitney Wills watched Mr. Murdock and Mrs. Field every step of the way to the elevators, and was relieved when they disappeared without any show of affection. He was not certain what he would have done if he had witnessed funny business. From a drawer at his waist he removed a hand mirror to check his appearance and saw that he was blushing.

Going up in the elevator, Elvis Mahoney opened the newspaper enough to study the front page, skimmed the headlines, the raw smell of newsprint rushing up at him, crowding out Franny Lott's warm perfume. He saw a dull, bleak photograph, a shape on a gurney amidst a crowd of anxious men. It appeared to be raining. There was another photograph to the right of it, an inch-square picture of an old guy in a hat that appeared to be a file photo, something AP or UPI could punch up on a computer in seconds, along with most of the information that appeared in the story. Something about this old mobster being shotgunned in a bakery.

Franny Lott yawned. "This heat," she said. "Anything interesting?"

"Nah. Some gangster back east got shot."

A bell rang, the doors parted, and Franny Lott stepped out. "I'm going to take a nap. What I said about Del, that's between you and me, okay? Deal?"

He patted her hand, doing a very good job of not laughing out loud. "Deal," he said solemnly.

Going back to his room, he thought: Del, a little on the wild side? Yes, you could say that. After all, the guy did fifteen years for killing a man. Shot him point-blank was the whisper.

Chapter 7

Before you entered the bar proper, there was a small, dark lobby presided over by a bleached blond slouched on a stool behind glass cases and a cash register. She wore a black one-piece costume with silvery glitter in it, essentially a bathing suit with fitted lifts for her boobs and some extra material that fanned out from her hips, like louvers. Her face was made up to be seen in very little light. Her legs were sheathed in sheer stockings with a black seam clear up to her fanny, visible and endearing when she turned around to reach out a package of Gauloises for Del Rebus. The costume she was wearing struck him as a throwback to the fifties, a conscious effort to imitate the look of Vargas, when *Playboy* was daring stuff. But the availability of French cigarettes impressed him. Inside the case expensive cigars in individual glass tubes were fanned out on black velvet. There were Swiss chocolates too, and breath mints, briar pipes and ivory cigarette holders. Behind the counter, besides cigarettes, a variety of sports periodicals and tout sheets were displayed, along with copies of the major men's magazines. The woman had a wad of pink gum in her mouth and a talent for detonating it. It was almost eleven in the morning.

"Dollar seventy-five," she said, scarlet nails drumming the pale blue package on the counter. "How'd you say these were called?"

Del Rebus repeated the pronunciation. He looked forward to the raw bite of the tobacco. It had been more than fifteen years.

"Right," said the lady of the lobby. "We call 'em gollies. Just ask for gollies."

Del Rebus tried to think of a joke the girl might understand. He nodded instead and said, "I'll do that. Thanks."

"Mister?"

He turned around, about to touch off his lighter, and squinted at her.

"Your change?" she said. "You gave me a ten."

Six months out of Lompoc, and he still muffed the simplest money transactions. So many years of bartering for hard goods had dulled his understanding of currency. Wagering was one thing, a clear-cut deal, but in matters of purchase he was as awkward as an Apache. It was in instances like this one that Del Rebus lost his perspective a little and had a taste of the dregs of the bitterness that had brought him here.

"Keep it," he snapped.

The bar was doing business, even at this hour, and that picked him up considerably. The lighting was dim blue and the music being piped in sounded like the lobby lady's costumer had a hand in the selection: Sinatra, Clooney, Perry Como, an occasional Nat King Cole, a Dinah Washington number. Del Rebus could remember his father, an otherwise intelligent man, spewing epithets at a television screen when the King provided entertainment at a Republican presidential convention. His dad couldn't imagine a black man voting Republican. He forgave the King for it, but never forgot it. And never understood it. Del Rebus knew his father went to his grave believing there was a political party grounded in virtue, that they were called Democrats, and although most of them were shameless crap artists, one or two slipped through to fight the good fight periodically. So far as Del was concerned, and he loved the man, his father had bought into a myth.

Booths flanked the walls, there were tables with smooth black surfaces, and a kind of carpeted runway between the bar and tables with a waist-high partition upon which all manner of plastic greenery flourished. There was a stingy dance floor to the right, composed of enough parquet to accommodate a half-dozen sedated couples, tops, and beyond it an elevated and carpeted area where a baby grand, a full set of lounge drums, and two floor mikes gathered in the musty light. The bar itself ran off at some length edged with black padding that resembled what was current in automobile dashboards, although upon closer inspection, Del Rebus decided it was soft enough to sleep against. He walked the length of the bar and mounted a black padded stool at the end, next to the servers' station, where the waitresses picked up the drinks. It was a good place to listen for gossip. He laid his wallet, the package of Gauloises, and his lighter on the bartop, and waited with an easy smile on his face for the bartender to find him.

He wore the same pair of blue jeans that he'd worn the day before, upon arriving in Phoenix, the same comfortable, scuffed, camel-colored cowboy boots, a different shirt, but loose fitting like yesterday's and full of friendly color. The shirt hid the slight roll on his waist, but was less successful at concealing his biceps, which he considered respectable if not formidable.

Formidable was a word he saved for arms like the ones on the blond barkeep who hovered over him across the bar wearing a white shirt with ruffles down the front, a wing collar, no bow tie, short sleeves strained close to transparent by the sunburned musculature they encased. The keep's face was the same furious hue, the eyes a drained shade of blue, a pronounced lower jaw stubbed out with a day's growth of whiskers, a thick mustache over his upper lip so blond it resembled neon. His hair was longish and tempestuous on top, cut boot-camp close back from his temples, then flourished from his nape in a glorious, moussed profusion to somewhere in the middle of his back. Del Rebus, child of an era when there were straights and longhairs, marveled at the ingenuity of the look, wondered if it was purely a victory for style, or if it meant something. He requested a Bloody Mary, made spicy, and the hot-faced barkeep grinned. "You serious?" he said.

"Serious as a heart attack," Del Rebus said. "If you got the recipe, let's taste it."

"I sure do have the recipe," said the hulk, moving his face a little to wink.

Del Rebus glanced in the direction of the expression, expecting to find some long-legged wench at the servers' station, but saw instead a lean, dark, handsome animal, a dapper man in his thirties a few inches beneath six feet. The man's outfit, what Del could see of it, looked contemporary, casual, and costly. The sleeves of the pale gray jacket were shoved up on his darkly tanned arms, showing a thick gold watchband on his wrist, probably a Rolex there. Underneath the jacket he wore a collarless shirt that looked aqua in the light, and if not aqua, definitely expensive. The man's hair was cut fairly short, long enough to comb, and with abbreviated sideburns. The hair was a liquid black, like his eyes. The man leaned against the servers' station as if he owned the joint, but there was a humorless shine in his eyes, like that of a fortune-teller's. He was too small to be a bouncer, that was for sure, but he didn't have that gloat or air of concern to suggest proprietorship. Del decided he would have to watch that boy.

They called him Ruby because of the way his skin reacted to the sun, and he let the name live because by temperament he was not inclined to take offense. He was a naturally large man, who bulked himself into the supernatural out of a bashful ambition to become noticed, possibly even desired, and mostly to cover the fact (he thought) of his weakness for other men. He thought his inclination was still a secret when he was hired on as a bartender at Sport Time. He hadn't worked there six weeks before the owner, Paul Scorcese, took him home one night and made him a friend. Paul Scorcese was good to his friends.

So, as a friend, Ruby would remember exactly the time, nearly eleven-thirty, when he set the second spicy Bloody Mary in front of the old hippie, that the phone rang behind the bar. The old hippie chewing a jalapeño pepper with his Bloody Mary, rapping out some truly funny jokes so that several patrons moved over to listen, along with Paul Scorcese himself. Ruby finally comprehending the voice at the other end of the line, laying the receiver amongst the liquor bottles, bellowing at Paul to come quick, it was about his father.

Del Rebus left off midsentence, saw the elegant gentleman in the pale gray jacket move behind the bar, seize the phone, listen.

"Pauli?"

"Yeah."

"You know who this is, kid?"

"Yeah."

"They got to him."

"Father?"

"Nailed him in the bakery."

"Who?"

"C'mon, kid."

"*Who?*"

"We're workin' on it, okay?"

"I'll catch the earliest flight I can."

"No. Stay there. The family needs you where you're at."

"But if he's—"

"He ain't. Not yet anyways. You sit tight. I'll let you know."

"And Mother?"

"The girls are with her, and the grandkids. Don't you worry. I got it under control."

"God go with you."

"Just sit tight, okay?"

"Okay."

Del Rebus watched with half a jalapeño in his hand, sweat studding his forehead, as the slim, dark man cradled the receiver, his back to the room, his eyes in the mirror that ran the length of the bar behind the bottles. It was a face difficult to read at that distance. The barkeep, after answering the phone, had sounded quite agitated, but the one he had called Paul looked rock solid, pressing a finger along an eyebrow, then disappearing around a corner at the far end of the bar. Del Rebus eyed the hot-faced keep, deftly snapping the caps off Coronas, bantering with the clientele. His composure was back, or seemed to be. But my, he was an excitable lad.

Not like the one called Paul.

Someone jabbed his shoulder, a member of the small audience he had attracted. "C'mon partner, don't leave us hangin'. The pilot comes back . . . Hey Ruby, I'm buyin', set this man up!"

Del Rebus took another chomp from his jalapeño, felt the heat flare in his mouth, his lips go numb, his nasal passages suddenly flood, and loved every sensation, the sting of living once more. "Yeah," he said, mopping the sweat with a cocktail napkin. "He sees this priest, this rabbi, this black guy on the plane. He goes . . ."

Ruby finished his shift at four o'clock and went to the gym to work out for an hour. Afterward he sat in the whirlpool, showered, then drove to his apartment in Tempe, near the university. He phoned to have a pizza delivered, a large one with sausage and peppers and onions and an extra helping of mushrooms, then stripped down to his jockstrap and flopped on the foam-cushion couch, the standard brown complex model, popped the tab on a Bud Dry, and flipped through the channels on his twenty-seven-inch television with his hand-held remote, the TV and the gizmo both gifts from Paul.

He devoured the pizza watching *Entertainment Tonight.*

There was a segment on *ET* featuring a new Warren Beatty movie, something chock-full of action with outstanding sets. Ruby admired the graphics even as he winced at Warren Beatty in a trench coat, his collar turned up, machine-gunning automobiles packed with bad guys. It made killing look simple and necessary. Ruby could not believe murder was that easy a thing to do.

He spoke to some friends on the phone, then went into his bathroom, studied himself in the full-length mirrors of the closet doors, showered once again, toweled down, and applied an aromatic moisturizer to his face, his mammoth neck and shoulders, and his buttocks.

He donned baby blue bikini briefs, black spandex biking shorts with thick pink stripes down the hips, and a black tank top cut short halfway down his rib cage. He wore leather huaraches on his bare feet, size twelve. Back in front of the mirror once more, he admired the way the spandex showed off his business. He pushed his fingers through the still-damp hair on top of his head until he was pleased with the effect, then sprayed it with a mild setting agent. He drank another Bud Dry standing behind the sliding glass door to his balcony, overlooking the swimming pool, which was deserted at this hour.

He hopped into the used black Suzuki Samurai that Paul lent him from his dealership and sped across town to hang out in a west Phoenix club near Indian School Road, one that required a twenty-five-dollar annual membership fee and was five dollars a pop in addition to get past the bouncers. Paul owned the club and provided Ruby with a VIP Card, a thousand-dollar investment for free, unlimited, lifetime entry, in exchange for Ruby reporting on the management, any irregularities he might spot: watering drinks, shortchanging or in any way hustling the clientele. Ruby spent several hours at The Stallion Bar & Grill, shooting eight-pocket pool and dancing with several men, drinking club soda for the most part, downing an occasional Corona to show he was just another party animal. His outfit was a big success.

He made one phone call while he was there to report on a redheaded drag queen, a crystal freak suspected of drugging her johns and stripping them of their jewelry. Within a quarter hour two gentlemen, identifying themselves as friends of Paul, asked Ruby to point out the queen. They were guys in rumpled suits, like cops, but very polite, and thanked him, and left without making a scene.

Around ten Ruby departed the Stallion and tooled down to south Phoenix, pulled into Sport Time.

The bar was filled with players from the track. The musicians were on a break. The two keeps, friends of his, were definitely earning their money. He worked his way down to the end of the bar, beyond the servers' station, and was more than slightly amazed to see the old hippie still at the bar, although on a different stool, and apparently still conscious. Even more astonishing, he seemed to have attracted the undivided attention of the most beautiful woman in the establishment; Ruby watched a little longer and amended his opinion: she was the most beautiful woman ever to enter the establishment. Long dark hair, pulled taut to her head and held in place by combs, fanned out halfway down her back. She had high cheekbones, dark and sparkling eyes, full lips, something about the mold of her flawless face to suggest the Mediterranean, possibly a Gypsy ancestry. There was an aura about her, a calm bearing, and it was this, Ruby believed, that set her apart. There were some fine-looking women in Sport Time, and not all of them gaudy pop-star clones, but even the classier ones couldn't touch the lady next to the old hippie.

Paul Scorcese appeared suddenly at Ruby's elbow, to congratulate him for identifying the queen. He felt his ass squeezed affectionately. Ruby smirked and lifted his chin.

"You see that piece of gorgeous with the old hippie? What's he do, like own half of Camelback Mountain?"

Paul said, "I don't know yet. But I'll tell you this: he's got con all over him. He might as well be wearing a sign."

Chapter 8

They had agreed if Del did not return by seven, they would have dinner together at a small Italian restaurant Elvis had discovered in north Phoenix. Franny left a note on the night-stand on Del's side of the bed, and they drove the freeway north to Bell Road, then east to the restaurant. Because they did not have reservations, they had to wait in the bar after leaving Elvis's name with the maître d', a short, compact man with graying curls and a warm, enthusiastic manner.

There was seating at the bar for a dozen patrons, with several small alcoves where from four to six people might sit while awaiting a table. Elvis and Franny, after some negotiating, managed to secure two stools together along the brief bar. She ordered a glass of white wine, whatever was the house variety. He requested Russian vodka, a double, poured over shaved ice.

"I like this place," said Franny Lott, when the waitress went away. "The way Del talks about Phoenix, I despaired of finding anything remotely attractive, except behind the bars in the zoo."

"Good and bad in every city. You make trade-offs wherever you go."

"Not to hear Del tell it. It's very personal for him. His folks moved here when he was fifteen, from Ann Arbor, Michigan."

"That's right," said Elvis, "now I remember. His daddy was a professor at the university."

"English professor. They moved out here for his mother's health, and because his father wanted to open a bookstore, using a small family inheritance."

"Uh-oh. I never heard this part, but I can guess."

The lady bartender in the buttoned-up white blouse brought their drinks and set paper napkins beneath them. She hesitated, as if she wanted to inquire, but moved away, her eyes still on Franny Lott.

They touched glasses. Franny's eyes drifted, studied her wine. "Yes, I imagine you can. The business was in trouble from day one, but his father struggled at it for close to five years. Del was going to school when the store folded. He came back from Ann Arbor to sell what was left of the inventory from the back of a station wagon. After a while, he couldn't stand it, sitting at street corners beneath an umbrella, with the hand-painted signs and his father drinking bottles of cooking sherry." Franny Lott shrugged. "So he fled. He was a kid and he was tired of being bummed out. Now he's got this enormous guilt for abandoning his father, and he's laying it off on this city. That's why I asked you what this payback was all about. There's something very visceral about his feeling for this town. I just . . . I'm not into violence, Elvis."

He lowered his glass, letting the vodka filter through his system. "Well, chile, like you said: you can always walk away."

She looked at him with her eyes wide, full of surprise and hurt. "I thought we were friends."

"We are."

"I was trying to be honest."

"Me too," said Elvis. "Look: you think I don't know the guy's a handful? I got eyes, Franny. He talks a lotta stuff, too, about games he sat in on and how much he walked away with, since he's been outta there, and I have a brother, Bobby Muhammed, who's in a position to know, he checked out the stories, and guess what? According to my brother's sources, Del isn't telling the half of it. The man is awesome."

"I already told you that."

"So what you're saying, you want to protect me from the consequences of being his friend."

"Alert you is more like it," she said. "I guess I've always geared myself for contingencies. That way, when boredom and contempt coincide, you can walk out on a marriage into the arms of a man like Del and know it was a right move, even if it most likely won't last. People born into money have the luxury of thinking that way, Elvo. Or maybe it's the obligation."

Elvis Mahoney let the remainder of his vodka muddle through him before he could respond. "You?" he said.

"My family owns racetracks, thoroughbreds, estates in Kentucky, Florida, and a summer place in the Hamptons. I am not a romantic like Del. I don't have that kind of courage."

The maître d' approached, both hands in the air, inviting them to descend from their stools.

Franny Lott said, "That's our second secret. I promise not to burden you with more."

The waiters were attentive and the food was magic, vanished from their forks. The maître d' visited them with a crystal pitcher of ice water, inquiring as to their satisfaction, and departed with a smile from Franny Lott that made him ache with desire.

She was saying, "Seriously?"

"Honest. I'd spend hours back there reading cookbooks, imagining meals like this. It seemed like a saner use of my time than dreaming about ladies."

"How about the violin?"

Elvis made a sound of dismissal, sucking through his teeth. "I got into my body as an instrument," he said. "Of survival."

"You aren't going back to your music, then."

"Chile, I got to do what I got to do. Me and Del, we don't have no racetracks in the family. We're just trying to get on. He's got an idea, and I bought into it, and that's all this is about. Maybe I'll make enough to open my own restaurant."

She looked at him across the bright white tablecloth
and closed her eyes, and opened them. "I hope so."

The waiter came up with a dessert list, but they balked,
ordered cups of espresso instead. They eyed one another,
sorting things out. When the waiter returned with the demi-
tasses of espresso, he set beside each a crystal cordial glass
containing sambouca. "Compliments of the maître d'," he
explained. "And he apologizes to the lady, whom he is certain he has seen in the movies, but cannot remember her
name."

"Please tell him there is no need to apologize," she said.
"I am not an actress. Although he's a shameless flirt. But how
else could he be, being Italian?"

Across the crowded tables Franny Lott caught the attention of the maître d' and silently mouthed her apprecia-
tion.

"Will that be all?" asked the waiter, and when Elvis expressed his confidence that it would be, the computer-
printed tab was left facedown beside his plate, the bar bill
enumerated on the backside.

"On me," said Franny Lott. She opened her wallet and
pushed a sheaf of twenties across the table. "I don't want to
be embarrassed if your plastic's no good."

"Del says, long as we pay the minimum, we're home
free."

"Del is a charming, and charmed, man, but God he is
not."

She wrinkled her nose at him.

Elvis Mahoney touched a napkin to the corners of his
mouth. "No, he ain't. But the man delivers."

Finished with her liqueur and coffee, Franny Lott said,

"I'm going to phone the hotel. If he's not there, I want to see what shape he's in. Will you come with?"

"I wouldn't have it no other way," he said.

Inside the Charger in the Sport Time parking lot, the engine on and the Freon fighting the heat, Elvis told Franny Lott, "Case you haven't noticed, this is a white-bread city. Means a black man and a white woman together get noticed. Whereas a nigger by himself in a place like this is just another loser. You go in and find Del. I'll be in there, case there's any problem, but otherwise you don't know me from what's left in the ashtrays."

He waited five minutes after she'd left, punching the options on his radio, running the FM gamut. He picked up on a Wynton Marsalis piece piped in from a Globe station, Globe being a copper town, a company town that the company, Dodge, all but shut down. Bayou jazz piped out of a dying ore district: there was poetry, thought Elvis. There was stretch. That was even reason to believe there was something to believe in, if the something could be identified. Elvis called it Del Rebus.

He had learned some of what he hoped to learn, and he was content, having tapered off the booze without calling attention to it. He had bullshitted with several attorneys, aides to state legislators, an assistant to a U.S. senator, and a flock of lobbyists, and had accumulated the kind of details that were especially persuasive when dropping names. Del Rebus had done his work for the night. He was trying to ease off, edge around the bitterness that in all honesty had brought him here, the main attraction, when a vision of something at last right in his life touched his shoulder. Franny.

She tugged on the sprout of hair at the nape of his neck. "You lonely, soldier?"

"Frances, you don't know the half of it."

"You mind?"

She settled on a stool beside him and they kissed. It was a long, exploratory kiss.

She explained where Elvis was and why, and he nodded, approving.

He stroked her cheek tenderly, with something like amazement. "Buy the lady a drink?" he inquired.

"A glass of ice water would be delicious."

"Not the water from the taps in this town. How about some of that French fizzwater?"

"Lovely." She took his hand in hers and kissed his knuckles. "Darling, have you eaten anything?"

"Hamburgs. Real goddamn ones cooked on a grill."

"I thought I tasted onions in that kiss. My God, I don't believe I've seen this many bola ties in my lifetime."

Del glanced around. "People do fancy them in this town."

"I hate them." She pushed her fingers above her eyebrows. "They look like something designed for Nazis."

He touched her cheek once more, then turned his head, hollered at the nearest barkeep, calling him by name. Her glass of sparkling water arrived with a twist of lemon in it. It surprised her that he ordered nothing to drink for himself, as there was no glass in front of him, only a package of ciga-rettes, his lighter, and his wallet. He lit one of the cigarettes, and the smoke almost made her gag.

She put down her glass. "What in the world are you smoking, road kill?"

"Gauloises," he said. "Haven't had one for years. Picked up a taste for them from my father. When we lived in Michi-gan, he'd smoke one after breakfast with a second cup of coffee, a book open at his fingertips. And one before dinner with a martini with my mother, the two of them trading campus gossip. Smoked a pipe the rest of the time. You have to understand something, Frances, they had a son and daughter into their teens when I sneaked up to surprise them. Abortions were still a dicey business back then. My mother was forty-one, no longer an active ballerina, but thank God still healthy, when I was born. My father was sixty when I first tasted tobacco. Smoking a Gauloise the way my father did, that was the epitome of civilized. It was a perfect blend of desire and discipline. Am I losing you?"

"Not for an instant, darling."

"He had thick silver hair. He was the picture of an aristocrat."

"I'm certain he was, given a son like you."

"He was a fool, Frances. He equated intelligence with understanding. He didn't have a fucking clue."

"You mean Phoenix? He moved here for love. Your mother's health, wasn't it?"

"Yeah. I guess so. Anyway, it's a good excuse for defeat."

She put her face close to his. "Del? Did you have any trouble in here earlier? There's a blond creature over your left shoulder, at the end of the bar, he's giving us some pretty intense looks."

Del Rebus dropped his chin, raised it, let his eyes drift, and drift, until he recognized the day keep, down by the servers' station, the guy with the birthstone name. Ruby. Yeah, Ruby. And whoa . . . look at this: right behind the behemoth, *intimately* behind the behemoth if his jail time counted as education, stood the sleek, composed gent by the name of Paul.

"No," said Del Rebus. "No trouble. The blond muscle is a bartender here. He likes boys."

"I like men," whispered Franny Lott. "If you're free for the night, soldier, let's go back to the hotel."

"I like your style, Frances."

"I like all of you," she said.

"You drive," he said, leaving a twenty-dollar bill on the bar as a tip and handing her the keys to the rental car.

"Follow them," said Paul.

"The old hippie and his lady?" said Ruby.

"Yes, Ruby. Yes. Call here when you have an address."

"You mean follow them in the Suzuki."

"Yes. And if they stop somewhere and get out to walk, you stop and get out to walk. You got the idea now? I'm a little shorthanded at the moment, or I wouldn't ask. You think you can help me?"

"Sure, Paul. I sure can."

Fifteen minutes later the phone was ringing at Sport Time, Ruby on the line for Paul. Paul picked up in his office beyond the kitchen. "Yeah?"

"They're staying at the Hoyt on Adams. I know a guy on the desk. They're in a bridal suite. A Mr. and Mrs. Irwin Field."

Paul Scorcese thought about that, smoothing an eyebrow with his middle finger. "Thanks, Ruby," he said at last. "You kept your distance, they didn't spot you?"

"No way. As soon as I saw it was the Hoyt they were going into, I didn't, like, get close to the place for a while. My roommate Whitney is the desk guy."

"The Suzuki, Ruby? Tomorrow I'll sign the papers. It's yours, sweetmeat."

"Like, for real?"

"What'd I just say?"

"Yeah. Wow. Uh, you, like, did you, should I come back there or what?"

"I got a business to run, Ruby. Not tonight. But we'll talk. We'll talk soon."

"Whatever."

In the phone booth next to the one Ruby used in the Hoyt, Elvis Mahoney cradled the receiver and watched the blond hulk shamble across the lobby, disappear into the night. He ascended in the elevator, knocked on the door of the bridal suite. Franny Lott answered in a nearly diaphanous gown, the room dark behind her. Elvis Mahoney lowered his eyes and looked away. "He still awake?"

"Taking a shower. Elvo, what is it?"

"Somebody had you followed from Sport Time. A big blond guy. He made a phone call from the lobby."

"A black tank top, pink stripe on his shorts?"

"That's him."

"Jesus." Franny Lott slapped the door. "I knew it. I knew it. What the hell's Del doing, Elvo?"

"Just making friends, far as I know. But tell him in the morning. Meantime, somebody knocks on this door, don't you answer it. Call me instead."

"Why?"

"While I was in Durango, I found out my eye-hand coordination wasn't too bad. I picked up a three fifty-seven Magnum."

"You trying to scare me?"

"Alert you is all," he said. "It's what friends are for."

He was halfway between the elevators and the suite when he heard her say, "Flamingos in Phoenix, right?"

Elvis Mahoney waved a hand at her without turning around, uncertain of how much he agreed with the remark. Or if he did. That was the trouble with a lady like Franny Lott: she mucked up a man's thinking. But he had done jail. He would survive Franny Lott, too.

Chapter 9

Doctors prohibited the police from interviewing the Baker close to four weeks, in spite of repeated personal requests from the Queens borough president, the district attorney, and the chief inspector of homicide, Moriarity. While the time passed, the city of New York paid uniformed officers to stand beside the door to the Baker's hospital suite. Standing along with them around the clock were people from the Scorcese organization. There was some tension at first, but within a few days policemen were seen venturing as far as the phone booths to call out for a delivery of coffees and Danish, hamburgs, a pizza with the works.

On the morning of the second Monday in June, Lieutenant D. James Cox and Detective First Grade Wallace Fitzsimmons gained entrance to the wing where Joseph Vincent
Scorcese resided. They were ushered by a candy striper to an
alcove where there were two bench-hard couches facing one
another, and some chairs done in a tweedy gray fabric, with
an elevated television beyond them that was located at an
awkward ninety-degree angle to the seating. Cox, before sitting, hiked up his trousers to prolong the life of the knees.
The walls of the alcove were painted a cheery melon color,
and there were framed prints hung on them. Some tall green
broadleaf plants in ceramic tubs had been strategically
placed amongst the chairs to provide the illusion of privacy.
The various flora held no attraction for Cox. The broad
leaves reminded him of obedient patients asked by the doctor to say, "Ah." Wallace Fitzsimmons, having flopped on the
couch opposite him, got one of his menthol cigarettes going
and cocked his head, drawn by a morning-show interview
with an actor known for his megadeath movies. Cox re-
viewed the notes he had made in a small spiral notebook,
pausing to remember the conversation with Takimoto, the
guy's excitement or hunger, that edge that made him a valu-
able cop. One that still cared, believed. Cox, knowing his
clout was nil, swore to himself that he would call in some old
accounts, find someone to be Kenny's rabbi, boost him. He
popped a disc of dried plum and scratched away with a
ballpoint, reworking some of the questions he intended to
ask the Don.

He had dressed for the interview with purpose. The
pale gray suit with chalk-color pinstripes and a pale gray
fedora, this was a look of respect without being funereal. His

tie was a flat charcoal of some woven material. The shirt white, the nails manicured, the beard and hair professionally cut: Lieutenant D. James Cox was going to give it his best shot. He had never probed a man of the Baker's stature.

Another candy striper, a young blond girl barely out of high school, with braces on her teeth and a pair of zoom-bobwahs Fitzsimmons couldn't take his eyes off of, led them into the presence of possibly the most powerful man in the state of New York. Passing the police officer in blue and the family rep, Cox at last got a glimpse of the man, a frail hump of hips and legs beneath a white sheet, wearing a maroon silk bathrobe, white hairs visible on his chest, the hair on his head cartoon-ink black.

There was a woman on a chair beside his bed, a small woman with magenta nails, different-colored eyes, the general aspect of a fortune-teller. She was swathed from ankle to throat in a black dress with no sleeves, plenty of silver in evidence—bracelets, earrings, a pendant between her breasts, a lump of amethyst set in a shield of it pinned to the black turban that hid her hair. Her skin was pale white and there were freckles on her arms. She rose on the far side of the bed and lifted the old man's hand in hers and brushed it with her lips, whispered something. Cox and Fitzsimmons stood with the candy striper at a respectable distance, in an anteroom, waiting for the small woman to come around the end of the bed. "Grazie, Juanita," they heard the old man croak.

"Tia," she said. "Tia Juanita is how I am called, Padrino."

"So be it, child. So be it."

Lieutenant Cox lifted his fedora and nodded as the small lady passed, perplexed that he couldn't identify her, because he was certain he'd seen her before. Possibly the costume confused him, or the circumstances. Fitzsimmons leaned down over his ear and hissed, "Wild. You notice one eye is blue, one green?"

On the near side of the Don's bed, that they couldn't see until they entered the room proper, sat the *consigliere*, the Don's second son, Lorenzo ("Hey, call me Larry, know whaddime saying?"), a Park Avenue tax attorney whose legal skills and degree had been honed on the island of Grenada, at the college there. What he did, so far as Cox understood it, he owned a firm of Ivy League legal minds whose primary endeavor was to protect Scorcese assets, and occasionally, for publicity purposes, to take on the case of some schnook battling the bureaucracy in an effort to establish legal precedents.

Lorenzo stood up when the cops came into view and shook hands with them. He was dressed in a silk suit, the cut and tailoring of which suggested that Cox's outfit possessed all the sophistication of a loincloth. He was a short man with the matinee-idol looks of his younger brother, Paul, but with the edge in his voice that he could put there at will, the quiet malice. His black hair was cut very conservatively and not a whisker on his cheek had escaped the razor. A dry, brusque cologne hung in the air after the handshake, the scent of a man serious in all matters. He indicated two chairs to the right of his, away from the bed, and said, "Gentlemen, please, be seated. We are prepared to cooperate in any and all ways, but as I'm sure you can understand, conserving my father's energy is a priority. He lost a good deal of blood.

The trauma to his system cannot be underestimated. There are gaps in his memory. Worse"—and here Lorenzo glanced back at his father, whose eyes were closed, his head in a pile of plumped-up pillows, the clear plastic pouches of IV solutions feeding him even as he slept—"the old bastard is losing his grip. He's like a child, know whaddime saying? Can be talking quite normally, and all of a sudden—like that—he's whining for some chocolate ice cream. The doctors describe it as protosenility, an early stage hastened by the trauma of the attack."

Lieutenant Cox, who sat next to Lorenzo Scorcese, said, "You mind I get something clear?"

"By all means," responded the *consigliere*.

"It's your position, or it's gonna be, that this particular victim of a shooting on the fourteenth of May, in a bakery on Metropolitan Avenue, that this particular victim is incompetent as a witness to that assault?"

"We will answer any question we can, Lieutenant."

"Lemme talk to him," Cox said, coming out of his chair.

Lorenzo Scorcese rose with him. "He is a weak and tired old man, Lieutenant. Please be so good as to sit down. There aren't going to be any station-house shenanigans, know whaddime saying?" He unbuttoned his suit coat to show them the slender recording device in the pocket of his monogrammed white shirt. "As you gentlemen know, it's perfectly legal to record one's conversations."

Cox, still standing, glanced over at his partner, Fitzsimmons, to see if he appreciated the joke here, the game that was being run on them. Fitzsimmons sat impassively, an ankle resting on a knee, stroking his handlebar mustache, his eyes off somewhere, beguiled by the contours of a candy striper. Cox grinned ruefully, pulling up his trousers to sit down. To be saddled with Fitzsimmons while a clock-watcher like McClanahan partnered with a young cop of Takimoto's character seemed so unjust as to be pathetically funny. Not so funny, but cute, very cute, was the strategy being employed by the Scorcese family.

"You mind if I talk to your father?"

"Not at all. Ask me anything."

"So that it's you and me that's having the conversation, right?"

"My father's command of English, since the tragedy, it's not so good. I can translate."

"I heard him a few minutes ago. He sounded fine."

Lorenzo Scorcese shrugged, opened his hands, palms up. "What can I say? He has his good moments. But the point is, I'm not going to permit you to stress him out."

D. James Cox slipped a wafer of dried plum into his mouth and tugged on his nose, took out his spiral pad and touched the tip of his ballpoint to his tongue. "What the fuck," he said, "we're here. Let's at least go through the motions."

An hour later a disgusted D. James Cox flipped his spiral pad shut, thanked the Don via Lorenzo for his time, and slapped Fitzsimmons on the shoulder with the back of his hand, jarring him awake. They stood up. Lorenzo stood up. The Don's eyes were closed once more and he appeared to be breathing through his mouth. D. James Cox adjusted the hat on his head for the longest time.

"You mind I ask," he said at last, "the pretty little lady was in here ahead of us, who was that, Lorenzo?"

"Larry."

"Right. Larry. Who was she?"

"I wish I could help you, Lieutenant."

"You're just jam-packed with good intentions, aren't you, counselor? That's all I listened to for a fucking hour."

"Honestly, Lieutenant. The little broad claims to be a psychic. Says she can identify the guy who put together the hit on my father. Turns out she's totally out to lunch, know whaddime saying? My father humored her to get rid of her, just as you witnessed. That's all that was about."

Lieutenant D. James Cox jogged the brim of his hat one more time, sneered, and said, "Lorenzo, if things don't work out in the business you're in, look to religion. The Jesuits could use a boy like you. I should know. I was almost two years in the order myself. So don't waste your time and mine trying to shit a shitter, okay?"

Once the room was empty of police, Lorenzo Scorcese addressed his father in the language of the land where he was born. "You heard?"

The old man's eyelids fluttered. "The fat one, Cox, do not ever trifle with him. He is a serious man."

"And the little fortune-teller?"

The old man's eyelids closed, and he emitted an audible hiss. "Is that business in your shirt pocket turned off?"

"Of course."

"Put it in my hand, ZoZo."

"Yes, Father." The *consigliere* placed the device in the Don's palm, then got up to turn on the television, entered the private bathroom and twisted the tap so that the cold water was gushing full force. He leaned over his father, who was completely awake now, his small black eyes glittering. "I don't like the little broad's description," said Lorenzo. "I don't like what it's got me thinking."

"It is not a matter of what we like. It is a matter of preserving the family. You understand this?"

"Yes."

"Then you know what to say to Paul."

"Nothing."

"Exactly. Now I want you to arrange for my release. Hire some nurses, whatever I require. I do not want to be breathing this hospital air by tomorrow."

"It will be done."

"Oh. And my son? Tomorrow night I wish to have a conversation with Vacanza. Alone."

Lorenzo Scorcese patted his father's small, dry, crabbed hand, the fingers bent up from the knuckles from something the doctors called Dupuytren's syndrome. It had been diagnosed at the Mayo Clinic in Rochester, Minnesota, and surgeons that the clinic recommended cut away at tissue in the Don's palm, to alleviate the condition. Aesthetically, the effect of the surgery was nil, the fingers were still crimped, but some manual strength had been restored, and the Don could handle a knife and fork, sign a check, even withstand a handshake, if it was gentle.

Kissing the crippled hand, Lorenzo Scorcese said, "Patience before discipline, Father. It is always what you taught us."

The Don's eyelids fluttered momentarily. "Then do not waste my time by reminding me. Go. Do as I say to you."

Tia Juanita took the F train out of Queens, transferred at Lexington Avenue to an uptown IRT. Because of the hour of the day, there were no seats in the car, so she gripped a pole, preferring that to the uncomfortable stretch of hanging on to a hand strap. The air-conditioning, if it was operating at all, certainly did not measure up to that on the F train; within a minute she could feel sweat percolating beneath her turban, questing from her armpits, from the underside of her breasts. At the Eighty-sixth Street stop enough people departed for her to find a seat. Sitting back on the hard plastic, a large black leather purse in her lap, her toes barely grazing the floor, she surveyed the car through enormous dark glasses. The inhabitants were predominantly young, predominantly black and brown.

Tia Juanita was forty years of age, with smooth skin and a supple figure, which she attributed to her diet (plenty of fresh fruit and nuts, steamed vegetables and brown rice, with tea or fruit juice). She neither smoked nor drank alcohol. She practiced yoga after a fashion. Concealed beneath the black turban was flame-colored hair and a temperament to match. She was exceedingly pale for a Puerto Rican, but it meant nothing on the island of her birth. There, unlike apparently anywhere else in the world, pigmentation was a matter of indifference. To be Puerto Rican was to be part of an extended family.

Tia Juanita, staring without seeing into her large dark purse, reflected upon this aspect of her heredity and took comfort in it. For a woman whose bouts with endometriosis had finally ended in defeat, or so the doctors told her, saying that childbirth was out of the question, the cohesion of family had a particular allure. She had known Luis Cortez was trouble when she took him into her bed, but as many women do, she succumbed to the idea that good loving equated with good therapy. She had long ago recognized she was wrong, even if the physical business between them continued, albeit sporadically. But however stupid or evil Luis Cortez had been while he lived, he was still family. It was not the place of outsiders to determine his fate, and that was what galled, what hacked at her heart. It was *she* who should have either ratted him out, or murdered him in his sleep.

Because she knew.

Because she experienced in her nightmares, having listened to him in his, the barbarity that was becoming routine to him, in exchange for walking-around money.

Because he had bragged to her. The opportunity of a lifetime if he didn't blow it. A chance for him to make the kind of money that if he used it right, he wouldn't have to perform those tasks that woke them in the night with the sweat and screaming. And all he asked of her was to cast his horoscope for a propitious day to take action.

Because she had stalled him with false readings, in an attempt to learn the details of the deal. Luis Cortez only mentioned in passing that his new employer was a big man with a single brow of hair above his small eyes, like the pictures of primitive men in newspapers. Not from Luis Cortez, but from people in the street, she acquired a rough description of a meet that took place the day before the attempt on a Mafia don. In a Chinese restaurant. She cultivated the place by herself, left large tips. After a couple of weeks, she probed the waiters and waitresses. Their descriptions so aptly matched with the vague one from Luis Cortez that she felt brave enough to put through a call to the hospital.

"Mr. Joseph Scorcese, please, or whoever is empowered to speak for him."

Time passed. "Yes?"

"Mr. Scorcese?"

"This is Larry. Who is this please?"

"I have information."

"So does Ma Bell. I'm not impressed."

"Because this line is probably tapped, I'm not even going to try. To impress you, I mean."

"Go on."

"One of the boys who came into the bakery that morning, I know him."

"Room number four hundred, lady. Ask for Lorenzo. Expect to be felt up plenty before you're permitted in the room. Security takes precedence over manners, know whaddime saying?"

"Si. I do."

And she was.

And Joseph Vincent Scorcese, a man who had done well by his family, lay alone in a hospital room taking his nourishment from tubes, his old body hooked up to monitors and machines, left alone to contemplate the incomprehensible evil of a son who would attempt to murder his father.

Chapter 10

Field, Murdock Investment Consultants operated out of a suite of offices off Scottsdale Road, north of Camelback, in a complex anchored by a California bank. The company advertised in bold print in the 5100 section of the Sunday classifieds, under the heading of Business Opportunities. What Field, Murdock offered, depending upon the requirements of its clients, were quick, lucrative returns on speculative ventures or vehicles by which income could be legitimately sheltered. On file, for any client's perusal, there existed a rainbow array of four color prospectuses. This was not a company that serviced a client who had a thousand dollars saved from a year's labor—no, fifty K was the minimal sum necessary before the shiny potentials, spelled out in numbers, were shown on the shiny, four-color paper. But what especially attracted investors was Field, Murdock's paltry service fee of 1 percent. Most firms charged 5, 6, even 8 1/2 percent. As Field, Murdock explained it, their strategy was based upon confidence in a high degree of success, so that while they required a minuscule sum for service up front, if the deal flew, they would participate in 10 percent of the profit, *not the principal.* Who would not pay a dime for a dollar of profit?

The offices, a reception area, and two spacious rooms done in mauve and plum with pale gray carpet occupied a niche on the second floor. At each end of the floor were rest rooms for the tenants with key-only entrance. The suite overlooked a parking lot bordered by fan palms. Beyond the fan palms was a small greenbelt with a shallow reflecting pool, part of the grounds of an adjoining hotel complex. Gazebos roofed with orange tile had been erected at either end of the pool, presumably to encourage private conversation, suggest a place for lovers to rendezvous, although in the heat of a July afternoon it was doubtful even the most passionate couples would venture to spend five minutes out there. This was the time of year when the desert prevailed over the spirit, when the inhabitants of the city, their emotions rubbed raw in the blunt air, reeked of menace and aberration.

With a fraudulent five-hundred-thousand-dollar letter of credit created by the same jail contact that had put together the bogus Master/Visa cards, Del Rebus negotiated six months of free rent, given the lousy market in commercial property, in exchange for a signed lease of five years, with a five-year option to renew. The landlords, a California consortium, were so desperate for tenants that they even subsidized the improvements, the paint and carpeting, the brass lettering on the door. The improvements, according to the lease, would be picked up in the CAM charges (Common Area Maintenance), which included all sorts of unanticipated and incontestable costs. It was a form of subtle extortion that a small business was helpless against.

Unless that small business happened to be Field, Murdock, a company designed not to be honest and industrious, that is, the screwee, but, addressing the real world, had strictly organized itself to screw the screwers.

Not all of Elvis Mahoney's time in the prison library had been devoted to poring over cookbooks; indeed, he had developed, as a result of his predicament, a rather keen interest in the law. It seemed, initially, to be a body of machinations constructed over the centuries for the benefit, chiefly, of a single fraternity of individuals: lawyers. On the particular charge responsible for putting him away, he read the case law, tracing the key case, *Solitro v State*, 165 So.2d223. He tracked down every avenue of appeal his reading suggested, and every one of them wound up in a dead end. But he found the reading of law fascinating, like a score of music, the play of nuance and interpretation. When he mentioned this during a walk in the yard, Del Rebus asked him if he had ever read a stock prospectus. Elvis hadn't. Del said he had a ton of them, because his daddy had done some investing, how about Elvis looking them over, since he had the ability to translate legalese into English. Elvis did. Elvis told him that a prospectus, boiled down, consisted of puffery with plenty of figures to support it, and a convenient covenant that released the issuers of the offer from any financial responsibility, should the venture fail. Del Rebus simply nodded.

On the day after Elvis's release from Lompoc, he and Del went to the beach, Franny preferring to spend the morning at the zoo. They rented a beach umbrella and sat in low-slung canvas chairs with a cooler full of ice-cold Michelobs, several cornbeefs on rye, dill pickles and cucumbers sliced lengthwise and wrapped in aluminum foil. Del Rebus wore a navy blue duckbilled Chargers hat, and they both wore shades, their eyes all over the beach, drinking in the multitude of feminine charms. Elvis said that if he had had the sense to wear a hat, it'd be resting on his crotch, so that he could relax and let his dick take its natural course.

Elvis waded out and dived into the surf, dived again and again and again. He came out of the cold water into the sun feeling cleansed, and full of purpose. Del snapped a cap, placed a chilled bottle in his hand. Radios from nearby blankets favored them with everything from contemporary pop to salsa to soul to rap to vintage Dead to eye-in-the-sky traffic control. Del told him a joke about a German and a Finn who had just become acquainted in a bar.

Then he leaned out of his beach chair, his forearm on the cooler that rested between them beneath the umbrella, and said, "You know what we are, you and me, we're two guys who've been royally fucked."

Elvis Mahoney looked out at the surf, thundering and creaming as it broke, uncertain about his response, how to phrase it. He tilted the bottle to his lips for a long, deep swallow, then belched. "You saw my jacket, but I didn't do the kind of time you did to have that kind of juice. I heard . . . the whisper was you did a guy."

Turning, he saw Del Rebus lift his dark glasses and park them on the bill of his cap, pinch the bridge of his nose, his eyes closed. Something, a brief trembling, surfaced in his face, and was gone.

"I did what was necessary to survive in there," said Del. "Some of us are more imaginative than others. Remind me to tell you about it sometime."

"How about now?"

Del Rebus repositioned the glasses on the bridge of his nose. "I'll tell you this: I killed a man. I thought it was the right thing to do at the time, and I still do. Just like it was the right thing for you to do, breaking that biker mother's arms with a tire iron. The judge and the jury and the attorneys, *they weren't there, in your skin.* At the trial, did anyone address the life-and-death situation you found yourself in? You know they fucking didn't, Elvis. They argued the applicable law. They fenced over words in a book. You weren't a person, you were an opportunity for some assholes to get into a bloodless argument, see who could be crowned smart guy for a day."

Del probed for a cold bottle, cracked the cap, and sucked up the hops. Del's hand, the one holding the bottle to his lips, shook visibly, a display of emotion that Elvis had never before witnessed and thought it prudent not to push.

"You got that right," Elvis said. "It's one thing to get fucked. It's something else, getting fucked as if you aren't even there."

When the entirety of the bottle had dropped down Del's throat, he took it from his lips, lifted the top of the cooler, and gently disposed of it, with a manner that suggested he was launching a model boat. He was the old Del once more.

He settled back in the canvas chair, scraped his fingers in the sand, and rolled his face in Elvis's direction, his lips curled up at the corners, with the knowing, nasty grin. He leaned over and spit in the sand. "I don't give a hump for the law anymore. But you know what I'd like?"

"Justice?"

"Too late for that, Sparky. No, what I'm looking for, partner, I'm looking for payback. Compensation. I'm willing to do it any way I can, even working for it. But card playing, good as I am, isn't enough. Gambling is all a matter of edge. It takes a lot out of you. Gamblers, truly disciplined ones, might have slightly longer careers than athletes, but not by much. What I'm saying, while I've still got that edge, I want to get back into living as fully and fast as possible. There's fifteen years of schemes between these ears. I've got a master counterfeiter did ten years with me operates a tattoo parlor in San Francisco, he's in; he's the guy that'll put together all our ID, plus letters of credit. Another guy I jailed with that got sent up for computer theft will take care of providing us with credit cards, create and document our backgrounds. So all that I'm lacking is someone I can trust who can read, write, and talk the legal bullshit. You, Elvis. How'm I doing?"

"You're scaring the shit out of me is what you're doing. I'm one day out of the joint, Del, and you're proposing what?"

"That you will remain anonymous among each other, known only to me, so that if we blow it, I'll take the dive, solo. Only we aren't going to blow it. It's going to be a thing of beauty."

Elvis glanced at him beneath the umbrella, saw still the old Del, but no smile on his lips, his eyes locked on the horizon. The man was putting himself on the line. Elvis did not doubt him for an instant.

"Del," he said, "how much we talking about?"

There was the smile again, curling up at the corners. "Seed money, Sparky. In three to six months, I guarantee we'll snag between a mil and ten times that. Seed money for a life. Think about it."

One of the tax shelters offered by Field, Murdock that had proved most popular in the five weeks of the company's existence involved purchasing shares in pedigreed greyhounds. The animals were all qualified runners registered with the state commission, and Field, Murdock even went so far as to grade the offerings like bonds, so that a particular dog could receive anywhere from a triple-A rating, down to a B. Nothing lower than a B-grade creature was recommended by Field, Murdock. The higher the rating, naturally, the more the investor paid per share. Half of the investor's share in the winnings would be returned on an end-of-month basis, and the other half of the investor's share of winnings would be applied toward upkeep of the animal. Because it was a high-risk venture (after all, some dogs *were* dogs, as the prospectus candidly joked), the investor could take a 10 percent tax credit on the money he or she had invested. The beauty of the offering was that, in a worst-case scenario, a winless wonder, every bit of the money could be written off. As against the possibility of buying into a winner, which meant not only an immediate return, but the enormous profits to be reaped in stud service, greyhound shares were selling briskly. Ads in *The Wall Street Journal, Barron's,* the Sunday editions in New York, Los Angeles, Chicago, Detroit, and Dallas had already paid for themselves, plus the cost of purchasing an 800 number and a recording machine for the weekends.

Field, Murdock was also doing a keen, if minor, business selling shares in dairy cows, offering the same 10 percent tax credit. There wasn't the sex appeal of a big score, but the calls and credit-card numbers trickled in from Missouri, Kansas, the Dakotas, and Texas, even from as far as upstate New York. The milkers were all blue-ribbon stock, registered with and endorsed by the National Dairy Farmers Association.

Any investor could check out his particular four-footed investment, in order to corroborate the information in the prospectus, and would find that indeed the animal was so registered. What the prospectus neglected to mention, and was legally not bound to mention, was the fact that registrations were updated on an annual basis, beginning with the calendar year.

Field, Murdock specialized in marketing shares of animals already completely depreciated. Recently deceased dogs. Decomposing cows. Phantom shelters.

Besides setting up the office suite in Scottsdale, Del Rebus had signed a lease, with the letter of credit as collateral, for a house in Paradise Valley, off Doubletree Drive. The house was a four-bedroom adobe with washed-out sautillo tile throughout, an indoor spa off the master bedroom, an Olympic-size pool, and two clay tennis courts equipped with lights for play at night. It occupied an acre and a half of land that required the services of a professional landscaper on a weekly basis, at a cost of approximately one thousand dollars a month. The house, fully furnished, rented for ten times that amount, but it had been sitting tenantless for five months, so when Del Rebus said he'd agree to seven five a month, in exchange for signing a year's lease, the managing agent for the property experienced something like religious ecstasy. She knew that the Japanese bank that held the paper on the house would have settled for half what Del offered. She could feel her star rising in the realty firmament, and on the strength of it purchased a cellular phone for her black BMW 320 coupe. What she did not know was that neither she nor the bank would receive a single penny in rent. The landscapers, a husband and wife by the name of Lopez, were promptly paid, as were the cook and housekeeper, a pair of young Swedes by the name of Inge and Rolf. But nobody else.

In the two months they had been situated in Phoenix, Del Rebus had become a fixture in the bars of the tonier golf courses in the Valley, Paradise Valley and Orangetree in particular, although he felt a certain nostalgia for Sport Time and would periodically drop in there, chatting up the clientele and watching his backside to see if he was followed. He never was, and came to the conclusion that Elvis had suffered from an overdose of imagination—possibly to impress Franny.

Elvis had composed a routine for himself: upon waking at dawn, he jogged from the house on Doubletree down to

Camelback Mountain (something of an exaggeration of terminology), up the slope and down, and back to the house. Laps in the pool and then half an hour pumping weights on the patio with Del. Franny Lott would accompany Elvis on bicycle down to Camelback and back when she was in town, but she had flown east in June for a nephew's bar mitzvah and was currently in California, huddled with attorneys attempting to finalize her divorce.

In her absence, Del became, if such a thing were possible, even more gregarious. It was as if he could not be comfortable alone in any other condition than passed out. Several nights around the midnight hour, Elvis was summoned to Sport Time, Del knowing he was incapable of negotiating the drive back to Paradise Valley. It was some consolation to Elvis that Del, even in a bad way, had the presence to know it; the man's behavior was stupid, but not reckless. He understood his limits even in a state of derangement.

And the next morning he was there on the patio when Elvis returned from his run up the mountain, a cup of coffee at hand on the glass-topped table, smoking a cigarette with a book open in front of him (he despised the papers), waiting for Elvis to finish his laps. Currently he was reading *The Origin of Consciousness* by a guy named Jaynes, a white paperback that he laid down spread-eagled to the page he was on as soon as Elvis climbed out of the pool. They took turns spotting one another with the weights. Then they showered and had breakfast. Elvis motored over to Scottsdale to work on a prospectus, liaison with the printer, while Del took a taxi to the parking lot of Sport Time to pick up his car.

Usually Del returned to the house off Doubletree, spending the remainder of the morning on the telephone, schmoozing with clients, unless he was part of an early four-some. Del, if he made an appearance at all, seldom came into the office much before two or three in the afternoon. So on the July day that Elvis Mahoney peered down upon the re-flecting pool and gazebos, trying to imagine lovers crazy enough to rendezvous there, and at the same time wondering what he should do for lunch, the voice of their secretary, Shelley, very distinctly greeting Mr. Field, spurred him to cross from the windows to the door and yank it open. He looked down the hall and saw Shelley behind the charcoal gray kidney-shaped desk, her platinum hair and perfect nails, her spacey blue eyes enlarged behind oversized lenses fixed within ruby plastic frames. She was talking on the phone with the receiver caught between her cheek and shoulder blade, scrutinizing her nails in the light, but she must have heard the sound of his door disengaging. Swiveling ninety degrees on her chair, she spotted him leaning out the door and winked, gave him a tiny wave. Nobody else was visible, but the door adjacent to the end of her desk was closed. Del's office.

It was barely noon.

Elvis Mahoney emerged from his office, thumbs hooked in his striped suspenders, face cocked to one side.

Shelley's mother was on the line with her usual noon-hour recitation of complaints, which dwelt upon her internal organs, her husband's habits, the rude butcher at Safeway, the outrageous behavior of movie stars as reported in *The Enquirer*. Shelley, with Mr. Murdock approaching her desk, cut short her mother's opinion of an actress who was suffer-ing complications from a boob job gone awry: "Ma, can we talk about her tits later? I've got a job here."

And hung up. She scratched away with a ballpoint on her memo pad, barely getting the ink to run, practicing her signature there while she prepared a smile for Mr. Murdock. She liked Leslie. Mr. Field was a crack-up, always making jokes, but there was something hard about him behind the banter: something she couldn't put her finger on, but scared her to death. Leslie was different. Growing up in Phoenix, Shelley had not had much contact with black men, most of it coming from movies. And when she first described her bosses to her mother, her mother grew so agitated, she thought she might have to phone for the paramedics. But Leslie was nothing like what she'd been led to expect: he dressed conservatively, spoke better English than most of the people she knew, was polite and professional, much more so than Irwin Field, who called her Sherry as often as he remembered Shelley, and even sometimes called her Shirley or Sally. Leslie had a way of speaking to her not as a boss to an employee, but as if they were partners in an important enterprise. He did not squeeze her cheek or make sexual innuendos, but when they spoke, he looked her in the eye. And he noticed things: a new outfit, her jewelry, the cut of her hair, when she was down or just plain beat from a late night of dancing. One day she hit upon it: Leslie Murdock treated her exactly as a woman desires to be treated—with respect and a degree of tenderness. Yet he made no moves on her. Their relationship remained very much business. The man confused her in a very tantalizing fashion.

"Unless there are ghosts in here, Shelley," he said, "I'd swear I heard you saying hello to Mr. Field."

"No ghosts."

"Chile, it's not even noon."

"Mr. Murdock, what can I say? Wonders never cease."

"Those new earrings?"

"My boyfriend."

"Sapphire?"

"Aquamarine. He got them on sale for our third anniversary."

"Three years and he hasn't proposed, what kind of stiff is this guy?"

Shelley dipped her head, soaking up the compliment. "Not years," she murmured, "three months."

"Oh." Elvis released his suspenders, let them snap against his chest. "Is Mr. Field alone in there?"

"With a client."

"Well, well, well. And as early as this. It's too hot to go out. I'm thinking about sending out for Chinese. If that sounds good to you, it's on me. What do you think?"

"Why thank you, Mr. Murdock. Gee."

"Their wonton soup tastes homemade, order us some of that. And whatever else strikes your fancy. Within reason, of course," he added, dropping a twenty-dollar bill on her desk. "Just none of that Hunan. That's Irwin's thing. I want to taste what I'm eating, not be eaten alive by what I'm tasting. Hellfire's got to be a picnic next to eating Hunan."

The first spoonful of wonton approached ambrosia, and Elvis, sitting at his desk, loosened his tie and prepared for a visit in heaven amidst the varied scents and textures borne in the white delivery cartons. Across the desk Shelley Mars sprinkled flattish chow mein noodles into her soup, then squirted duck sauce and hot mustard into the concoction. Different strokes, Elvis thought, watching the knob turn, the door to his office open. Del's face, the wicked little grin there. "Smells terrific," he said. "Les, if you could spare a moment, there's a client I'd like you to meet. He's already down for fifty on the greyhound proposal, but he'd like to hear about the gene-splicing formula prospectus you're working on. It'll be just a minute. Sherry, just arrange the cartons so they can see you, I guarantee it, Les, the food'll stay hot."

Elvis touched his lips with a paper napkin, drew the knot of his tie tight, and rose, tucking his shirt in at the waist. He told the receptionist to relax, enjoy her meal. If there were any phone calls, she could take them at his desk.

Out in the hall, the door closed behind them, Elvis Mahoney said, "Fuck you talking about? I don't know shit about genetic engineering."

Del Rebus gripped him by both shoulders. "This guy doesn't either. He saw an article in yesterday's paper. You read the rags, don't you?"

"I remember something about it."

"Okay." Del leaning into him, his breath suggesting a diet of early-morning beers, said, "I plucked this bird out of Sport Time. He's like a live turkey. The guy bought into the dogs with cash. Fucking cash, Elvo, you believe it?"

"It's Leslie," Elvis said behind gritted teeth. "And no, I don't believe it."

Del dug into the pocket of his blue jeans and produced a pile of thousand-dollar bills that looked real enough. He fanned them for Elvis, then draped his free hand over his shoulder. "You got to have more faith in old Del, Sparky. Now what I'd very much like you to do is blow some smoke, use your legal jargon to get this old fart salivating. Give him that stuff about anticipated exponential returns on invest-ment."

"Irwin? The guy's walking around with fifty K in his pockets cash?"

"Sure." Del Rebus grinned, softly slapped Elvis's cheek. "Of course not, you butthead. He's old-world. I drove him up to his house, which by the way, isn't far from ours, a little south and the other side of Tatum. You have to drive past a guard station, the works. It's up on the cliffs facing Camel-back. Very secluded. He left me in the company of a friend of his son's. And let me tell you, the kid mixed a mean margarita."

Elvis nodded, acquiescing. "Okay. Let's not keep the gentleman waiting."

In Del's office, which also overlooked the gazebos and the greenbelt, as well as the parking lot directly below, the wall behind Del's desk was decked out in bookcases, filled to the brim with the spines of impressive books, all of them purchased from an interior decorator. There were plants in the room, all of them silk, and a twenty-seven-inch television connected to a VCR, in order to show tapes of offerings. There were three cushioned, charcoal gray chairs equipped with casters in front of the desk. And behind the desk was a high-backed chair covered in gray leatherette.

A small man with ink black hair occupied one of the charcoal chairs, the one nearest the window. He wore a white cotton shirt buttoned to the throat, a bola tie cinched with a silver clasp emblazoned with a turquoise inlay of a thunderbird, baby blue trousers with an elastic waist, and glossy white shoes. Dark glasses covered his eyes. The skin hung loose along his throat. He was a tanned old man, darkly spotted with potential carcinomas, the insides of his elbows etched with as many folds as a map of a delta.

Elvis extended his hand to the old gentleman, even as an indefinable unease washed in. The fingers on the man's hand were crippled in a strange swaybacked fashion; his grip had little more strength than that of an infant. "I understand you're interested in the future of genetics. I'm Leslie Murdock. I share your interest, sir. I think it's going to be a fascinating, lucrative field of endeavor. Mr. Field here indicated you might have some questions about our offering. Please, feel free, fire away."

The old man remained in his chair and hung on to Elvis's hand. A thin string of spittle inched from a corner of the man's mouth. As if suddenly sensing it, he pulled his hand away and brushed the spit with the back of his hand. "You speaka so good for a colored man. You went to one a them ivory league schools, I betcha, huh?"

Elvis and Del traded looks. "You got my number there, sir," said Elvis. "Harvard, class of eighty. Then a year at the London School of Economics. MBA from Wharton. Us coloreds just trying to do it the American way, sir."

The old man in the dark glasses wagged a bowed finger. "I like you," he said. "Hey, mister blue jeans, you gotta good one here. So, Mr. Murdock, what is this company you got is gonna be able to make the babies we want, create the future?"

"It's a little more complicated than that."

"It's okay. I'm a listen."

"Well, to begin with, Mr. . . . I'm sorry, I don't believe I caught your name."

"Joe," the old man said. "The name is Joe Scorcese."

Chapter 11

Fear begins with a jolt of adrenaline, body parts suddenly behaving all by themselves, a profusion of liquids surfacing, and in extreme instances, the anal sphincter unlocks. Elvis Mahoney experienced all but the last humiliating symptom the moment he heard the new client's name. He spoke, but he could not remember what it was he said. The small man with the bent fingers and dark glasses complimented him again on how well he talked, following this by saying he would have to speak to his son, but the investment sounded most promising. He reached beneath his chair and settled a panama hat on his head that was the color of a newspaper left in the sun for days, that probably was new before Panama became a drug mecca. Del Rebus fawned over the guy, practically begged to carry him down to the white Mercedes stretch limo waiting for him in front of the western gazebo.

Elvis stood in the office working a handkerchief around his collar, across his brow, watching Del gentle the old man into his automobile. The limo departed and Del turned, ever the showman, swung his arm beneath his waist and bowed. Then threw both arms up, thumbs extended.

Elvis opened a door beneath all the interior decorator books. The door concealed a refrigerator. Elvis filled two glasses with ice cubes. He poured Jack Daniel's over both of them. He spritzed water from a unit on the refrigerator. This was going to be their adios cocktail.

The intercom beeped, and Elvis settled into Del's high-backed chair to pick up the phone. "Yes?"

"Mr. Murdock, you were so long, I closed up the cartons and stuck 'em in the fridge. Just whenever, let me know, I'll nuke 'em in the microwave. And Mr. Murdock? Hey thanks for the lunch. It was delish."

"My pleasure."

He put down the receiver and took a long swig. It didn't taste all that wonderful on an empty stomach, but it did back the tension off a turn or two. Beyond the door Del's voice suddenly brimmed with infectious sound, the man wired on a strange kind of revenge: not against an individual, but a place, the site of his father's defeat. It wasn't something he came right out and talked about, but the man made remarks, insinuations, sneering asides. Elvis didn't entirely understand it, and in his more lucid moments, especially in the early morning, pushing himself up and down the side of Camelback Mountain, he wondered if Del wasn't just a bit crazy. All of which was moot now, given the cowflop they both had just embedded their feet in.

The door swung slowly in, Del Rebus entering backward, pinching tears of laughter from the corners of his eyes. "I love it! Shirley, you ever hear the one about the young lumberjack, he's in the woods for three months, he's gotta get laid."

"Irwin."

"Steals a Jeep and drives sixty miles to the nearest town."

"Irwin!"

"Hang in there, partner. Take time to smell the roses, okay?"

"It ain't the season for roses, if you get my drift. Man, we got to talk."

When they were alone, Elvis lifted the glass toward Del Rebus, Del graciously thanking him. "That was some kind of inspired presentation, Sparky," he said, bumping glasses. "The old dude can't get over the idea of a black man speaking better English than he does. I thought he was going to make me an offer for *you*, for chrissakes."

The room, because of its southern exposure, was filled with light, although the brightest seemed to spring from Del's smile. He bolted his drink and snapped his fingers, too wound up to sit still. He paced between the windows in blue jeans and sandals, in a loud loose shirt, rattling off numbers. "This guy, Joey Cheese, he's our thirtieth sale."

"Scorcese," said Elvis, still in the high-backed chair, feet on Del's desk, waiting for the man to come down off the mountaintop.

Del waved him off. "Whatever. You were beautiful in there. Tell you what, we're going to be out of here earlier than even I expected, partner."

"You got that right."

Del Rebus stopped pacing, struck by the tone of the words. He moved his face slowly, in mock search of the room. "Is this one of those what's wrong with this picture deals? You look good, I know I feel good. We just pocketed fifty big ones in cash, plus our one percent. Why is it I don't hear the voice of a happy camper?"

"Because the man we just scammed is a fucking Mafia don out of New York. I thought he looked vaguely familiar, and when he said his name, shit, I *knew*. You don't read the papers, but some guys tried to hit him a couple months ago, and every one of them is dead, except him. A goddamn don."

Del Rebus stopped midway between the windows and drew himself up and silently mouthed the last three words Elvis had uttered, and when Elvis nodded solemnly, Del drove a fist into his open palm, then, pumping his elbows, did a little jig, his face lit with a wicked grin. "Why this is fanfuckingtastic!"

Elvis reacted as if someone had just taken a Louisville slugger to the soles of his shoes: he was on his feet in an instant, his senses reeling. "Say what?"

"You tell me he's an old mob guy, I say, all the better. Payback is one thing, but poetic justice, now there is a sweet taste of something I never expected."

"Excuse me?"

Moving his glass aside on the desk, and leaning over, Del Rebus glanced over his shoulder, as if somebody outside the windows might be listening. "Let me explain something.

Franny mentioned she told you about my father's disaster in the book business. This was supposed to be a franchise operation, the old turnkey promise. He paid a deposit up front for the company to select and negotiate a location, supply him with inventory, and link him up with a warehouse for new product, for which the parent company would receive a small percentage of the gross sales per month. At the time my father bought in, there were ten successful corporate stores, and about sixty franchise stores. Within a year there were more than two hundred franchises, all of them started up with used books, like my father's store was, and the promise of new title deliveries that were sporadic at best. The company stores were bought en masse by a conglomerate, and within a week of the sale, the so-called warehouse filed chapter thirteen. It was a mob laundering operation, and what it did, it sucked up fifty thousand dollars, most of our family's life savings, plus my father's spirit. He fought and worked like a madman to save that store. He watched my mother die in the process. And his heart went south. He became a bitter, defeated man, just waiting for directions to the dead-end street. A gentleman—and a gentle man—this is what he gets for bumping up against the likes of Mr. Scorcese. Scoring off sewage like Scorcese, that's a fucking delight, Sparky."

"I don't think so. It's a prescription for a short life is what it is. Del, man, use your head."

"C'mon, he's on senility row. He drools when he isn't babbling. He's basket material. Don't worry about it."

"Don't what? Jesus, Del. You aren't serious, are you? His people find where his money went, they're gonna schedule us for open heart, and it won't be surgery. Franny too, if she happens to be around."

There was a period of time when Del Rebus didn't move, just exercised the bridge of his nose with his thumb and middle finger. "Elvis, look: I got too much going on to walk away from it now. Far as I'm concerned, if he is who you say he is, he's just a Lester with a different accent. You remember Lester, don't you?"

"Yeah, like I'm ever going to forget."

Del Rebus's lips curled at the corners. "I believe he threatened me, that first time you and me met, didn't he?"

Elvis nodded. "Yes he did."

"Because he outnumbered me."

Elvis was grinning. "That was his reasoning."

"Yet look what happened. Next day in the prison shop he trips over his own feet, the clumsy dumb fuck, and startles an inmate using an acetylene torch. Guy swings around, whoosh, Lester's face takes off like charcoal briquettes."

Elvis laid a hand on this crazy good friend's shoulder. "You don't have that kind of juice out here."

Del winked, slapped his cheek lightly. "I still got the brain, Sparky. Next move is theirs to make. I say we wait. But if you want to bail out, I'll work with you on it. I'll be pissed too, but I won't do you the way the mob scum did my father."

Even as he tried to tick off the pros and cons involved in Del's position, Elvis was conscious of a difference between the friend he was accustomed to and the man before him now. Suddenly the man had a father instead of a daddy. Beneath the bitterness and bright patter lurked something that ran deeper than sorrow. Either that, or Elvis was light-headed from lack of sustenance.

"Okay," he said. "We'll wait and see."

"Done." Del Rebus was like a statue dissolving into fluid motion, fingers snapping, snatching Elvis's glass from the desk and bending over in front of the refrigerator. "So'd I tell you about the lumberjack, three months he hasn't been laid?"

Chapter 12

In less than twenty-four hours after the attack by the crazies, as he called them, Angelo Scorcese had seen to it that his father's bakery in Middle Village was restored and operational. It was a matter of pride, and every member of the extended Scorcese family congratulated him upon it. Even the affiliated families and independents, like Jimmy Capistrano, applauded his decisiveness, his quick assumption of responsibility. And when the Don, upon gaining his release from the hospital, personally removed Lorenzo as *consigliere*, installing Vacanza, as a veteran of previous wars, Angelo Scorcese couldn't have been more pleased with his position.

Mai Lee concurred. She believed her husband better off with an old brute than with Lorenzo, someone in the family who had brains. She was meticulous in overseeing the meals the two men shared in Howard Beach. After a few gatherings, she felt, if not at ease, at least in control of the old dinosaur. Finally, subsequent to a meal that featured her recipe for sautéed kidneys and calves' hearts, she seized an opportunity to bump into him, prior to the descent to the game room, the rounds of billiards. "Monsieur Vacanza, I understand the need for precaution. But let me ask you. Is there any way I might be able to slip into the city to view the new exhibit at MOMA?"

He squinted down at her, making a fist of one of his hands to scratch the underside of his nose. He wore a white shirt buttoned to his throat, and dark trousers hung from black-and-red-striped suspenders to eliminate the necessity of searching for a belt that could circumnavigate his prodigious waist. His face, with a jaw full of dark jowls, narrowed as it approached his hairline, suggesting diminished intelligence. He had coarse dark hair and stubble for eyebrows, small dark eyes, and a nose that ballooned out from the bridge at a faint angle toward his right cheek. She considered him an intellectual cipher, but dangerous because of it. He smelled of sweet fruit fermenting.

"MOMA," he said. "My apologies, Mrs. Scorcese. I don't know that club."

"It is not a club. It's a museum, monsieur. The Museum of Modern Art, on Fifty-third Street off Fifth Avenue. There is a showing I should like to see. If you could arrange the security."

"A picture gallery, you mean. I gotta check with Angelo, see what he says. You unnerstand?"

"*Oui*, I do," said Mai Lee Scorcese.

It was early July, and a succession of sultry days at the
beach together with unfulfilled nights, with Angelo on the
go constantly to solidify alliances and turf, had taken a toll.
Mai Lee ached for something more than a pat on the ass, or
the infrequent, sudden assaults in the morning when she was
still groggy from an agitated night's sleep. Day upon day she
ferried the children to the shore in the Hamptons with two
carloads of security, a black van in front of her and one
behind her. On the beach, the older security guys maintained a distance, but kept her in view with binoculars and
sound devices attached to their beachware—the collapsible
aluminum chairs, the umbrella. The younger security personnel wore swimsuits, but shouldered colorful beach bags that
contained Mac 10s and .357 Mag autos with fifteen-round
clips. Once the entourage had settled at a suitable proximity
to the surf for the children, Mai Lee smoked a cigarette,
standing to peer up and down the shore. Then she went into
the water, came out with her hair still dry, but her suit cling-
ing, her nipples tensed against the material, and walked in
the wet sand, her face erect and proud, enjoying the sensation of being undressed by men's eyes as she moved up the
shore. As she paraded herself, her toes squeezing the volup-
tuous sand, she longed not so much for a specific man as an
avenue of escape (because she had no illusions concerning
that option), but rather for some indescribable experience,
some temporary excess to restore the flavor of life, to alleviate her isolation. Because she had little more freedom than a

creature in a harem, her dreams in the hot light of the sun drifted inexorably in the direction of a friend who drove a sapphire Jaguar.

It was only a matter of time before she managed to slip away for a few minutes to make a call on a pay phone, to arrange a rendezvous.

The billiards room in Angelo Scorcese's house was subterranean, equipped with the best jamming devices available, or Manny Saperstein, of Mad Manny's Tip Top Tech, had been promised a final resting place in a car trunk. The entire premises at Howard Beach were swept daily, at irregular times, by a technician from Tip Top. The billiards room contained a bar at one end with a double-wide refrigerator and a stove, closets for dishes and seasonings. At the opposite end was a fifty-inch television screen hooked to a satellite dish and several arcade games. Between were two immaculate slate-surfaced tables, one for true billiards and the other for pocket pool. The floor was covered in carpet of a green to match the baize on the tables, in a thickness to rival anything in a corporate boardroom. But only three men congregated here: Angelo Scorcese, Luigi Vacanza, and Cato Dellacroce, demoted since the assassination attempt to gofer for the Don's eldest son.

The game was eight ball. Vacanza, shooting solids, had only a six ball remaining. Shooting stripes, Angelo Scorcese stroked in a nine ball dead-on, and the English on the cue ball brought it back up the table upon impact, stopping a few inches shy of the eight ball. Angelo screwed the cue tip into a cube of blue chalk, called the pocket, and poked the eight ball home. Creasing a one-hundred-dollar bill lengthwise, Vacanza snicked it off his palm and watched it drift down to the slate. On the bar, with Angelo's permission, Cato had set up an old phonograph given him by the Don and was practicing dance steps to the strains of the Dorsey Orchestra, also courtesy of the Don.

Vacanza, as loser, racked the balls while Angelo Scorcese stood at the opposite end of the table, chalking his cue intently. "Two months, Lou," he said. "Two fucking months, and we still don't have a clue who did the number on the old man. Nobody's made a move on us, Lou. How do you figure?"

The *consigliere* lifted the triangular rack with a flourish, as if he had performed a piece of magic. "I ain't figured. I hear it could be Colombians, outta Jackson Heights. And don't forget, I think we had some business we were doing with the spooks."

"The jigs? Lou, shit, Jimmy Lord handles the cooze for us, but he wouldn't fuck with Joe, you can take that to the bank. Lord's the only nigger I met didn't think with his dick."

"Not them kinda spooks. I mean the ones down in Washington, them spy fellahs."

Angelo, who had been sighting his cue for the break, stroked it slowly to one side of his target and laid it to rest on the baize. "Spy fellahs?"

"CIA types."

Angelo Scorcese gazed off, digging at the crotch of his trousers. Damn boxer shorts. "What are we doin' in bed with those guys, Lou?"

"Got me. I just picked up the drops."

"I guess maybe Lorenzo forgot to fill me in on that, the slippery little shit."

Vacanza pulled on a knuckle, cracking it, and stared up the room. "Fuck he think he is, Michael Jackson?"

The two men shared a bout of laughter, as Cato Dellacroce, graceful as the swell and ebb of an ocean, concocted steps with his invisible partner, under direction of the Dorsey trombone.

Given the mood, Vacanza thought it a prudent time to introduce Mai Lee's request. To his surprise, Angelo Scorcese seemed calm, even receptive. He asked intelligent questions with regard to her security. Then he issued his permission as long as she was held to a strict, accountable schedule. He did not want his wife returning home before he and the Dutch nanny, a tallish (at five ten) and amply busted redhead, had finished having fun in the hot tub. The nanny part was not mentioned to Vacanza; that was Cato's field of operations. He was in charge of being the impenetrable veil between Angelo the husband and Angelo the man. Between Angelo the Catholic and Angelo the man of catholic tastes.

From the phonograph came the lilting music of "The Blue Danube." Cato Dellacroce waltzed on the green carpet as quiet as a wave at sea.

It was a Saturday morning, a little before noon when the white Lincoln limousine with the smoke-colored windows glided to a stop in front of the entrance to the Museum of Modern Art. It was trailed by a black van with similarly treated windows. Cato Dellacroce, all 280 pounds of him, emerged from the shotgun side of the Lincoln, made eye contact with two men outfitted as joggers bent over gathering breath on either side of the entrance, and pulled open the rear curbside door. A size-five turquoise heel planted itself on the concrete, in the shadow of the huge man holding the door. A head of long black hair and a face impeccably made-up appeared, the eyes concealed behind large dark glasses with white frames and broad white bows. She wore a sleeveless dress cut along classical lines, snow white against her tan limbs, and over it a bulky, lightweight turquoise jacket, the sleeves bunched at her elbows. A silver necklace and bands of slim silver stacked along her wrists. Turquoise studs for earrings, three on the shell of her left ear, one on the lobe of her right. Even in the heels she was barely five five, and Cato Dellacroce loomed above her like a thunderhead. But he followed her only as far as the entrance, stopped to remind her of the time she should be prepared to be picked up, and then strolled with an easy gait back to the limo.

Inside, Mai Lee Scorcese did not pass through a turnstile, but entered inconspicuously through the VIP entry, escorted by a museum hostess, a squat black woman in a blue blazer with a name tag that identified her as Darla.

"Damn," said Darla, curled fingers to her lips, "but you like a piece of heaven. Mind I ask, wha' perfume you be usin'?"

Generally, black women in this country rubbed Mai Lee wrong, given their outspoken disrespect for authority. They seemed to behave as a law unto themselves. But something about Darla's candor cut through her impression: there was an element of spunk, a trait without which Mai Lee might be swabbing toilets in Saigon as a form of moral rehabilitation. For a moment Mai Lee, an orphan and opportunist, experienced sisterhood. She dug into her turquoise-and-rawhide-colored leather shoulder bag and pounced upon the vial of Chanel No. 5.

Mai Lee pressed it into the lady's hand and strode away. Within a few minutes she had bumped into a gentleman in front of a Matisse exhibit, a canvas of huge colored cutouts. The man wore a monogrammed white shirt open at the throat, washed-out jeans, Reeboks on his feet. The sleeves of his shirt were rolled up just beneath his elbows, and the veins swelled still on his powerful right wrist, from a morning of tennis. Black hair stood out on the back of his tanned hands. He was a lean-waisted man who stood close to a head taller than Mai Lee, his hair and mustache prematurely gray, a beard trimmed to five-o'clock-shadow length, and bright brown eyes. He had a narrow nose that in profile resembled a scythe. He was a graduate of Brandeis, with a Harvard MBA, who harbored a desire to become a stand-up comic. He was a stockbroker by the name of Jay Rose, and he had introduced Mai Lee to laughter, and later to adultery.

The spontaneity and joy of Matisse's work had an impish effect upon Jay Rose: standing behind Mai Lee, he leaned over and whispered, "Thinking about you cost me the price of a second admission ticket. One for me, one for the love muscle."

Turning slowly to face him, her eyes unblinking, she addressed him first with an acidic smile, then said, "I'm sorry, you must have mistaken me for someone else," and walked off down a wing of the museum, her turquoise heels striking the parquet floor like gunshots. Jay Rose's Reeboks bleated behind her, gaining upon her, until she felt his hand on her shoulder, coaxing her to slow down, to stop.

He brought his face down to hers, breathing a little unevenly. "What is it?"

She drew a deep breath through her mouth and said, "Please, take your hand off me. Someone may be . . ."

Jay Rose did so, tucking both hands in his armpits, a look on his face of mock fear.

"Darling," she smiled, and this time genuinely, "I do love you. But not every meeting is an occasion for jokes. Try to understand that. And I am not some aspiring actress. I have yearned close to two months for this moment, and I won't have it cheapened by one-liners."

Jay Rose nodded, his arms still tucked, and asked if she'd seen the Jackson Pollock exhibit.

The hot tub was located off the master bedroom, a marbled jade green shell fitted with six jets and a rheostat to control the temperature of the water. Angelo Scorcese and the Dutch nanny resided on a bench, their naked bottoms bobbing gently in the heated turbulence. Angelo's fingers drifted down and played in the lady's furiously colored pubic hair. Her name was Gretchen Hartsook, but she answered to Gretta. She had come to the States with a boyfriend, who was putting together a drug deal that never materialized, and when the boyfriend vanished, presumably back to the Netherlands, she took up with a young sculptor with Salvador Dalí eyes, who was enrolled part time at the Art Students League. Discovering a few weeks later that the sculptor earned a living by performing in gay porn films, she counted herself blessed to have landed a waitressing job on the upper East Side, in a place called the Comic Club. A patron there, a real gentleman, had befriended her, upon learning her story in the wee hours after the club closed. The next day she applied for the position of nanny at the house in Howard Beach, and couldn't believe the salary that was offered. Gretta owed Mr. Jay Rose big-time.

Several months later in the hot tub she still could not believe her luck: being paid a salary as nanny, plus a bonus from Mr. Rose to report on Mai Lee's contacts, *plus* the recent virile attentions of Angelo Scorcese, whose gifts were generous, to say the least.

About to straddle him a second time in the hot tub, Gretta uttered a single word, which rhymed with *ice*, but in Dutch described a bodily deposit. The phone, a separate unlisted number, was tweeting. Picking up the receiver, Angelo said, "This better be fuckin' good."

"Tell me how soon you can make eight. I'll do five."

Angelo, with this lovely young flesh accommodating him, her hips moving, stirring him, leaned forward to nuzzle an eager nipple, and said, "Gimme thirty minutes."

Where immediate information needed to be transmitted candidly, the Scorcese family, unlike most American families, had a problem, insofar as any line registered to them had a tap on it. This was simply one of the headaches of business. For long-distance communication, they relied upon a code updated weekly through the mail, public phone booths identified by number only. Because of the urgency in his younger brother's voice, Angelo Scorcese, upon getting his rocks off a second time, bolted from the hot tub, toweled himself off roughly, dressed in sweats and running shoes, shades and a Mets cap turned backward, roared down the driveway in his wife's Mercedes convertible. He drove to a phone booth in South Ozone Park, not far from the Aqueduct racetrack. The nearest he could park was around the corner from the designated phone booth. He stepped up to the pay phone just as it began to ring.

He snatched the receiver, turned around to study the street from 360 degrees, then brought it to his lips. "Go ahead."

"It's the old man, Ange," said Paul Scorcese, at a pay phone inside Paradise Valley Mall, wearing neon pink shorts, no shirt, loose leather huaraches on his feet, the din of a yuppie throng passing by in air-conditioned comfort, triple-digit sneakers squeaking on the polished granite flooring. Porsche shades with black arms hung from a neon pink cord in the black hair of his darkly tanned chest. "He's worse than you said."

"Whadda ya mean?"

"He met somebody at the dog track here, or the bar nearby, he's a little confused, but the sharp sold him on a business investment. The old guy brought him up to the house here, pulled out fifty thou five hundred in cash, to buy some shares in a group of greyhounds. It's a write-off, the old man says. I said, Pop, we don't need write-offs on cash that's already clean. He says, They got a real interesting proposition with genetic engineers, this colored fellah talks like music, he's so smooth. Sharps took him off, Ange. You give the word, I'll handle it."

Right outside a liquor store, Angelo Scorcese watched

two black men, obviously drunk, erupt into a clumsy fight, the two men slurring their words and swinging lethargically. He chuckled as the men staggered away, arm in arm, good buddies once more. He said at last, "Yeah, go for it. Get our money back plus interest. Then bury 'em."

"Bury 'em?"

"That turd town's surrounded by desert, you oughta be able to find a place. Am I right?"

"Yeah," said Paul Scorcese, smoothing an eyebrow with a middle finger. "It can be arranged."

"One thing: keep our people around you. Find some dumb cowboys and farm it out."

"I hear you," said Paul Scorcese, absently scruffing the hair on his chest. "Hey, tell me, how's Mother doing?"

"Whadda ya want me to say? She's an ace, kid. She's doin' fine. Believe me when I tell ya."

"I love you, big guy."

"Geddoudda here."

Angelo Scorcese cradled the receiver and pulled at his nose, his eyes moving over the street. He grinned, detecting on his fingertips the faintly lingering scent, he would swear to it, of the opulent Gretta. He glanced at his wristwatch and saw that with any luck he had time to pull off a sexual trifecta.

Turning the corner off Lefferts Boulevard, Angelo Scorcese spotted two black men, former pugilists, dashing east with Mercedes wire hubcaps under their arms. The convertible top had been slashed as well, and the Blaukpunt sound system was but a memory. Angelo spat in front of his feet. The fucking lowlifes.

* * *

A little more than an hour after she had made the lady's acquaintance, the museum hostess Darla was confronted with an opportunity to respond to Mai Lee's generosity, the gift of perfume. A whitely handsome white man, stylishly groomed and smelling sweet, approached the hostess, assisting the beautiful lady, who appeared indisposed, and asked if there might be a room or area of privacy, as the woman had fainted. The man identified himself as a doctor. Darla, knowing the director's suite would be vacant for the weekend, employed her ring of keys to introduce them to an airy room with an enormous ebony desk, much African statuary, a Picasso on one wall, and lush white carpet, divans, chairs of a size for two. She left them with a walkie-talkie to contact her when the lady recovered. Jay Rose walked her to the door and thanked her once more, locking the door behind her.

He swung around to face a suddenly rejuvenated lover. "You are a fox, Mai Lee."

Already out of the turquoise jacket, her shades on top of her purse and her heels kicked off, she said, "Undress me, please. We have an hour." And she showed him her back.

Chapter 13

The first light of morning was seeping amongst the crags of Camelback Mountain and across the palatial grounds of the homes in Paradise Valley as Elvis Mahoney scooped empty soda cans and beer cans into a thirty-gallon plastic trash bag. He hauled the cans to the garage and loaded them into the back of the Charger. The .357 Magnum was holstered on his hip, and several boxes of cartridges, purchased the night before, were in the sack that he set on the shotgun seat, along with two canteens filled with water. The garage door rolled up electronically. Elvis started the Charger, flipped on the headlights, backed down the drive, activating the garage door with a transmitter, so that it closed and locked.

A minute later he was winding north on Tatum Boulevard, the windows rolled down, the headlights stabbing the dusky air. Of what traffic there was, most was headed opposite the direction he was going. Paradise Valley existed as an independent town within the city of Phoenix, a turf where the rich wouldn't have to risk rubbing elbows with anyone other than the rich. Foreign ambassadors had compounds there, as did the heirs of old Arizona wealth and new California money; it was home to doctors by the score and (or so it seemed) to lawyers by the hour; real estate whizzes lived there, along with entertainers, pro athletes, gangsters like Joe Scorcese, who were just about housebroken, and even a football coach or two. And scam artists, what the city of Phoenix invited, according to Del, and rewarded, and deserved. Del had led Elvis down a small private road south of the Paradise Valley Country Club some weeks ago to show him house upon luxury house that was empty, abandoned. "See this?" he had said. "This is the soul of this city. There's no economy here. It's all a shell game. This is the fucking Third World, Sparky. Tell you how big a shell game this is, there's more lawyers in this state per capita than any state in the union. Now all we're here to do is play the game: fake out the fat cats, stick it to the shitballs. Then blow this pop stand."

The breeze, such as it was traveling at fifty miles per hour, brought little relief, even at that time of the morning. Emerging from Paradise Valley into Phoenix, Elvis shuttled amidst shopping malls and housing developments, apartment complexes and low-six-figure residences. There were hills, aspiring mountains, visible in the distance, charcoal in color and tapering to an altitude of a few thousand feet, that seemed within reach in minutes but were in fact close to a half hour away, and only if you exercised a heavy pedal. Topography in Arizona, Elvis was beginning to discover, begat illusions. Nothing was as it seemed. He could understand, a little now, how the land and heat could conspire with disillusionment to forge the kind of bitterness that animated a man like Del Rebus.

He could understand it a little, but not entirely. Nothing that Del had said or shown him, or that he himself had experienced, quite explained the torque of the man's passion. In his cups, Del could become flat weirded out on the subject of this town.

But it was also something of a bore. Elvis suspected Franny Lott had dashed off to California, not only to participate in the strategy for her divorce, but to escape the malevolent (if sometimes hilarious) monologues on the topic of Phoenix.

He took Tatum as far as Union Hills, traveled west to Cave Creek, then bore down on the desert. The last fleck of purple had dissipated from the sky, and now a smooth crown of blue arched over the landscape. Headlights off, windows rolled up, Freon fighting the environment, the Charger edged off the highway north of Jomax Road, followed a wash bordered by scrub and ocatillo, piñon pine, some paloverde that were lime green, their branches shaped as if by static electricity. Elvis parked on a sandy flat littered with tires, beer cans, a mattress. Shards of shattered glass bounced brownish light around.

He piled the tires along a bank of the wash, the sand there so fine as to be almost powdery. He arranged his targets methodically, without any particular excitement, because handling a gun did not touch off the boyish enthusiasm most men seemed to exhibit. For him, the big Mag was an instrument of death, period. Hitting what he aimed at did not fill him with thrills or pride, it only constituted a security check, something along the order of a man going through his house before bedtime, making sure the doors are locked, the windows secure.

Pacing off fifteen yards, he drew down on his targets in a two-handed stance, two fingers of his left hand wrapped on the trigger guard, the rest supporting his gun hand, drew a breath and let it go slowly . . . squeezed off six rounds, the cans bouncing, the tumult of the gunshots crackling out over the alien land. He popped the chamber, his ears struggling to adjust to the six concussions, replaced it with a second chamber of loads, and repeated the process, watching the wrenched cans tumble. Four of them at any rate . . . He inserted earplugs.

An hour later, his right wrist smarting, Elvis stood in the shadowless heat swallowing the last water from his second canteen. He was wearing cowboy boots, washed-out Levi's, and a tank top, and not an article of clothing was dry. He could almost feel the constant trickle of sweat down his spine and into his briefs. Tiny green lizards, close to the color of the paloverde, flicked about the litter, appearing and vanishing. He practiced, not quick draw, but bringing the Mag up fast from the region of his waist and firing one hand, by instinct rather than sighting. He surprised himself, hitting more than he would have believed possible, three out of twelve. His hand smelled of discharge, an almost metallic odor.

Because he had been shooting, he did not hear the Sturm und Drang of two Harley Hogs, homing in on the Charger, but turning around with his reloaded chambers, he saw the two white men astride their bikes, the kickstands out and the men climbing off. The bigger of the two, around six foot and two-fifty, wore a dusty black T-shirt, dirty jeans, and black boots, his long black hair wrapped in a red headband. A salt-and-pepper beard suggested that he hadn't shaved in the last six months. His partner was blond, lanky, and shirtless, with a stringy blond beard. The hair on his head was no longer than a quarter inch and was shaved clean in a wide swath around his ears. There were brownish nicks in his teeth, and what looked like holes from fillings lost. Both wore silvery glasses with reflective lenses, a style favored by Los Angeles motorcycle cops.

Elvis Mahoney, walking away from the tires, casually dropped a reload onto the spindle and snicked the cylinder home. If mentality could be cloned, he was looking at two of Lester's offspring. Hanging by its chin strap from the handlebar of the blond boy's Hog was an abbreviated black helmet of the sort favored by young Nazis. Elvis strolled toward them, in spite of the forty-fives displayed on their hips, trying to draw upon Del's showmanship, when to feint and when to act.

He forced himself to grin, and said, "How you doin'? Talk about timing, I got all these cans left to shoot at, but no more ammunition. You guys are welcome to 'em."

The blond biker had a thin pinkish nose that twitched, like a nervous tic accompanied by hisses. "Hear that, Rayce?" he said. "Boy's leavin' us all his pop cans."

The one called Rayce stuck a cigarette into his beard,

struck a match off the zipper of his grimy trousers, and grunted.

"Ain't that mighty white of him?" The blond biker bared his bad teeth in the enjoyment of his wit. "Ain't it though?"

Rayce had to think about that. In the meantime, he hooked his thumbs in his belt loops and hitched up his pants, which promptly sank back where they had been, given the protrusion of his belly. "Bullets is expensive," he said at last. "I don't hanker to waste 'em on tin cans."

"Actually," said Elvis, taking a step forward, trying to put the Charger between himself and the two bikers, "the cans are aluminum. Shoot the shit out of 'em, and then you can sell 'em for recycling. Guys, I'll even leave the bag." He took another step and bent over, behind the fender of the car, brought up the limp brown plastic he had tucked beneath the tire. "Guys?"

The blond biker had a stovepipe chest, not much definition, but standing maybe fifteen feet on the far side of the Charger's hood, even shooting by instinct, Elvis didn't see how he could miss. He held the Mag leveled at the skinny biker from behind the brown plastic.

"Guys?" sneered the blond. "Who you think you are, boy? One of us?"

"We're all humans," said Elvis. "But after that, it's a matter of degree. Also, in case you skipped class that day"—and now he lifted the plastic sack enough to show both men the barrel of the .357—"being human, we're all mortal."

The blond biker approached the Charger. "You're outta ammo, remember?"

Elvis moved the barrel away from the biker with bad teeth and chanced a round, a blast that devastated the front tire of Rayce's Hog and left the Harley heeled over in the sand. The big biker spun, yanking off the mirror glasses, to stare at his machine. Elvis tugged on his earlobe. "I lied," he said.

The big biker screamed, "You shot my fucking Hog!"

"Well, that's the bad news. The good news, Rayce, the way to look at it, is I didn't shoot you."

"Boyd," the big biker moaned, "you see this? You're right: it's what the country's come to, lettin' the goddamn niggers have guns."

"Equal rights and in my sights," said Elvis Mahoney, his free hand on the hood of the Charger as he moved around it. "What're you guys, twenty, twenty-five, somewhere in there?"

"Yeah." From the shorthair, Boyd, his pink nose hissing.

"My uncle was a marine. He fought in Nam, Boyd. He earned a Purple Heart and re-upped, and got his face blown away in the house-to-house of taking back Hué. Just exactly what is it about black folks with guns that disturbs you? Go ahead, jump in. This is an extra-points question."

They were close enough now that Elvis could see sweat on Boyd's upper lip and the blackheads beneath his jaw. With the hammer of the Mag cocked and the barrel pointing directly at Boyd's manhood, Elvis liberated his .45. Rayce yielded his weapon without waiting to be persuaded.

With all the visible hardware in his possession, Elvis retreated to the Charger and climbed inside, started the engine. He paused, catching sight of a hawk in the high air, to watch it swoop and swerve, scouting the hard land for prey, for sustenance. He followed the creature with mixed emotions, unlike his feeling for the specimens of rat dirt that he had just disarmed. The feeling: blowing their brains out would at least improve their IQs.

He rolled down the window. "Time's up, Boyd. Afraid you lost those extra points. But it's still your lucky day. Because the thought of my uncle dying for the likes of you angers me to the point where shooting you dead would be a fucking upper."

Elvis Mahoney popped the clutch, and the little front-wheel drive buffeted backward, braked, and spun off alongside the wash. In his rearview mirror he saw the two men congregate over the fallen Hog, hands on thighs, as if hatching some dim-witted conspiracy.

His mind still on the bikers (to be honest: still scared shitless from the encounter), Elvis failed to recognize the intersection with Union Hills, and so cruised on toward the next major thoroughfare, Bell Road. Spotting a bar off to his right, just before the intersection, he pulled into the gravel lot and made his way inside. It was spacious and dark and rank smelling, like any bar at that hour of the morning. Waylon Jennings emoted from the jukebox. Ceiling-mounted fans on black stalks whirred without effect. A pool table, several arcade games, and a dart-board area took up one side of the room. There were wooden booths along the opposite wall and tables strewn about and a homely bar with a dull wood finish, plenty of scars in the wood, wood stools for a score of imbibers. Elvis counted six inhabitants, the barkeep included. Everyone but the barkeep wore a cowboy hat, a Stetson or some straw variety. The barkeep was on the phone to someone, attempting to get service on his air-conditioning unit. The hats sipped their drinks with an air of accustomed resignation. Elvis straddled a stool and waited for the barkeep to finish his business.

The hat next to him was a white man with sun-drenched skin, heavily lined, and long black sideburns with a little gray detectable in them. He sat staring straight ahead hunched over the bar in a faded blue-and-white-checked shirt with pearl buttons that snapped, drinking from a long-necked bottle of beer. His hat was black and stained and rested just over his eyebrows, so that when he cocked the bottle to his lips (still staring straight ahead), the body of the bottle bumped the brim. The man drank with a certain honky-tonk élan that fascinated Elvis: bringing the mouth of the bottle to his unmoved lips, and upending the bottle to suck leisurely at its contents, his Adam's apple bobbing. Emptied, the bottle was set smartly on the bartop, and the keep quickly resolved his conversation. The keep had reddish hair that was thinning fast and milk white arms thickly infested with red hair, even on the backs of the hands that he flattened on the bar. "Another of the same?"

"That'd be a good idee." The black hat stared straight ahead. "They's a gentleman to my right been waitin' patiently."

The keep glanced at Elvis, back at the hat, then at Elvis. "Can I help you?"

"Yeah, you can. I'd like a Jack Daniel's neat, and a beer chaser."

"Jack and a chase. You got it."

The keep sifted away, and Elvis leaned over the bar, cocked his head. "Can I buy you a round?"

The man with the black hat did not move his face. "You sure can."

Elvis heard a familiar quirk. "This town, it's interesting. People seem to be sure of everything, what they know and don't know. Real positive people, you Phoenix folks."

The man pursed his lips, but waited until his hand was folded around another sweaty bottle, the contents ice-cold, just the way he liked it. "I lived in this town near to sixty years. Attitude is about the one thing you can be sure of hangin' on to. Even if you're flat busted, and a lot of us has been, and looks like we will be again, least we got that. Might not be shit to cheer about, but we sure do know where we're at. Most a the time it's about four blocks north a hell."

Elvis backed the shot glass to his lips and jammed the Jack down, trickling cold beer after it. He closed his eyes, feasting on the sensation. "Oh yes," he murmured, and shivered.

"You hadda scare, huh? Some dumb-butt driver."

"Close. Two of them."

The man had turned and was looking at him, his left eye visible and vague, with a spear-colored look of glaucoma about it. His other eye was warm and brown and direct. "Come again."

Elvis recounted briefly the confrontation in the wash.

"The one's a skinhead. They's a bunch of 'em hang out south a here, in Sunnyslope, where I live. You coulda done me a favor by shootin' the little lizard. Goddamn punks with swastika tattoos march around like Nazis, all this goddamn garbage pouring out their mouths. My father fought in the

Big Two, survived Normandy. I sure don't understand why there ain't a law against 'em. We fight a whole war with the bastards, then say, but go ahead an' organize here, it's jake. Country's run by snakes and ruled by Eyetalians." The man paused to scarf the last drops from the bottle. "Ned," he commanded, "let's do it again."

The balding, red-haired bartender moved quietly and efficiently. Refilled glasses and a fresh bottle were back within seconds.

Elvis said, "I heard a man the other day say it was the Japanese that owned the country."

A dry chortle escaped the man in the black hat. "They just think they do. You take the bullshit on Bell Road, the construction there. They's little businesses, and some big ones too, losing their asses. Mom and Pop's gettin' blown out every day, because there's no access to their place of business. City or county or state give a shit? Fuck no. Eat shit and die, little guy. But they's all kinds of set-asides from our tax dollars for the landlords of the dead malls. Many of 'em Japs. And who's bein' paid tons more tax dollars to rip up Bell Road every year since the invention of macadam? Who sells the city the road crews and heavy equipment and cement sewer drains and asphalt, and who drags out the whole goddamn deal to get cost overruns? It all goes to the Eyetalians. Okay, maybe some Mormons make a buck too, in this town, but what they take in millions is just enough to fill a wop's watch pocket."

"You seem to have studied the matter," said Elvis, trying to strike a politic note.

"You would too," said the man, "if you was one of the simple bastards being bulldozed outta business."

Somebody at the bar was a very slow study, Elvis thought. "You own this place," he said.

"I sure do. For as long as I can hang on."

"People will come here," Elvis tried to assure him, "just to listen to your wisdom, to say nothing of the good service."

The man with a black hat removed it and brushed a checked sleeve against his upper forehead, amid a widow's peak of stranded black hairs. He settled the hat and said, "Son, the public is like water, seeking its own level. Where there's an obstruction, it vanishes. Don't matter whether the obstruction is in front of a nugget a gold or a pile a shit."

"You remind me of a guy," said Elvis, leaving money for the drinks and easing off the wooden bar stool.

"Sure nice talkin' to you," said the man in the black hat. He stared straight ahead, the bottle tipped to his lips, without offering his name or a hand to shake.

Back out in the sunlight, the glare like a slow, constant drubbing, Elvis could feel the beer and whiskey cushion his senses, but in a pleasant fashion, his metabolism restored. Even with the windows left cracked open, the air inside the Charger had a gathered weight to it, as if on the verge of combustion. The cardboard sunscreen that unfolded in segments to cover the windshield, in theory to provide shade for the dashboard, the steering wheel and gearshift, gave off a dry, burnt smell, and the whole screen itself was friable, about to crumble at the folds. Elvis climbed inside and fitted dark glasses over his eyes and started the engine, leaving his door open and letting the engine idle awhile, then rolled up the windows, juiced the engine, and flipped on the a.c.

Bell Road east from Cave Creek swarmed with strip malls populated by marginal businesses. You had only to glance at the sparse number of parked cars. Even at the major intersections, empty space seemed to be a growth industry. Yet off the road on the undeveloped land that skirted Bell, independent entrepreneurs sprouted hither and yon. People operating out of vans, the trunks of their cars, off flatbed trucks. There were colorful throw rugs woven by untraceable Indian tribes from the Yucatan. Instant, free windshield repair. A Sabrett hot-dog stand, possibly the one true value. Row upon row of VFW-looking auction tables piled with designer jeans, two pair for twenty-five dollars. Silk plant and flower arrangements hung from a clothesline like Sunday's wash trailed out and around and back from the tailgate of a clean brown Chevy van. White poster-board signs fixed on metal tripods advertised the prices.

Elvis spotted one potential Indian face among the scraped, hard-luck white ones trying to make a buck: he pulled off the road to look over the man's sand paintings. The subject matter was clichéd, but Elvis was taken by the technique, the subtle coloration, and so he purchased (without dickering, a southwestern practice that he despised) a rendering of a wild stallion, a runner in a herd that still exists in the arroyos and canyons of northern Arizona, the barrel-chested and beauteous mustangs. The man reached into the hip pocket of his jeans for a thick sheaf of bills, peeled off change for Elvis's twenty. The man counted silently. The bills were hot and moist and smelled as if they'd been buried in earth. Without a word the man walked off to crouch in front of a weathered Ford Fairlane, his ten-gallon straw hat throwing shadow over his eyes.

Farther down the road, right where it intersected with Tatum Boulevard, Elvis pulled off onto the shoulder, the bleached-out red clay and gravel there, to inspect a flatbed advertising two tagged saguaros and three ocotillos. There was nothing so very special about the ocotillos, except that they grew spiky green tentacles slowly from the ground to a height of twelve feet or more, a whole clutch of them as thick in diameter as ten feet, although the root balls on these were about a yard thick. Elvis had been struck by them when he first drove out in the spring, because of the flame-colored clusters that drooped from the tips, gaudy as a magic act. Like the ocotillo, the saguaro was protected by native plant laws, hence the necessity for tags. The saguaros formed the columnar cactus phalanx he had encountered on his descent into Phoenix, many with an elevated arm or two, as if offering surrender. Towering from twenty to fifty feet high, they left an impression. A single arm, Elvis had learned since his arrival, did not bud before the cactus had achieved sixty to seventy-five years. As he walked around these strapped-down, vulnerable desert giants, he made a point of studying the tags. It was the liquor acting upon him. And maybe too several conversations with Franny Lott, the wildlife advocate, unless the wild life being talked about applied to humans.

A blond guy climbed down out of the cab from the driver's side wearing blue jeans, scruffy no-color boots, and a blue-jean vest, no shirt. He was deeply tanned and wore his hair pulled back in a ponytail, and what looked like self-inflicted artwork carved in blue showed up faded on his left forearm. Letters and crude shapes. A kind of puffy smiley look on his face that Elvis recognized. "Help you?" he said.

"Just dreaming," Elvis said. "Wondering how a guy goes about getting tags for natural wonders like these."

The blond with the puffy smiley face shrugged.

"Probably the same place," Elvis said, "he gets that righteous herb he's been smoking."

They looked each other in the eyes.

"You got a warrant?" said the blond.

"No."

"Then don't get me mad."

"I don't think I want to do that," said Elvis, walking back to the Charger, settling himself behind the wheel. He leaned across the shotgun seat to roll down the window, then started the engine. "What I want to do is call the law. Is nine-one-one still the operative number?"

Gravel sprouted from the front tires.

What Elvis Mahoney loved about the tall strange plants was the soft and alien sound of their names. *Oca-tee-yo, sa-war-o.*

It did not occur to Elvis Mahoney until he turned off Tatum onto Doubletree, that of the several score vendors he had passed, given an earlier time, one of them might have been Del's father. Just one more guy scraping by. With no more dreams.

Fuck 911.

Chapter 14

Elvis entered the house through the garage with the holstered Mag in his hand, the empty canteens slung from straps across his shoulder, the sand painting cradled in his arm. He crossed bleached sautillo tile through the rec room, empty of any amenity, and down a hall and into an open kitchen with a breakfast nook overlooking the pool, the tennis courts beyond it. In the nook sat Del and Franny Lott, cups of coffee and saucers in front of them. The wide-brim straw hat tipped over her ear looked like the same one Franny was wearing the first day she and Del arrived in

Phoenix. No dark glasses, but the sleeveless white dress looked familiar.

Depositing the empty canteens and revolver next to the sink, Elvis approached the table and laid the sand painting face up on it. "Welcome home, chile," he said, and leaned over to kiss her on the cheek. Her perfume was airy and sweet.

"What's this?" said Franny.

"I'll tell you what it is," Del said. "It's a bribe. I told him you were flying in this morning, and he's tired of doing all the cooking, since we fired the Swedes."

"Fired them?" Franny looking incredulously from Del to Elvis and back to Del. "But why?"

Del said, inflecting his voice with a faintly mocking tone, "They overcooked his fresh spinach, they undercooked the omelets, they wouldn't know sauté from a sauna. I miss anything, Sparky?"

Elvis shrugged, pulled on his ear. "I thought I could do better. I found out I could. So did he."

"Sparky ain't lyin' there. We've feasted on fresh trout and scallops, Chinese and Italian, stuff on the grill. Fresh salads. Homemade bread. This man can cook, Frances. But there's this other, less glamorous part of the deal, and that's what I think he thinks he can foist off on you, tempted by this . . . this unique work of art."

"It's a sand painting. I liked the colors and the gritty texture. It's just a simple thing done well. And yes, I got it for you, Franny. It's a mustang. For our lady of wildlife."

"It's lovely." She looked up at him and smiled, but there was no animation in the expression, none of the light and joy he had come to associate with her.

He glanced at Del, but learned nothing. He opened the refrigerator and poured cold bottled water down his throat, then found a cup and saucer for himself and poured some coffee. Maybe sober, he would discover he was wrong, that he had misread the solemn, decisive look in her eyes.

When he had pulled a stool up to the table, Del pushed his cup away and said, "Our lady of wildlife. I like that, Sparky. You believe it's a hundred ten outside and we're going to the zoo? Me, going to a goddamn zoo. Some kinda way to spend a Saturday."

They backed their chairs from the table and excused themselves, very polite about it. Franny's fingers trickled over his shoulder, and he listened to the sound of their heels on the rough tile, the lazy gait of lovers in no hurry to be anywhere, content with now. Elvis finished his coffee watching the light play off the surface of the pool, the water looking ethereal, a place for angels to frolic, and maybe the few mortals that could measure up to Franny.

He picked up cups and saucers and washed them by hand in the sink, gazing out over the pool and beyond the property, dwelling upon the spires of ash green eucalyptus, red plum and junipers, the jacaranda fluttering, stripped of their lavender spring flowers, the gushes of untrimmed oleanders. He needed a woman, bad, and something other than what Del had arranged for him in San Diego.

Once Del and Franny had reestablished their situation, they would talk, Del and he. He wanted a date, an X on the calendar announcing the end of the gig, so that he could begin to have a life.

He spotted a scarlet hummingbird drifting in the air, its needle beak prodding one of the sugar-water feeders Franny had bought and filled and hung from wires along the patio. It was the optimum time to watch for them, when they zipped in for the shade and sweetness, and Elvis headed off down the hall, toward his bedroom, for the materials to clean the revolver. That way he could sit in a swimsuit under the patio, minister to the Mag and delight in a show that exceeded magic.

He almost stumbled over the luggage. A pair of matched buckskin suitcases with dial locks. He recognized them as belonging to Franny. He snatched the thick straps, intending to deliver them to the master suite that she and Del occupied. But set them back down.

And thought: *He already knows!*

The flamingos, enjoying an afternoon siesta, slept with one leg tucked beneath their bosoms, gorgeous brush strokes of pink in the deep shade. Franny Lott, from behind her dark glasses, watched Del Rebus look them over, a finger idly brushing the side of his nose. "Your kind of bird, Frances. Beautiful, odd, dreamy, and vulnerable. An exquisite creature."

She made a fist and lightly touched his shoulder. "They can be tough when the need arises."

"Yes. I suppose it goes without saying."

They strolled in the heat past the caged creatures, and Franny Lott sensed indulgence more than interest, until Del struck up a conversation with a gentleman operating a food stand within the park. The stand was little larger than a sizable travel trailer, with a shallow wooden awning over the counter. The man sold soda and beer from the tap, as well as boxed popcorn, potato chips in plastic sacks, slender franks in buns, and ice cream on a stick. They bought hot dogs and beer in paper cups from the man and a young dark-haired girl standing on their feet in the heat and smiling. The man's last name was Assoud, and he was an immigrant from Lebanon. The girl was his daughter, quiet and polite, with the eyes of a startled animal, the contours of incipient womanhood. Yielding to Del's way, Assoud boasted of his daughter's industriousness, and how, though barely fourteen, she would make a fine wife for a proper suitor. His own wife had remained behind in the port city of Tyre, with two younger daughters, until Assoud could afford to send for them. To Del's solicitous query, he responded that during the winter he was able to set aside money every week, but the summer, with the heat that drove people indoors, was hard on his business. Del complimented Assoud on his operation and suggested he explore the feasibility of offering frozen yogurt. Assoud dipped his head, offering many thanks for the idea.

They found shade across from an enclosed, grassy knoll upon which an amorous pair of Galápagos tortoises were conducting themselves in a slow and fumbling fashion.

"If they're any example," Del remarked, finishing his hot dog ahead of Franny, "I can understand why evolution took so long."

Franny laughed, a skittish sound of amusement, and touched a paper napkin to the corners of her mouth.

"I'm having another beer," he said. "Assoud needs all the business we can give him. Frances?"

"No. Thank you. I'm fine."

When Del returned with the tall cup of beer, they spent

some silent minutes together, watching whatever interested them. Breaking with habit, Del had donned a bright red T-shirt and white shorts and a pair of rubber thongs. His long and hairy, but not especially powerful legs stretched out from the shorts with an institutional pallor. He broke the silence by remarking, "You look at those legs? I could pass for one of your effing flamingos."

Franny Lott hunched her shoulders and leaned forward from the waist, her face cocked in Del's direction. "You don't like it here, do you?"

He sighed. "It's the cages, Frances, not the creatures."

Finished with the beer, he crumpled the cup and flung it with a snap of the wrist. She retrieved the balled container and dropped it into her handbag. She hugged her shoulders for a moment exchanging looks with him, then spun and walked off, her low heels stumping along the asphalt. He caught up with her easily. "Frances? It's too hot for dramatics. I understand why we're here. It's neutral ground, and very public."

She raised her hand, her fingertips tenderly graced his cheek.

He blinked, then elevated his eyes and rolled them at the sky, sucked in his breath, and said, "Coming back from California with empty luggage ain't exactly encouraging."

"Let's walk," she said, and they made their way past leopards and ostriches subsisting in their restricted outbacks, past blue-and-scarlet macaws, African grays and blue-tipped Amazons and umbrella cockatoos, until they had reached the large, permanent concession area where she and Elvis had tried to consume foot-longs. Because of the way the wind was blowing, the lions' den made its presence persuasively known. They navigated amid the peacocks and walked down to the water's edge. Trees soared above them, and a single cage with a single green parrot resided there. As they approached, the parrot clambered to the top of his cage and unloaded a wolf whistle.

Del leaned over to Franny. "The bird has good taste."

"How do you know it wasn't whistling at you?"

"Isn't that what I just said?"

She cuffed him lightly on the shoulder, then stuck a finger through the top of the cage, and sure enough, the parrot bowed his head for her to scratch it.

"I told Elvis once I thought you were a little on the wild side, that I was lucky, because I could always walk away."

The parrot, whose eyes were nearly closed from an excess of pleasure, snapped its head erect, an eye tracking Del Rebus as he moved around the cage, until he stood opposite Franny Lott, hands jammed in the front pockets of his shorts. "Go on, Frances."

"David wants to attempt a reconciliation."

"I don't blame him. And you?"

"Evidently David's attorney hired a private detective to do some research on you."

"Yes."

Franny pulled off the dark glasses and dropped them into her handbag, from which she removed a white monogrammed hankie, dabbed with it at the corners of her eyes.

"His attorney told my attorney that the reason for your incarceration, what you were doing in Lompoc . . . that you killed a man. I . . . I guess I had assumed, given your intelligence, that you had gotten caught short in some high-risk venture and the feds made an example of you. Did you kill a man?"

Del Rebus studied his feet, then studied the blue afternoon sky through the shifting embroidery of leaves overhead. He said, "Yes," his eyes meeting Franny's.

Franny Lott blinked, tears running unfettered from her eyes now, her hands in fists above the cage. "Goddammit, Del. I'm looking at you, and I know I was wrong. It isn't that damn easy walking out on you."

"You want me to make it easier, Frances?"

"No! I want you to tell me it's a lie. A last-ditch fabrication."

"I can't do that," he said. He turned and walked a short distance from the cage, almost to the water's edge. He faced her across the shadowed stretch of ground. "The stuff my daddy told me, that's crap. I made it up. My father was a genteel and standoffish guy. He didn't mix well with the hoi polloi, if you know what I mean. Phoenix was no place for him. Neither was retail, when you get down to it. He came here with a dream and lost it. I just finished the job. I killed him, Frances."

The car that Del was renting was a white Oldsmobile Calais with red leather seats, full power and tinted glass all around. The leather was a mistake, as Del was reminded, slipping behind the wheel in his shorts. Even behind the dark glass, the upholstery had achieved a stove-top temperature. He clenched his teeth and turned the ignition, and they swept out of the asphalt parking area and onto the gravel exit road. The air conditioner labored mightily, and within minutes their skin ceased to smart from the heat. Franny sat rigidly, strapped in by her seat belt, her arms folded beneath her breasts.

Del turned down the volume on the radio, as a Rod Stewart number was unfolding, something about not wanting to talk about a broken heart. They were silent for a time soaring down out of Papago Park, the red buttes that Elvis had pointed out to Franny rising behind them, the distinctive, smoky sound of the singer weaving a lament that both listeners understood too well.

When the song ended, it was Franny who leaned forward, shutting off the radio altogether. "Come back to California with me. You can't get back what your father lost. This business with guns and muscle men following us home in the night, it's no good, Del."

He said nothing. Then he reached up where a package of Gauloise was pinched to the roof by the sun visor. He fitted one of the fat cigarettes to his lips, and Franny leaned over, snapping a lighter, the flame jumping to light the tobacco. He took a short, deep toke, depressed the switch to lower his window, and exhaled.

"Frances, I grew up in a literary, faintly bohemian household, but not much of it rubbed off on me. Numbers were my trip. Probabilities, statistics, any kind of problem solving. I could pore over batting averages and feel as if I had tapped into the fiber of life in the same way my parents did reading poetry aloud to one another. The thing of it is, we respected one another's interests."

"I see. I did not mean to be so insensitive as to love a man who has just told me he killed his own father. It must be the heat."

"Phoenix has that effect on people. The human compass goes all to hell."

"You are determined to be rid of me."

"No," he said, harshly. "But you have to understand how it is. I have my priorities."

"What? What are we talking about?"

"It's simple." Because they were at a red light, he took his eyes off the road and treated her to his knowing, roguish smile, then winked. "I'm going to walk out of this town a winner."

Doubts about him flickered, even as she was faced by the grin, the zest in his eyes, the determination too. "I think you're nuts," she said, and only half in jest.

He threw back his head to laugh at the remark, and when he was finished being amused, he opened up to her as he had never done. At the age of twenty he had fled Phoenix for San Diego, to enlist in the navy for three years. Most of it spent schlepping supplies from Japan to the southeast coast of Vietnam. Re-upped for another trio, partly due to his involvement with a Japanese lady. Mustered out into a society slightly hostile to Viet vets, and being one to accept a challenge, Del moved to Berkeley, where the hostility was still at fever pitch. He let his hair grow, but never relinquished his identity, spreading a strange brew of anticommunist caution about, insisting that the Cong and North Vietnamese hadn't cornered the market on morality either.

He opened a health-food restaurant in the same year that he ran for president on the Libertarian ticket against both Nixon and McGovern, losing big to both in Berkeley, but finishing second to McGovern in Oakland. Politics aside, over the next year he sold five franchises in San Francisco and was soliciting financial backers for the money to promote a push into the southern California market. He had become in a rush a longhair of some means living in Marin, a three-bedroom retreat with a cedar-shake roof secluded in sweet redwoods, a blanket of pine needles everywhere. And then he told her of the Thanksgiving eve, the reconciliation with his father after almost eight years, and how he had awakened in the night, alarmed by a sense of something gone wrong, and found the shell of the man he once knew sitting up in bed with a gun under his chin, shaking, mumbling words Del could not understand. The rest of that nightmare was still a blur for him, except that he could remember a struggle for the gun, and when it was pressed against the old man's chest, Del had cried, *You want to do it, do it right.* And then there was the explosion.

"I hauled him to the bathroom and washed him in the tub. The clothes in his suitcase were as ratty as the ones he had arrived in, so I got him into a robe of mine and carried him into the living room. I sat him on the couch against some pillows and put slippers on his feet. I had a framed photograph of my mother, taken when she was the age I was then, wearing a long dark coat with the collar turned up, with her hair brushed out over her collar, looking windswept. And her eyes. We used to tease her, the old guy and I, saying she had the eyes of a silent-screen vamp. I placed the photograph in his hands, so that it would be her he would see, if he could see anything. Something always happened to his eyes when he looked at my mother. Something . . .

After I got him all arranged, I mixed myself a dry martini, straight up, and lit a Gauloise, and tried to enjoy it all for him, one last time."

Del cleared his throat and swallowed. "The prosecutor scored big off that little detail."

Franny Lott could feel her heart beneath her breast, and her breath stammering. She squeezed the leather seat and stared out the window away from him, at the flanks of the Camelback, the stately slopes of contoured rock with high-ticket homes perched there for the privilege of looking down upon the world from a safe altitude. She said nothing.

And Del Rebus said nothing. They turned off Tatum and were soon purring up the drive toward the garage. He operated the transmitter to coax open the door. Inside the garage he turned off the engine and leaned forward, rested his brow on the wheel. "You know how many drunks it takes to screw in a light bulb?"

Franny Lott left him in the car and went quietly into the house.

Chapter 15

It was Sunday morning and Elvis was impressed, because he had fully expected Del Rebus to go into the tank upon Franny's departure Saturday.

Elvis had driven her in the Oldsmobile to catch her flight out of Sky Harbor. In the car they exchanged reminiscences from childhood, memories calculated to buffer them from the present. Franny recalled summers on a lake in Michigan, the lone Jewish girl in a neighborhood of goyim, whose closest friend was an Appaloosa that she rode for hours every day, and how, on the day of her bas mitzvah at age fourteen, she was awakened by a gunshot. She remembered running out onto the lawn amidst the tents erected for the guests, and across the street, and into the yard of the caretaker, seeing the rawboned man in bib overalls emerge with her father from the barn, the shotgun cradled in her father's arm. Her Appaloosa had been discovered in the corral, its foreleg unexplainably broken.

Elvis had memories of church socials in East St. Louis, the names of JFK and Martin Luther King, Jr., on everyone's lips; in Los Angeles there were no saviors, only the gangs. He was fifteen, sitting first chair in the civic orchestra, when his parents first heard him perform. The occasion was an attempt at Tchaikovsy's Symphony No. 5 in E Minor. The rousing finale in allegro vivace stumbled a little when the conductor lost control of his baton, sailing it past the tympanist's ear, but the orchestra charged on, making up in gusto for what it lacked in finesse. His father, a diminutive man given to large silences, said nothing after the performance for the better part of an hour, before declaring himself impressed, as a man who had just experienced the very gates of hell flung open.

At the departure section of Terminal 3, Elvis popped the trunk and a skycap, after asking which airline Franny was flying, hefted her suitcases off toward a check-in counter. Elvis joined Franny on the curb, and she pressed a card into his hand. "It's my lawyer. You can always get in touch with me through him."

Elvis tugged on his earlobe. "Like if I need a recipe for fresh salmon almondine, something like that."

"No, fancy cooking, that's your department, Elvo. You know what I mean."

Elvis glanced at the skycap, a broad-shouldered brother

with a pencil stache, waiting with Franny's luggage at the counter, his impatience with her somewhat mollified by curiosity. Elvis recognized the look as one he had seen all over Phoenix, on faces white and black and all the colors in between.

He reached for Franny's hand and clasped it in both of his. "Yeah. I know what you mean. We all got our own ideas of what hell is, and I imagine this is Del's. But he's a big boy, chile. I guess he'll just drink himself through it." He let go of her hand then, placed a kiss upon his fingertips and touched her cheek with them. "Me, I'm going to sit down with the list of clients, make sure Del's sticking to the program. I got nothing against a little redistribution of the wealth, but not the way Keating did it. How 'bout you? Once the divorce is final, what, you going back east to check out your race-tracks?"

Clasping her hands and closing her eyes, she shook her head even as she contemplated an answer. Then she smiled her beautiful smile at him. "No. And another thing: I don't want anything more to do with country clubs and charity balls. What I've been dreaming of, you know what I've been dreaming about?"

"Tell me."

"Going back to school, Elvo. To learn how to do something, as opposed to just being what I am. To earn a degree in wildlife husbandry. Animals are the real innocents in this world."

"I wouldn't know about that."

"I'd like to make a difference, like Dian Fossey. But the reality of it is you have to be as crazy, or possessed, as I think Del is. Or she was."

Elvis leaned over to whisper in her ear. "You don't have to be like anybody to do the best you can."

"Thanks." She leaned forward and kissed him quickly on the cheek. "Elvo? Don't think too badly of me."

"Not a chance," he said.

She took a step back, away from him, and said, "Del . . . Del and I . . ." and turned swiftly, the hem of her dress snagging for an instant on her calves, before it snapped free to accommodate her stride.

A lady cop, maybe 130 pounds if you included all the accessories hanging from her belt, edged up to him and said, "Sir? Take a picture, it'll last longer."

"Pardon me?"

"Move the car, please. This isn't a parking lot."

Del surprised him by not leaving the house that night for the usual haunts. Instead they shared a subdued meal together, cornish hen and rice baked in a mushroom soup and onion concoction with stir-fried snowpeas and mushrooms on the side. Del drank ice water with the dinner, and when the cleanup was finished, he mixed himself a martini and took it to the patio and stretched out in a lounge chair and sipped it beneath a black sky radiant with the jewelry of distant constellations. After going through the list of clients, Elvis came up with two that bothered him, because of their addresses in Sun City, a retirement community, but it was a matter that could be deferred, no rush, not with Del doing whatever he needed to get past the loss of someone like Franny Lott. So it was Elvis, not Del, who drove down into the city to party that night and who struck up something crazy, and eventually passionate, with an America West stewardess.

And it was Elvis who awoke in the residence off Doubletree a little past sunrise, next to a warm feminine presence, resting his hand for a pleasurable instant on the lady's ass, right where it curved away from her spine. He pawed around in the almost charcoal light for his briefs, then wandered out to the kitchen to make the coffee. The coffee not only had been prepared, but was brewed, with two cups and saucers set out next to the pot.

Del Rebus was visible in the dusky beginning of the day standing next to the pool and sighting on the North Star with Elvis's empty Mag.

Elvis drank his coffee black at the breakfast nook, watching Del taking pretend practice shots. With his second cup he ate a slice of unbuttered pumpernickel toast and gobbled vitamins. Then he ambled back to the bedroom, pulled on a jockstrap, donned sweats, socks, and his Reeboks. Back in the kitchen he filled a canteen with water. He broke and swallowed a raw egg. Sliding open the glass door, Del came in from the pool and set the Mag in the holster beside the sink. "How was the coffee?"

"You got the touch."

"Believe it or not, I know a little about the restaurant business."

"There isn't anything I don't just believe you wouldn't know a little something about. Long night?"

"I got some sleep. Kind of a jangly sleep without all the liquor in my system, but I expected that. Ready to run?"

It took Elvis a moment before adding it up: the bulky gray sweatshirt, the red shorts, his stick legs planted in good jogging sneakers. "You serious?"

"I'm going to give it a shot."

Elvis led the way onto the patio, where they loosened up for several minutes, bending and stretching, Del repeating between groans a convoluted joke that Elvis had heard him tell a half dozen times.

They trotted down the drive and up the asphalt, matching stride for stride almost to Tatum, before Del fell back after about a mile and, gasping, announced he would be waiting for Elvis beside the pool to pump iron.

When Elvis loped up the drive, entering the house through the garage, crossing the sautillo tile breathing through his mouth and inhaling deeply, his whole body jelled with sweat, he encountered another surprise: his lady friend, Heather Tamara Lee, ensconced in the breakfast nook with a cup of coffee and a gorgeously rolled egg omelet embraced by an arm of fresh strawberries sliced lengthwise. A crystal glass of Dom Pérignon resided beside the coffee. "The white gentleman named Del," she said, smiling, "is he your press agent?"

"No."

She snicked a finger against the throat of the champagne bottle. "You might want to think about hiring him."

"I'd kiss you," he said, "if I hadn't run so far I probably smell worse than my own jockstrap." Elvis slid the door open to the patio and slid it shut. Del occupied a lounge chair still laboring over the book about consciousness. "Del?"

He pushed his sunglasses onto the top of his head and

laid the book on the cooldeck, splayed page down where he had left off. "Ah, Sparky. Time to pump some iron."

"You been holdin' out on me. You lay a flashy plate like that in front of Heather, but all the time I'm cooking, you act like you don't know broccoli from brussel sprouts."

"I said I knew a little something about restaurants."

"More'n a little something," grunted Elvis, dropping down next to Del on the cooldeck to do push-ups.

"Okay, I owned a few. Tell you about it sometime."

They did three reps of fifty each, rolling onto their shoulders between sets to rest for one minute, arms flat at right angles to their torsos, knees above their heads and toes touching the cooldeck. Then they moved beneath the patio to take turns spotting each other with free weights. They worked together for close to an hour before Del dived into the pool to do laps, while Elvis, feeling almost otherworldly from the exertion, strolled inside in the direction of the bath. Heather met him when he emerged from the shower, toweling off, and in a very short time elevated him from otherworldly to celestial. After which they both slept until early afternoon.

Elvis awoke first and padded through the house in his briefs. He found Del in the same lounge chair, in the same red shorts, asleep in the sun. He cupped water from the pool and whipped it in the direction of the prone figure in the lounge chair. Del opened his eyes.

"You got to watch your intake of ultraviolet, white man."

Del blinked and touched his chest, his belly, his thighs below the hem of his shorts. "Yeah. Thanks."

"Maybe if you read someone who could keep you awake."

Swinging his feet onto the cooldeck, Del pushed his fingers through his hair and looked sheepish. "Frances gave it to me. Pretty rich stuff, actually. The man argues that the gods, including the big Guy Himself, originated in auditory hallucinations. The two lobes of the brain weren't in sync yet, so reactions that are automatic to us were transmitted a little slowly, in the form of voices. One lobe 'hearing' the other. It's rich stuff, Sparky, really. But the thing is, the writing, it's like one of the lobes is transmitting in German to the lobe that's doing the writing in English, with assistance of a Chinese translator."

"Slow going."

"Like tramping through quicksand in cleats."

Elvis squatted in front of him, butt between the backs of his calves, forearms on his thighs, and grinned. "You reading not just to learn, but to learn about *her.*"

Del sighed. "You just might be right. Back there, all you thought about was survival, getting over. I got—I have a lot of catching up to do. It's a little more complicated out here."

"You say that again."

"You know what you do? Keep your dreams simple. Mine's as simple as a silver dollar: one side, there's what we're doing here; the other side's Frances."

"It's the sun, Del. You better come inside."

"Wrong, Sparky. Now I understand the way my father looked at my mother." Del Rebus stood abruptly and clapped his hands. "I'm going to shower and head downtown. Maybe check out the crowd at La Mode, or Rex's Thing. Leave you two alone. Shit, maybe I'll make a run at Sport Time. But you won't have to come get me, you got my word."

Elvis placed a hand on his chest. "No. Not Sport Time. You just did business with a don in there. Don't go soft in the head on me, Del."

The twinkle went flat in Del's eyes. "You running the show now?"

"I thought we were partners."

Del put his head down, pushed his fingers through his hair. "We are. I guess nostalgia got the best of me. Like the place would be a way to . . . hold her a little longer. But okay, no Sport Time. Thanks, Sparky."

Del squeezed his shoulder, picked up towel and book, and passed through the sliding glass door.

For the first time in twenty-four hours Elvis felt good about things.

Chapter 16

It was Ruby's first visit to Paul's office. The room beyond the kitchen in Sport Time surprised him by its Spartan decor. This was the man's theater of operations, or so he had been led to believe.

The walls were forest green and without adornment save a dart board. The pale gray carpet yielded comfortably underfoot, but Ruby had walked on plusher—walked and cavorted too. Paul Scorcese sat behind a slender ebony desk in an ebony chair with sloping, sinuous arms, a stern piece of furniture that appeared to be the descendant of some Oriental device of torture. There was a single ivory phone on the desk fitted with buttons for several lines. Nothing else on the desk, not even a pen. An expensive-looking sound system occupied one side of the room next to a large-screen television backed in a far corner from the desk. In the corner behind Paul's left elbow stood a black steel safe with chromium dial that was almost the size of the television set. Paul sat with his back straight and leaning forward, his brown ropy forearms at rest on the desk. He wore a white knit shirt, what tennis players used to wear, and no jewelry whatsoever. The shirt was buttoned to his throat.

Paul nodded affably at one of the two torture chairs facing the desk. In the other chair, once he had sat down, Ruby recognized one of the guys that had come to The Stallion Bar & Grill the night he identified the redheaded drag queen. A guy in an off-the-rack suit in need of pressing, with a look about him—mostly the eyes—of a cop.

This was the short one, with the stocky frame and the spray of freckles under small agate eyes and the corrugated nose. He was chewing gum, maybe the same stick he was working on the night he came into the Stallion, digging around in his ear with his pinkie finger asking Ruby what he knew about the queen. It was a different suit this morning, but still off the rack, a dark blue with white stitching, possibly a top-of-the-line item at Pic'N'Save. The knot of the man's prune-and-yellow-striped tie hung well below his throat and looked thick enough to stop a small-caliber bullet. He sat with an ankle hiked on a knee, a creased, black, highly polished shoe visible, also a white sock. His nails were clean and his chin was shaved and his stomach under the white cotton shirt lounged over his belt. The man looked soft, but only next to a leather truncheon.

Paul stood up when Ruby sat down, lifting his chair away from him, and came around the desk until he was standing midway behind Ruby and the cop-looking guy. "Ruby," he said, his arms extended to them, "this is a man you may call Mr. Johnson. Mr. Johnson, Ruby. Okay, so far?"

"Sure," volunteered Ruby. "Whatever."

The fellow in the suit kept chewing his gum and sneering at Ruby.

Paul Scorcese smoothed his eyebrow with a middle finger. "Mr. Johnson?"

"Yeah. Sure."

The guy in the suit went on chewing.

"Thank you, Mr. Johnson. If you'd wait in the bar, Ruby will be along shortly."

The man called Mr. Johnson pushed himself leisurely up from his chair, his small eyes and pulsing jaws suggesting a lowbrow's arrogance, even contempt. He struck Ruby as the kind of man who, if he smoked, would drop more ashes outside the ashtray than in. "I hope this ain't gonna take too long," he said at the door. "I gotta job, you know."

Paul did not even turn around to acknowledge the man's remarks, but his face sharpened for an instant, a definition that left no doubt about how dangerous a man he could be. When the door clicked shut, Paul moved down the room and manipulated buttons on the sound system, and a low wave of symphony music washed over Ruby. He knew nothing about such music except that you couldn't dance to it.

"Mozart," said Paul, settling in his chair across the desk from Ruby. "I find listening to Mozart one of the quickest ways to sanitize the air after having to share it with the likes of Mr. Johnson."

Ruby nodded, sensing that he and Paul were on the same wavelength.

"Ruby, I need a favor. You've met my father. You know he's not . . . he's not playing with a full deck anymore. Well, to get to the heart of the matter, he got hustled, Ruby, the end of last week. Took him for fifty grand."

"Jesus, Paul. But how can I help you?"

"You know the guy who hustled him."

Was it an accusation? Ruby was totally lost, and terrified. "I swear to you, Paul," he blurted, "I don't know. I don't know anything about this."

"No, no, no. Relax, studball. I meant that you could identify him. Irwin Field's his name. Irwin Field, Ruby."

The surge of adrenaline left Ruby drawing a complete blank.

"The man I had you follow that night back to the Hoyt, where your roomie works."

Now he had it. "The old hippie. With the beautiful wife. Funny guy, always telling jokes. Still comes in every now and then."

"That's him."

"How could he hustle all that kind of money from your father?"

"Trust me on it, Ruby, he did. I told you the man had con written all over him. I know these types. I know what buttons to push. This is not a stupid man, so he will listen to reason. I am a reasonable man. You will explain this to Mr. Field, that while I am upset about his abuse of my father's trust, I am a reasonable man: for one hundred thousand dollars, we will forget all about it. He made a mistake; to err is human. You will see: he will be only too glad to redress the situation. Once the money is paid, you thank the man and leave. I am going to give you a number to call when you're out of there."

Standing, Ruby didn't quite know what to do with his hands, pocketing one, squeezing a pec with the other, then joining them to crack his knuckles. "Paul?"

The quiet man in the tennis shirt had found spiral pad and pen and pushed them across the desk for Ruby.

"Paul, there isn't going to be anything like guns, or anything like that is there?"

Paul Scorcese shook his handsome head slowly from side to side. "This isn't the movies, Ruby, this is just business. Now write down the address and phone number I'm going to give you."

Ruby copied the information in a script he could barely recognize as his own.

Mr. Johnson took his time finishing his mug of coffee before acknowledging Ruby standing behind his bar stool in his black T-shirt, bleached jeans, and navy blue boots. Mr. Johnson didn't drink the coffee, he sipped it noisily, and when he was done, he swung around on the bar stool, wriggling his little finger in his ear, his eyes going lazily up and down, as if measuring Ruby for something, which probably was not a tuxedo. "Gotcher marching orders, kid?" he said.

Ruby patted the hip pocket of his jeans, where he kept his wallet. The man dug for change in the pocket of his suit jacket and left silver on the counter along with what appeared to be sock lint. It was ten o'clock in the morning and the voice of Nat King Cole melted into the stale air with the sweet strains of "Unforgettable."

Outside in the parking lot, in the nearly 100-degree sunlight, Mr. Johnson broke an immediate sweat but did not remove his jacket. "We'll take your car."

"You sure?"

"Sure I'm sure. Lead me to her, before I fuckin' ignite."

"You might want to take off the jacket," suggested Ruby, certain now the man had a piece clipped to his waist, that he was a cop.

"Why's that?"

"My car's got a canvas top, no windows, no air."

They climbed into the Suzuki and strapped on the seat belts. Mr. Johnson did not remove his coat. "Drive fast," he said.

"You won't feel any cooler," said Ruby.

"I know that. But we'll get there sooner. Or is that too tough for you?"

Ruby cranked the key and the engine leapt.

"Paul said two guys would be coming along."

"Bar on Cave Creek," said Mr. Johnson. "Take a left outta here, pick up Squaw Peak, be the quickest way."

They drove for a while, Mr. Johnson nixing every station selection on the radio, until Ruby accidentally switched bands from FM to AM, picking up a call-in show, something to do with home improvements. A man wanted to extend his patio by twenty feet, and having never worked with cement, he wondered how many bags he would need to mix. Mr. Johnson clucked disdainfully. "You believe this dummy?"

Ruby just drove, the air scraping him like a dull razor.

The host of the show, after a mild chuckle, suggested the man purchase premixed in a rental mixer, pick it up as early as possible, around sunrise if possible, and have plenty of help, or expect to be dead of exhaustion by noon.

Mr. Johnson leaned over and rapped Ruby lightly on the shoulder, shouting into the wind, "I bet your boss could give lessons in how to mix cement. Whaddaya think, kid?"

Ruby shrugged.

"Hey!" shouted Mr. Johnson, cupping one side of his mouth with a hand. "If you're uptight on my account, don't be. I got nothin' against wops. Or fags. Tell you the truth, I like you boys because it means more women for us normal guys."

They went through Dreamy Draw and onto Thirty-second Street, Ruby swinging west onto Cactus. His passenger was expounding upon the subject of Italians, the men in particular, and how they had a passion for gold jewelry, and just because Paul didn't appear to be gold happy, who the hell did he think he was fooling?

Ruby said, "Could be he doesn't like jewelry."

"He's a wop, kid. C'mon."

Ruby realized he was out of his league, but a certain defiance prompted him: "You don't show much respect for a man who's paying your salary."

"He ain't payin' my salary. I do favors for him time to time. He helps me, I help him. All there is to it." Mr. Johnson took a pinkie finger away from his ear and studied the nail. Then grinned at Ruby: "Sweet jumping Jesus. You got the hots for him, huh?"

"I don't know what you're talking about."

"Sure you do, young pudlick. You know zactly what I'm talking about. But like I said, don't be uptight on my account. Your secret's safe with me."

The bar on Cave Creek was a little north of Cactus Road in one of the strip malls struggling to survive. A half-score enterprises paid rent and CAM charges for the privilege of sitting back from an asphalt and nearly deserted parking area. A sign in the bar's window, lettered in black felt tip and faded by the sun, was legible within a few feet, and it encouraged motorcyclists to park behind the premises.

They pulled up in front, directly in front of the hand-lettered sign with the black curtains behind it. There was a tripod sign before the door that identified the establishment as the Cowpoke Tavern. Ruby noticed within the strip a gun shop with iron bars in the windows, a memorabilia store, a small animal hospital, several unleased, vacant spaces, a used-clothing operation, a pet shop with aquariums in the window, a self-serve gasoline station at the end that seemed to be doing business on a regular basis, in contrast to the rest.

Exiting the Suzuki, Mr. Johnson ambled around the vehicle to confront Ruby. He held out a pudgy hand. "Gimme the keys, kid. When your business is done, you make your phone call, and I'll pick you up."

Ruby dropped the keys into his hand. The man's shirt, drenched with sweat, was so thin he could see the gross belly beneath. Ruby's mouth was dry and suddenly incapable of uttering a sound.

From a pocket in his suit Mr. Johnson fished out a stick of gum and stripped off its silvery wrapper and let the wrapper flutter from his fat fingers. His hard jaws worked the gum around in his mouth. The small agate eyes stared at him, unreadable as the eyes of reptiles. "What're you lookin' at, my pud? Like to give her a lick for good luck?"

Ruby wanted to belt Mr. Johnson right there, with his head back and his hands plunged in the pockets of his trousers, but the man was a cop, and something you didn't do was hit a cop. Not in this town. Not if you were gay. Not if staying alive was a significant desire.

Turning away, Mr. Johnson reached behind the driver's seat of the Suzuki and fetched the narrow black attaché case. "Don't forget this," he said, handing it to Ruby. "Now you just trot on in there, kid. Your playmates are waiting. You'll like 'em on account they're real salt a the earth. Ask for Boyd or Rayce."

Chapter 17

The morning was another bright one, promising a temperature in the triple digits even as Del and Elvis finished their
session with the weights on the patio. Both men felt more in
tune than they had in months. Elvis, because he had experienced sensual bliss in excess of anything he could remember.
And Del for the simple reason that his definition of priorities
had shifted.

On the way into the office in the Oldsmobile, Elvis
volunteered the information on the card Franny Lott had
given him. Del, who was dressed in a suit for a change,

flicked the card with a thumbnail, thanked Elvis, deposited it in the recesses of his coat. They found a parking slot at the east end of the building and left the Olds there, for the late afternoon shade. Their receptionist, Shelley, passed over a sheaf of printouts, names and phone numbers of respondents to the 800 number who had called in over the weekend, activating the message machine. The lenses in the large ruby frames that Shelley wore locked on Del, the double-breasted pale gray suit, lavender shirt, and tie composed of grays and plum. Elvis and Del, Mr. Murdock and Mr. Field respectively, divided the list of prospects and departed for their separate offices.

Shelley cupped her mouth with her manicured fingers and addressed the retreating back of Mr. Murdock. "Is that the real Mr. Field, or someone he hired to dress up to look like him for the morning?"

With his hand on the doorknob to his office, Mr. Murdock turned around, grinning, and winked. "Scary, ain't it?" He came back across the carpet and leaned on the kidney-shaped desk. "Something like this happens, who knows? A black man could run for governor of Arizona."

Shelley's blue eyes stretched beyond mere magnification.

Mr. Murdock leaned closer. "I didn't say he'd be elected."

The phone call came about the time Elvis was beginning to think about lunch. Shelley contacted him on the intercom to relay Mr. Field's request to come to his office. Immediately would be fine. Something about the phrasing of the postscript put Elvis in mind of the Mag he had left unloaded in his bedroom.

He could only hope he looked composed emerging from his office and vanishing into Del's.

Between the two windows that looked out over the parking lot, the fan palms and the pool with gazebos, Del Rebus stood with his suit coat off, his tie loosened, and one hand in his change pocket, the other behind his head toying with the stubby ponytail. Seeing Elvis, he put on a lavish smile and rolled his head back, elbows at his sides, palms up, impressario fashion, and said, "Have I got a surprise for you."

"Yeah?"

"Oh yeah." Del moved behind his desk, settled into the gray chair behind it. "Somebody claiming to be the son of Joe Scorcese called to say a friend of the family was on the way and that it would be very smart to listen to what this friend said."

"Anything else?" Elvis, from habit, strolled toward the windows.

"Nope. You know how these strong, silent types like to come across. Short and sweet."

"He's going to want the money back, plus interest. I think we ought to pay the man."

"And get what?" Del Rebus sneered.

"Time to move the hell out of here."

"Sparky."

"Oh, shit. You got something else in mind."

"I do. A thing of beauty."

Through the window Elvis recognized the muscled blond with a black attaché case, gazing across the parking lot from the perimeter of the pool. He also recognized the two rudely dressed creatures standing with him in the shade. And while he didn't completely understand what was developing, he knew that he wasn't witness to mere coincidence. "I hope so," he said, "because something's coming down. The friend of the family isn't alone. Check it out."

While Del was doing that, Elvis stepped out of the office and, with as much calm as he could muster, asked Shelley to visit the ladies' room, lock herself in there until he knocked.

"Mr. Murdock, are you sure?"

"Move," he said.

Ruby didn't want anything to do with the situation he found himself in, but what Paul had put in motion had taken on its own energy, so that the young bodybuilder, even as he carried out his part, experienced the trek from the gazebo across the hot parking lot almost as a spectator. He had seen the bikers, Rayce and Boyd, reach into the saddlebags on Rayce's Hog and come out with guns in cloth holsters, colored green and brown, and stuff these deadly ensembles down their spines, beneath their shirts. The skinny one with the shaved head and bad teeth, who did most of the talking, gave him a wolfish grin. "I don't think this old hippie's gonna fuck with someone like you, but if he does, Ruby, that's what we're here for. Hippies. Jesus, you talk about your Martin Luther Coon lovers. I tell you what: I had only one bullet, and it's a choice between a hippie and a nigger, I think I'd shoot the fuckin' hippie. On account he's a traitor to his race. Ain't the nigger's fault he's born what he is."

Ruby climbed the concrete stairs and knocked on the

outer door and was asked to step inside, by a black man, as it turned out, an altogether handsome man sitting behind the receptionist's receptacle.

"And you would be?" asked the black man behind the kidney-shaped desk.

"A friend of the family," said Ruby, exactly as he had rehearsed it in Paul's office. "Here to see Mr. Field."

"Oh, yes," said the black man in the tailored suit and burgundy tie, "we've been expecting you." He stood up and showed him to the door nearest to the desk, pushed it open for Ruby, and stepped back deferentially. "Mr. Field, a friend of the family to see you, sir."

Standing backed to the wall next to the doorway, Del Rebus swung a blunt toe in the direction of Ruby's testicles, but missed, striking him just above the groin, but hard enough even there to drop the lad to his knees. Elvis, plowing in from behind, forearmed him across the cheek. They used their expensive ties to bind him at his wrists and ankles, and Del shoved his silk handkerchief into Ruby's mouth. They rolled him over on his back on the carpet in front of Del's desk. Elvis straddled his chest and pressed a fist against Ruby's windpipe. "You ever jailed, boy? Close your eyes once for no, twice for yes."

The blond eyelashes descended once.

"I thought so. Now we want some honest answers to our questions, or in a split second you will never be able to speak, ever. I will pulverize your Adam's apple. Blink if you're understanding the situation here."

Ruby blinked.

"Good." Elvis Mahoney withdrew the pressure on the man's larynx.

Del leaned above Elvis's shoulder, his lips puckered. "I have to tell you, kid, we're sorry as hell about this, but we're operating under a little bit of a time crunch. We happened to notice the pair of goons you were conversing with down there. It did not inspire confidence. For example, they could be carrying. Are they? I think we can take the hankie out, let the man speak."

Elvis did that, but put his fist back on top of Ruby's throat, not pressing, just to let him know.

Ruby took a moment to work some saliva into his mouth, then said, "Yes. Pistols."

Del said, "I see. The message is?"

Ruby explained it, his eyes moving from Del to Elvis to Del.

"A hundred thou," said Del. "And then what?"

"Then nothing," squeaked Ruby. "The money's there, Paul says it's just a misunderstanding. You're a man in business, and a very clever one at that," he repeated, as he had rehearsed it. "And he said to say, 'Salute.' He wishes you good health."

"Really. Somehow the boys down by the gazebo don't quite match up with that sentiment."

"It's what he said. He said between you and him, it is business, and that you would be smart enough to understand that."

Elvis looked over his shoulder at Del, trying to hold his eyes, but saw that Del was beyond negotiation.

"Ruby, we're going to break precedent in your case. I'm sure you're aware of the traditional reaction when a messenger delivers bad news. And believe me, asking us to fork over one hundred big ones kind of falls under the heading of bad news. You understand what I'm telling you?"

Ruby's eyes filled with more white, as the focus shuttled between Del and Elvis, even as the black man removed the pressure on his throat and rose to his feet.

"Don't piss your pants, boy. What the man's saying, usually the bearer of bad news is handed his head. Killed, Ruby. We ain't about to do that. You carrying?"

"No."

"Give me the key to the attaché case."

"In my billfold."

Elvis rolled him onto his stomach, dug the wallet from his back pocket, and handed it to Del. The key was inserted and the mechanism moved smoothly, the lock releasing with a sound they could all hear. Del worked two more latches and looked inside. *"Nada,"* he said.

Ruby could feel the knots being worked on at his ankles, and in a short matter of time he was no longer staring intimately into carpet piling, but was standing, his wrists still bound behind him, some bourbon trickling down his throat, the bottle held by the black man. The drink was the idea of the white guy, Del, who apologized for putting a foot in his belly.

"Ease the pain a little?" he inquired.

"A little," said Ruby. Standing, he experienced some double vision, but the tremors of nausea had subsided.

"Good," said Del. "Now tell me, how well do you know the goons? And what do they know about us?"

* * *

There were two porcelain urinals in the men's room for the second-floor offices, and two stalls, one of them oversized for the handicapped, with stainless-steel rails for the walking-impaired to hoist themselves from the wheelchair and onto the toilet seat. Its functional value was somewhat diminished by the fact that no elevator, escalator, or ramp connected the ground floor with the upper. The office jocks worked out in there during the lunch hours, employing the railing as parallel bars, but otherwise, it was a generally neglected area. It was here that Ruby found himself sitting bare-assed on the toilet, his wrists lashed with neckties to the railing, his jeans and briefs down about his ankles, bound by his own belt, and almost a whole roll of toilet paper stuffed in his mouth.

Elvis Mahoney, his hands on his thighs, leaned forward. "Don't fight it. It's almost lunchtime. You won't be in here fifteen minutes at the most."

Then he locked the stall from the inside, slid beneath the partition into the next stall, left it, and tested the knob on the outer door. Del, who was waiting for him there, descended the concrete stairs nearest to where they had parked the car. Elvis strode the length of the wing, knocked on the door to the ladies' room. He heard Shelley's voice: "Who is it?"

"Me, chile. Mr. Murdock. Listen. Sit tight five minutes more, then come out. Take the rest of the day off. We'll be in touch."

"You're scaring me."

"Yeah, well." Elvis pushed his forehead against the bathroom door. "Do it the way I say it. Okay?"

"Okay," she said. "Yes. Okay."

Elvis went back up the wing and down the steps that exited on the north side of the office complex, the side opposite the fan palms and gazebo-bound pool. Del was there in the Oldsmobile. Elvis climbed in the front and a few seconds later spotted the motorcycles belonging to Boyd and Rayce parked at a rakish angle near the front of the complex. Del accelerated. The bikes exploded off the grille and right fender of the rent-a-car, tumbling across the asphalt and landing sidewise, fuel lines spewing gasoline. Rear tires caught and squealed as Del dumped gears into reverse and backed at the prostrate Hogs with a vengeance. He whipped the wheel hard to avoid hitting them once again, braking right alongside them. Del glanced at Elvis, a book of Sport Time matches cupped in his hand, then ran his window down, struck a match and tossed it. The match flared, but failed to hold its flame. A second one ditto. Elvis said, "Shit. Trouble coming my way, Del. Coming fast."

Del struck a third match and lit the whole book.

They started running the instant they heard the sickening wrench of raked steel, knowing instinctively that their machines were at the mercy of some maniac. Boyd led Rayce by a good twenty feet at the end of the pool and increased the distance across the grass, digging hard in his heavy black boots and feeling it in his lungs. He saw the white car with the tinted glass idling at a crazy angle beyond where the bikes had been parked, and dropped to one knee at the edge of the asphalt, prying the recently stolen Ruger from his waistband.

Rayce came hauling up behind him and tried to stop,

but his heel sailed out ahead of him and he wound up butt-side down in the grass, the piece in his hand discharging into the sedate Scottsdale sky.

At the same instant the white car swerved away, the tires screeching, while flames flowered from the mangled shapes of their Hogs.

"Shit," said Boyd, squeezing off a round at the car.

"Shit."

"Shit."

"Shit."

The car had disappeared down the side of the building. Lumbering to his feet, Rayce came abreast of Boyd. "Lookit they done to our fuckin' Hogs!"

Boyd started running. "You got insurance?"

"Fuck's that?"

"Me neither. Here, gimme the gun."

Boyd skinned on his back beneath a parked BMW 325i, stuffed the weapons and holsters above a gap in the exhaust manifold. Scrambling back out, he took off his boots and leather trousers and convinced Rayce to do likewise. They attacked the fire, beating down the flames with their pants, shouting at one another. There was no way they could hear the sound of the engine of the white car that had circled the complex. The white car that had crept up behind them, that they suddenly noticed. The white car out of which climbed the white man and the nigger, the nigger a typical nigger, walking away from a fair fight, two on two, reaching into the popped trunk and coming around the car on the white man's side, the white man closing the door and approaching with a tire iron in his hand.

"Boyd and Rayce," he said, "isn't it?"

The bikers stood there in their socks, in their baggy white underpants, straddling the smoking remains of their motorcycles, and tried to comprehend how this suit with a tire iron knew them by name. The way Mr. Johnson laid it out, they were simply anonymous enforcers. But now it was personal. The light broke earliest for Boyd. "The nigger," he muttered. "It's the nigger from the desert, Rayce. That shot your Hog."

"I be goddamned, it is. It sure is."

They all heard the sirens approaching.

"Guys," said Del, "much as I'd like to stick around to beat on you. Rayce, you take off your briefs, then get under that Buick there. Do it, before I start breaking bones. Now!" He pointed to a red car parked beside the BMW. "Boyd, you want some of this?"

Rayce crawled where they told him to, and while he was doing that, they bound Boyd's arms and ankles with leather trouser legs and stuck Rayce's underwear into his mouth and hoisted him into the trunk. They emerged onto a side street, just as two police cruisers powered their way into the parking lot of the complex. The police found Rayce bare-assed beneath a Buick Regal, his face smeared with smoke and so bone-mad he could barely utter a coherent sentence. They booked him for indecent exposure.

The bottle blond in the black gussied-up bathing suit was propped on the stool behind the glass cases, fidgeting with an emery board, her hand moving in little mincing motions. She cracked her gum and glanced up, a tentative expression on her face. "Sir?"

"Package of gollies," he said.

She started to reach for them, hesitated, then smiled. "I didn't recognize you in the suit. You sure do look . . ."

"Respectable?" Del Rebus suggested.

"Aw, you know what I mean. Different." She plunked the package of cigarettes on the rubber mat on the counter-top, added a book of matches, and said, "That be all?"

He handed her the amount plus a dollar gratuity, no longer the extravagant tipper that he had been upon his first visit to Sport Time. He cocked his head, listening to the music sifting into the lobby, an instrumental piece that he finally recognized to be "Unchained Melody." He said, "Percy Faith?"

The woman, leaning against the stool, paused with the emery board. "What's that?"

"The music," he said.

"Oh. Is that the name of the group? The music gets played here, it ain't even hip enough for elevators. You know what the bartenders call it? Wheelchair music."

"Different strokes," he said, feeling for a burning instant the entirety of his age. "Helen, that's your name, isn't it?"

"Uh-huh."

"Helen, what I'd very much like you to do for me, I'd like you to step into the bar and find Paul Scorcese, and tell him a friend of the family would like to see him, out here."

"I'm really not supposed to."

"Lock up your register and cases. Go ahead. You won't hurt my feelings. I understand." He fanned five twenties on the rubber mat. "And you can hang on to this, darling, in case you come up short when they count the tittie maga-zines."

Helen eyed the money, the emery board frozen above a fingernail, then dropped it on the counter, snatched the five bills and did exactly what Del Rebus suggested.

It was easier than she had anticipated, because Mr. Scorcese was visible at the far end of the bar in his white Izod shirt buttoned to his throat, in conversation with a fat, freckled man who bought gum from her and never tipped, and a taller, kind of scary guy by the name of Chub. Chub had short black hair except for the first inch or so back from his forehead, which was completely white. He had black eyes and a cleft palate and a manner of speaking that confused Helen, adding to her fear of the man. Fear was probably a healthy attitude, given the fact that Chub was born to a gin-loving streetwalker whose idea of therapy was to tie the child up and tape his mouth shut, which bred in the man a decidedly dim view of women. He was Mr. Scorcese's driver and always wore a suit, nice ones too, winter and summer. After apologizing for the intrusion, Helen delivered the message from the man in the lobby and saw Mr. Scorcese's eyes move in the direction of the fat guy chewing gum. "Gentlemen," he said, and the three of them, with Chub leading, followed her down the bar and along the aisle to the lobby.

The grimy creature perched on her stool was as speechless as she was, because his mouth was stuffed with something unpleasant looking. Tears streaked his dirty cheeks. He was bound hand and leg by something wide and black, but that's all she could tell, because Mr. Scorcese quietly ordered her to go back into the lounge. The good-looking guy who smoked French cigarettes was nowhere to be seen.

She heard the freckled fat guy say, "Sweet jumping Jesus."

"Shut up," said Mr. Scorcese, without raising his voice. "Chub, clean up this mess, will you?"

And that's all she heard.

Chapter 18

Elvis Mahoney was not crazy about the stunt, dumping Boyd in the lobby of Sport Time, but given the alternative Del was considering, to take the skinhead out into the desert and strap him to a saguaro, he agreed to the prankster approach. It was not far from his thinking that Del had already killed one man, and once they were out in the desert, in the solitude there, murder might tempt him once more. Things were already out of hand. Killing someone, even pond scum like Boyd, was not something Elvis was quite prepared to be a part of.

He drove the Olds from Sport Time back to the rented residence in Paradise Valley, careful to obey the fluctuating speed limits, Del in the bucket seat beside him talking nearly the entire time, scheming. Clearly pumped.

In the house, the familiar sautillo tile and bare walls, the view of the pool fit for angels, this desert idyll among the slopes, Elvis experienced the gradual slowing down of his senses. He shook, and he shook with laughter too, collapsing onto a chair in the breakfast nook. He could not believe the madness of the past hour, and yet he had no choice: it was real. Somebody had tried to kill them. It was as real as fucking Kmart.

Del Rebus said, "I'm having a Corona, how about you?"

Pushing himself out of the chair, Elvis said, "Gonna go load the Mag."

"Then what?"

"Pack."

"And miss all the fun?"

Elvis went down the hall in the direction of his room. "Just put together numbers. Show me what you figure I got coming, I won't hassle you none. You're crazy, but you're not a bush guy."

"Thanks," said Del Rebus. "I'll include it in my résumé."

Joe Scorcese paying cash to buy shares in a deceased canine was not merely the exception, but an aberration, which Elvis believed Del should have picked up on immediately. However, his preoccupation with vengeance had blinded him. Elvis did not object to the scam so long as they were clear-headed about it. He owed the man, but he wasn't going to take a fall for his private devils.

So far as the money, Elvis was confident it would be there, because Del had been completely straight on the mechanics. The five- and six-figure checks made out to Murdock, Field were deposited in an account bearing that name, allowed time to clear, then dispersed in amounts less than ten thousand dollars (to avoid attracting the scrutiny of the IRS), to accounts in two-score banks around the valley, portions of them drawn out daily by Elvis and Del using false identification, thanks to the tattoo artist in San Francisco. Most of the money was there, in cash, in the house in Paradise Valley. Close to three million, if Elvis's calculations were correct. The original split had been twelve-five/twelve-five for the quiet guys, twenty-five points for Elvis, and one half for Del.

Thinking it over as he folded his clothes and filled suitcases, he wondered what amount Del was shooting for, for himself. By the terms of their understanding, he was already approaching a million five. And Elvis, almost three-quarters of a mil. He ceased folding, his eyes moving to the window, to the stunted slopes out there looking like huge efforts in papier-mâché, the dull greens and cardboard tints, the gray of stone and shadow, the glimpses of brick-colored rock like hints of the predominant hue of the Camelback to the south. The sky a perfectly smooth and dreamy wash of blue. So deceptive the beauty that he witnessed, at once alluring and forbidding, and also so elemental, as if it had sprung whole and intact from the Bible. Memories of East St. Louis came crowding back on him: his father, the church, the faith in a tangible deity, the socials, the trust. And the bond, born of shared suffering. He was reminded of the flat twang of a midwestern white man. The low-key sound of him saying, *What's this, a little exercise in Aryan superiority?* The bond.

The man had been there for him, and now what was he doing, washing his hands? Elvis Mahoney clutched two suitcases, with the Mag in its holster slung from a belt over his shoulder, and hauled everything up the hall and into the kitchen . . . and left the bags and gun in a heap beside the sliding glass door.

He found Del beside the pool, taking in the rays on the lounge chair, just a pair of red shorts on and dark glasses, the clear bottle of Corona half-emptied sitting in the shade beneath his butt. Del said, "Less expenses, you're looking at something over seven hundred thou. It's itemized, along with the money, in the tan suitcase lying on the backseat of your car."

"Del."

"I couldn't believe it. I spent more'n fifteen grand on your clothing alone."

"Hey, I don't want to walk out on you."

"Why not, Sparky, it's the fashionable thing to do."

Elvis Mahoney leaned over, his hands planted on his thighs. "Could be it's not a matter of fashion," he said, "but common sense. I been thinking. Way I figured it, your share, right now, is a million five. Pack it in with me, and I'll make your share two million."

Del Rebus lifted the dark glasses away from his eyes and parked the glasses on top of his head. He fumbled under the chair until he found the neck of the bottle, then lifted the beer to his lips, never moving his eyes. When he had drained the bottle, he belched. His lips curled at the corners. "I guess what my daddy said about making enough friends is true. Except he should have said making enough of the *right* friends. Yeah, I could retire, or at least cruise, on two mil. But it isn't just about money now. The same sort of scum that ruined my father tried to take me off. It's going to cost them big-time. This one's for my father."

"And not your ego?"

Del shrugged, swung his legs off the lounge chair, and flexed his bare toes on the cooldeck. "I guess I don't have to draw you a map to the garage."

"You don't even have a gun."

"No, unless you lend me one of those you lifted from the bikers."

"Just an attitude, that's all you got."

"Not an attitude, Sparky. A perspective. A way I hoped to build a game plan, with a friend. But I can buy help. Help's cheap in this town."

Elvis followed him into the kitchen, watched him bite down on the crimped edge of the bottle top and pop it with his teeth, spit the Corona cap onto the countertop. He leaned back against the sink, his legs crossed at the ankles, and raised the bottle in a silent toast, then tipped it to his lips.

"That where your game plan's coming from—a bottle?"

When Del Rebus finished swallowing, the bottle was empty, and after he had set it gently down on the countertop, he pinched off the moisture from the corners of his mouth and wiped his fingertips on his shorts. "No," he said. "I'm just trying to climb down off being shot at, same as you. Except your way is to become a little pissant."

Elvis almost stepped up and took a shot at the man. "Say what?"

"You heard me. Pissant."

That was it. Elvis took the step. He drove a fist at Del's cheek, a stupid punch for a shorter man to throw. Del leaned away and accepted a sting, as opposed to a solid crack, and wrapped Elvis tight with his arms, bound him like a package going UPS. Elvis struggled, though he kept it upper body, no jail moves. He heaved and breathed in furious bursts to break the lock Del's size and weight imposed, but to no avail.

Del said, "Now you want to hear the game plan?"

Elvis wriggled free as Del relaxed his grip. "Game plan," he gasped, working to recover his breath. "Going up against these kind of guys isn't a game. It's the real thing. Getting shot at is the reality when you mess with these people. I hate to say I told you so, but I told you so. Jesus. Do I have to go down to south Phoenix to find someone big enough to beat some sense into you?"

Del Rebus just grinned, his arms folded on his chest.

"Shit, Del. You gonna get us killed."

"*Us?* Did you say *us?* Sparky, you uttered the magic word. Let me show you how we're going to make enough money to open that restaurant of yours. Maybe a whole fucking chain."

Elvis glanced at the suitcases beside the sliding glass door, the Mag in the holster. But the fear of an hour ago, not to say the intelligence of his instincts, had been sapped by Del's easy confidence. Jail habits died hard.

"Maybe I best have a Corona," said Elvis, stripping off

his jacket and loosening his tie, "before you get too far ahead of me."

"You want a chunk of lime in it?"

He snatched the bottle and found an opener in the drawer. "Beer's beer," said Elvis, his voice edged with impatience, and possibly too a residuum of anger with himself for yielding to Del's mania. "Talk," he said.

It was late afternoon when they turned onto McDowell Road and sped toward the ascent into Papago Park, climbing among the great red rocks. Elvis Mahoney was driving the Charger, the a.c. blowing steadily a stream of relief that seemed to die inches from his face, even though the sun was descending behind them. In his rearview mirror he could make out the unspectacular profile of downtown Phoenix, a city without an architectural heart. Above it hung a thin halo of smut, a gift of congestion that the citizens had not yet seen fit to alleviate by building a beltway, or a truly useful form of mass transit. The layer of fumes looked like the work of a disturbed child with a crayon, a blur of brownish color. It was a place for sunlight to go to die.

Both men, in deference to the weather, wore shorts—Del the red ones, along with a San Diego Chargers jersey and cap, some rubber thongs for his feet, and Elvis a bright pair of pink and black, some abstract print, with his Reeboks and a black fishnet tank top. They cracked the windows and locked the doors in the asphalt parking lot of the Phoenix zoo. They walked in a manner indistinguishable from any other late-afternoon visitor, even loitering on the trestle entrance to watch a black swan assert its authority, flailing the green waters below. Del, paying for their tickets to enter, told the young lady in the glass booth a joke concerning an elephant. Elvis vaguely remembered hearing it before.

Once inside the zoo, they gravitated without a word being spoken toward the flock of flamingos, paused there, each with his own thoughts. "Something, aren't they?" said Del Rebus.

"Yeah," said Elvis, "ain't nothing like 'em."

A few minutes later Elvis was introduced to Mr. Assoud and his pert little daughter. Assoud was a small man, a few inches over five feet, Elvis judged, with a prominent nose and gleaming white teeth, his black silken hair beginning to diminish at the temples. He exuded courtesy to a degree that approached unctuous. Elvis ordered a Coors and a frank, handing the money to the daughter, who seemed at once incredibly curious and frightened by him. When she brought him his change and order, he thanked her, seasoned the frank with all the offerings, and ambled toward a bench in the shade, across from an exhibit of giant tortoises. He munched, watching Del gesture as he spoke to Assoud in back of the food stand.

After a few minutes, Assoud climbed back inside his place of business. Del fidgeted with the bill of his Chargers cap, surveying the area, until he spotted Elvis sitting twenty yards away. He pumped his fist, about hip high, his thumb raised. Elvis, his elbows draped over the back of the bench, nodded his head, acknowledging the success of the first phase of their operation. He wished he shared the man's enthusiasm. What Del looked upon as a magnificent dare to achieve a form of poetic justice, Elvis could not help but regard from an actuarial point of view as something akin to skydiving. A mood of banzai prevailed in his heart.

Assoud emerged from the rear of his concession stand with a ring of keys pinched in his fingertips. He and Del plodded off along the asphalt walkway and were quickly obscured by the flora and fauna.

Elvis turned his attention to the tortoise pen once again. One of the mammoth turtles was poised on a mound, a primitive eye directed in his general vicinity. Contemplating an alien intelligence intrigued him a little, and would have been a diverting exercise any other time. But between the thinking of a mobster and that of Del Rebus, he didn't have the energy, or the inclination, to mull the possibility of benign intercourse.

He sat there with the heat pouring all over him, the sweat stirring from his skin, and waited impatiently for Del to return, so that they could implement the next phase of the operation. Once they were moving, *acting*, he was all right. Action muffled the imagination, censored dangerous impulses to weigh and evaluate. Action, in short, relieved him of the responsibility to think. Just go with the flow. Do it Del's way. There was something almost religious about the sensation of letting it all hang out. . . . Elvis Mahoney lifted his eyes to gaze into a peerless sky and remembered the better world that existed before this morning. The one with Heather Tamara Lee in it. And yes, Franny Lott and her innocent flamingos.

Chapter 19

The humidity had to be up there neck and neck with the temperature, which was somewhere in the nineties, and standing outside in a phone booth on Pitkin Avenue, waiting for a call, Angelo Scorcese felt the sweat crawl from his pores, his boxer shorts adhering to the crack of his ass. He glared at Cato sitting in the brown van idling with the air-conditioning. Mai Lee had been on his case all weekend over the slashed top, the stolen wheel covers and radio: how could he be so stupid, leave a Mercedes 500 SL unwatched in South Ozone Park? Worse: going there alone, without a soldier. It was the kind of thing, she said, a man does who is thinking only with his dick, although she believed him, about the call from Paul due to the nonsense Old Joe had bought into. And finally, by this morning, she had forgiven him, sort of, blaming Paul for giving the old man so loose a leash, when he was clearly little more than a drooling child. Mai Lee, kissing him on his single eyebrow, said he could look forward to kidneys and calves' hearts for supper, one of his favorites.

She was a smart lady, Mai Lee, knew just where the edge was. Gave him shit right up to the point where another word would have been greeted with the backside of his hand, then eased off, all sweetness and light. The silken kiss, hearts and kidneys. The bitch had it together, he'd give her that.

Row houses with phony stone facades and pitched shingle roofs, two-story jobs with shallow basements, were built close to the sidewalks and jutted proudly away in every direction down the streets off Pitkin. These were family blocks, strongly Italian with some Irish and German mixed in, some Jewish. From habit Angelo Scorcese moved his attention slowly 360 degrees, checking out the terrain, the cars parked bumper to bumper, and then double-parked along the boulevard, like Cato was. A black Chevrolet, a four-door, eased out of the traffic and stopped behind the van just as the phone rang. Angelo let it ring. A young guy, Joe College with a fancy mustache, climbed out from the driver's side and dodged between parked cars, crossed the sidewalk to a liquor store. Angelo snagged the receiver with a big, sweaty palm. It was five o'clock in the afternoon, an hour before his supper, and the breeze—what there was of one in the heavy, steam-bath air—bore the unmistakable scent of the landfill to the south. "What's up?" he growled.

"Just checking in to see what Plan B is. Because Plan A went into the tank."

"Fuck you saying?"

"The guy that gets the cowboys gets two clowns instead. One is in jail, and the other has gone to seek his fortune in the desert. The sharps are still breathing, and we don't know where."

"We collect the marbles?"

There was silence on the line. Then: "No. We got zilch."

"Jeezus!" Angelo Scorcese cuffed himself above the single eyebrow, not believing it. "What kinda people we got down there, hire fucking clowns?"

Another silence, and then the voice with a little muscle in it: "Don't lay it on our people. You said to go outside, and I did. The guy is reliable help. So okay, he mucked this one up. But the sharps, we got license numbers on two their cars. They're being run through DMV even as we speak. We'll nail 'em. I was calling for some input, not to hear you get a hard-on."

Lifting the Mets baseball cap that he wore backward, catcher fashion, Angelo Scorcese pressed the back of his hand to his hairline and licked the salt of his own sweat. "Now don't go bitchy, little bro'. Tell you what: lemme sid-down with Vacanza, Lorenzo, few other people. I'll get back to you."

"That'll fly. How's Mother?"

"Same old same old. She's a trooper." Angelo glanced at the van, saw his father's ex-protector lip-syncing to whatever music he was listening to on the radio. "Maybe, whaddaya think, I'll fix her up with Cato for a night, take her mind off things. The grape seed, I swear to Chrise, it's about all he does is practice fuckin' dance steps. He's as fruity as the old guy."

"Call me. And give my love to Lorenzo."

"I'll tell you what I'd like to give the slippery little fuck, even he is my brother."

"Stick to business," said the voice on the other end, on the muscle again.

"We'll talk," said Angelo Scorcese, cradling the receiver, as someone else stepped out of the black Chevrolet parked behind the van. Angelo, digging the shorts out of his crotch, moved away from the booth to get a better look at the guy.

This was a guy, the one coming around the front of the Chevy, that looked like a bar brawler, a trim one if you stood him up next to Cato. Otherwise, he was just some ugly putz in an off-white suit, shiny white patent leather shoes, an off-white hat with the brim turned down all the way around. He wore a pale blue shirt and a wide tie that was almost indigo with splashes of jonquil in it. He walked as if the experience did not give him much pleasure. Angelo Scorcese watched him gain the curb, in no hurry, but clearly intent upon having a conversation, the focus of the small green eyes leaving no doubt about that.

"Mr. Scorcese?" the fat man in the suit said, sinking his hands in the front pockets of his pants.

"Not really." Angelo glanced at the van, saw Cato obliviously mouthing song lyrics, no clue to a situation developing. Soon as the old man croaked, Cato had a date with a car trunk. "Now my father, *him* you call Mr. Scorcese. What business is it of yours, friend?"

"Ah. The name is Cox, Lieutenant D. J. Cox, NYPD." He flopped open his gold shield. "Assigned to investigate the attempt on your father's life, back in May."

Angelo spread his legs and crossed his arms on his chest. "I awready talked to you guys. I musta talked to half the fuckin' dicks in the borough. Even this little gook sportin' a twelve-year-old's mustache, rolls his own cigarettes. Now you look like you can handle yourself, but Jeezus, don't they got any requirements for you guys anymore? Girls, little spics and gooks. Shit, when you gonna start hiring pygmies? As a taxpayer, I gotta tell you, you guys are a waste. You don't gotta police force, you gotta comedy club."

Lieutenant Cox dropped a hand into a pocket of his suit coat and brought a small red disc to his mouth, sucked it in. "The investigation ain't over, Angelo, I don't care how many people you talked to. By the way, there's plenty guys this borough calling *you* Mr. Scorcese. On account you done such a good job keeping the bakeries and pizza joints going. You done a helluva thing, the way I hear it."

"It was no big deal. The old guy had the program set up, and I just followed it. Any smart business, you plan for— what's the word? Like odds."

"Contingencies?"

"Yeah, that's the word. That's a Lorenzo-type word. My brother, Lorenzo, he's a lawyer."

"I met him," said Cox, "when he was your father's *consigliere*. Now that you're looking after your father's affairs, I understand that the man with your confidence is Mr. Vacanza, not your brother."

"So? The fuck is it to you?"

Cox delved into the pocket of his suit coat once more and fed himself a red wafer. He took a step toward Angelo Scorcese, his hands loose, a grim smile etched in his face. "*So*, asshole, I'm damn near fifty. I'm around long enough, I know Vacanza's been the man to your father through two wars. It's why you made him *consigliere* is what I think, except after the shooting in May, nobody's made a move on the family. And that puzzles the shit out of me."

Angelo Scorcese shrugged, pulled on a finger until the joint popped. "Life's that way sometimes."

"Yeah? You a philosopher too, Angelo? Your sheet says you're into everything else, but I missed that."

From the corner of his eye Angelo Scorcese watched the Joe College guy approaching with a bottle in a brown paper sack cradled in his arm. He stopped at the curb, a few yards behind Cox, and adopted a look of lazy interest in the proceedings. Young cops suffered from the same schooling as punks: they watched too many movies.

"Your boy's waiting. Cox—is that your name?"

"It's my name."

"You got anything to say, say it. I got no time to stand around and bullshit in this kinda day."

"Like I said, there's plenty guys this borough calling *you* mister these days. Which if I was your father, I'd kinda be thinking about it. You musta gone to a good Catholic school, the phrase *cui bono* mean anything to you?"

"Not less it's a relative of Sonny Bono."

"Well, your father ain't a witty guy like you. It might mean something to him."

Angelo Scorcese pulled on another finger, popping the joint. His grin was smug and dismissive. "Nothing means nothing to him anymore. Old guy's so out of it he oughta be wearing diapers. Now you got anything else to say, put it in writing and hand it to Lorenzo."

Circling the van, Angelo Scorcese climbed onto the shotgun seat and said, "Yo, songbird. Try to fuckin' remember you're being paid to cover my ass, not be Milli Vanilli."

Cato Dellacroce, who had lived little more than a year in the United States of America, engaged gears and steered into traffic. He understood from the tone of Angelo's voice that he was displeased with him, but wondered what it had to do with being a flavor of ice cream.

Mai Lee always prepared suppers to accommodate not only her husband's large appetite, but the possibility of unexpected guests. The children, except the two eldest who ate at the whim of their hormones, dined by themselves along with the nanny a half hour earlier. Mai Lee, unlike the mothers and wives and girlfriends and mistresses of the men with whom her husband associated, did very little of the actual cooking, relying instead upon a succession of Italian widows and spinsters paid for their culinary skills. But she did do the shopping, going as far as Sheepshead Bay, or Fulton Street in Manhattan, for the right piece of fish. She bought her veal exclusively from a butcher on Metropolitan Avenue, and her sausage from a vendor on Broadway, in Queens. The beef, prime Texan and Argentine, meat shipped north exclusively for Manhattan's pricey restaurants, resided cut, packaged, and identified in a Maytag freezer, one of two, in their garage. Vegetables and fruit were ordered by phone and delivered daily from a family-owned market.

Not Vacanza's, Mai Lee thought, *tant mieux*, recognizing the old brute on the security screen, standing outside the front door beneath the concealed camera. She pressed a button that electronically unlocked the door. Wearing a colorless suit, he greeted her with a hasty kiss on the cheek, with bloodshot eyes and in need of a shave, his hair combed with his fingers. He smelled of an impossible sweetness verging upon decay that reminded Mai Lee of her own confined yearning. It was just about six o'clock, and Angelo was downstairs shooting pool in the rec room. After Vacanza, she pressed the button several times more and began to become concerned not only about the timing of supper, but as to her ability to serve everyone. In the kitchen, over the butcher-block island outfitted with drawers and cabinets for all manner of utensils, Mai Lee and the cook, Therese, conferred, calculating portions, preferences.

Like the late widow Fratennella, Therese Sardello had lost her husband long ago in a dispute over cards at a social club on Metropolitan Avenue. Michael Sardello made the mistake of winning three straight hands of seven-card stud, the last one on a bluff, and when he refused to show his hole cards, a hotheaded first cousin to Luigi Vacanza shot Michael in the Adam's apple with a silencer-equipped .22-caliber Ruger automatic. Along with fifty pounds of lime, he was tucked into a shallow grave north of the city where he decomposed quietly within a stone's throw of the Major Deegan Expressway.

Therese said not to worry, she'd phone her brother-in-law, who owned a butcher shop on Pitkin, and while she did that, Mai Lee used the intercom to draft Cato for gofer duty.

The doorbell chimed. Mai Lee, entering the hallway, saw in the monitor that it was Lorenzo Scorcese, fashionably late as always, no doubt whistling some tune with his hands behind his back. Of everyone in the family, only Lorenzo treated Mai Lee with anything approaching familial affection, and he had done so from the moment she arrived at JFK and was introduced as Angelo's bride. The young one, Paul, observed all the courtesies, but remained distant, sensitive to the feelings of his mother, whose stance had inched from abhorrence to toleration, as Mai Lee bore Angelo's children, to the point of sharing the family pew with her at Sunday mass. Paul, for all his coolness, she still trusted more than Lorenzo, the difference bearing upon her sense that Paul would do what was right, and Lorenzo what was expedient. She opened the door, and he thrust a cluster of rose blossoms under her chin and leaned forward to kiss her on the lips. "Happy anniversary," he said.

"Larry," she said, "whatever are you . . . *Merci, merci.* But they are absolutely goddamn beautiful. What's the occasion?"

He must have just splashed on some cologne, because its scent was prominent on his cheek, along with the smell of good Scotch on his mouth. "You don't know?" he said. He was a handsome man, the type of handsome that she imagined had bones of porcelain and always someone around to wipe his ass.

She backed up in the hall, turning the bouquet in the

light of the glass chandelier. "Tell me. They're so beautiful, tell me."

"Today's the day I set eyes on you. At JFK. It's the first time I realized my older brother had brains. Find a princess like you."

The roses were salmon in color with an insinuating scent that approximated dry champagne. Lorenzo, as always, looked corporate smooth in the light from the chandelier, his cheek shaved and powdered, the black curls razor cut, his dark eyes full of amusement. He was dressed in a double-breasted Armani suit, a platinum-colored summer weight, with smooth-toed shoes to match, an impeccably tied crimson foulard with floral accents. He was about as close as any member of the family came to achieving an air of sophistication, which, even as Mai Lee enjoyed the little flirtation, she recognized as being on a par with that of telemarketers, certain evangelists, and glib, bromide-happy therapists. The way Mai Lee saw it: if Angelo was an American primitive, then Lorenzo was the perfect contemporary, all polished surface. And Paul, regardless of his heritage, had a quality of the Orient about him, a strict and cryptic code understood and enforced within a tight circle.

"Come," Lorenzo said, gently grasping her elbow, "let's find a vase and see how they really look. The florist was adamant about quickly getting them into water of the right temperature."

Mai Lee accommodated him, watched him fuss with the water from the kitchen sink as she stood holding the flowers and an elongated shape of fluted crystal. Satisfied with the temperature, Lorenzo snapped his fingers for the vase, and when it was one-third filled, he showed Mai Lee a packet of powder, tamping the contents into the vase. "Therese," he said, "where you hide the scissors?"

"I think I can do the rest, Larry," said Mai Lee, "really, thank you. Besides, Angelo's waiting. I promised him dinner for six o'clock, and here it is almost six-thirty. Really."

Therese handed scissors to Lorenzo, who in turn handed them to Mai Lee, with a wink. "Cut the stems on a forty-five-degree angle. It'll improve their longevity."

He leaned forward and kissed her on the lips once more, not making a production of it, only a simple statement, and whispered, "If longevity's something you think about, of course."

Mai Lee looked into his eyes but could decipher neither warning nor threat. His lawyer's lips held the contour of a smile for little more than a moment. Then his face was as intelligible as the smooth, fluted crystal.

She followed him out of the kitchen and into the hallway. "Larry?"

He took another step, dipped his shoulder, and pivoted gracefully, a ballroom maneuver, and greeted her with his arms outspread. "Princess?"

"Please, cut the clowning. That wasn't an idle remark, the one you just made about longevity."

"It wasn't?"

"Larry, all these men here tonight, something's going down."

He chucked her beneath the chin and winked once more. She despised him for the smugness behind the gestures.

"Yes, princess," he said. "In a far place that doesn't concern you. In fact, it's so far away, it won't put a dent in Angelo's appetite. Not that anything far or near could, short of death. And even that's moot."

Lorenzo Scorcese descended the stairs to the rec room whistling what sounded like the melody, "New York, New York."

Mai Lee ascended the stairs to the master bedroom and leaned over the bed, fidgeted with the dials on the intercom, trying to eavesdrop on the conversation around the pool tables. She could hear the children in their rooms, and Therese ordering Cato about the kitchen, and even the nanny, enjoying some private time on the telephone, saying, "Rosey, you're a crack-up. You should audition, honest to God. Go for it." But from the rec room, nothing, just a maddening continuum of static. She studied her face in the mirror in the bathroom, mainly to make sure Lorenzo hadn't messed up her lip paint. The man was shameless. And probably the remark was innocent, but given the recent meet with Jay, it touched a nerve, a vein of fear. Going back down the stairs, she had just about reassured herself. . . . *Jay*, she thought, reaching the hallway. Jay Rose, her lover, the man who made her laugh and even dreamed of doing stand-up: people in the clubs where they secretly had met *did* call him Rosey.

She hastened to the phone in the kitchen, where Therese was still bossing Cato about in the island patois, in time to see the lit button indicating the nanny's line go out, so that when she lifted the receiver, punching the button, all she heard was dial tone. It made her feel stupid: first, Lorenzo's remark, now this. As if she had lost her understanding of what it took to stay in control of things. The icy taste in her mouth was the taste of panic.

"*Signora,*" Therese suddenly standing in front of her, hands on her shoulders, "*Signora Scorcese, tutto bene?* Are you all right, child?"

A few moments passed. "Yes, thank you. I'm good. Cato, thank you for the run to Pitkin. Angelo would never forgive me if there weren't enough hearts to go around."

At seven o'clock, an hour beyond the promised moment, Angelo Scorcese convened his associates for a sit-down dinner in the formal dining room, which was unlike any formal sit-down the attending parties were otherwise accustomed to. Here there were no heavy curtains faded by the sun to the color of turkey wattles; no dark and brooding artifacts; no waxed fruit residing in Depression glass; no gilded mirrors or crucifixes or ancestral portraits. Here they dined at a table for twelve, consisting of an inch-thick plate of curved glass resting on a base of carved granite. The floor was pink marble, peculiar to a region in northern Italy. The walls were painted a stark white and adorned with artwork from the Caribbean, mainly from Haiti, crudely drafted figures brushed robustly in the primary hues, radiating exuberance. Track lighting enhanced the effect. For men accustomed to solemn, cathedral-inspired surroundings for their private repasts, the room was a little disconcerting, bordering upon the exotic. Lorenzo Scorcese probably spoke for all of the men invited to dine there when he ribbed Angelo about having to eat in Mai Lee's voodoo room.

When the men were seated, Therese distributed oven-warmed china plates, and Mai Lee, with Cato holding the stoneware platter, used tongs to serve each man a hastily thawed and broiled tail of rock lobster. Shreds of garlic swam in butter on the sweet meat. Cato reappeared with another stoneware platter, this one heaped with shrimps, chunks of squid, scallops, and mussels in their yawning black shells, bathed in a red sauce. Mai Lee again served from the platter, and when she had made the rounds, she said, "Gentlemen, *prego, godero*. Enjoy." Loaves of warmed Italian bread in wicker baskets were left around the table, along with the platter of seafood.

Cato slid shut the oak doors, sealing the men in their privacy, and stood with his back to the dining room. Mai Lee and Therese were visible, conferring over the butcher-block island. He could hear the smaller children squealing upstairs, running up and down the hallway. Remembering a Frank Sinatra tune, but not the name of it, he hummed the melody, a few bars anyway, and broke into a graceful cheek-to-cheek, dancing by himself in the lonely hallway.

The men oohed and aahed. The *calamaro* was exquisite. Had anyone anywhere invented a method to get all the sand out of the *cozza*? And who's fuckin' hoggin' the bread?

Angelo slammed the flat of his hand on the glass top of the table.

"We gotta situation to discuss," he announced.

"An irritation," suggested Lorenzo, sitting at the end of the table opposite his brother, "a little embarrassment."

"Yeah," said Angelo, "like Lorenzo says. We all know the Don ain't—he ain't playin' with a full deck. Not since what the shitballs done to him in the bakery. Okay? We all know this, right? Okay. So he's stayin' with our little brother down there in Phoenix, and you guys remember how he liked the track: Belmont, Yonkers, take a day and drive up to Saratoga?"

"He loved the races," opined Vacanza, sitting to Angelo's immediate right. Everyone concurred. These were responsible men, men who shored up portions of the Don's empire. There was Mike Carducci, the Appliance Prince of Flatbush Avenue, and an important man to know if you were in the market for heroin or cocaine, in bulk. Gino Maggliocca and his younger brother Rick—called Killer, not for his lethal skills, but for his success with the ladies—were there, important men to the Don insofar as the hijacking trade went, especially at LaGuardia and JFK. (It was to the Magglioccas that Jimmy Capistrano proposed the TWA sable theft, employing the Killer's slick looks to entrap a gay freight handler.) Old neighborhood guys were present, like Johnny the Geek, who owned escort services, modeling agencies, and who produced and distributed porn films for every conceivable taste; like Lunchmeat Louie, the muscle behind the Longshoremen's Union, a man who graduated from eighth grade when he was sixteen, already earning more at extortion than his teachers were at exhortion; like Bald Frank Francesi, the man to see about insuring businesses —especially nightclubs, bars, and theaters—against unforeseeable disasters.

Also present, but only to observe, because they weren't important men, or not yet, were Vacanza's hotheaded nephew, Bennie Focoso, an accomplished bone breaker, and Bald Frank's eldest son, Marco, who handled some of the family's legitimate interests. And there was Metzenbaum, the single trusted foreigner, affectionately known as the Wizard.

Metzenbaum was the youngest man in the room, at thirty years of age, and possessed a waist that in inches doubled that number. His bitten fingernails spent a good deal of time resting reflectively on the apex of his girth when they weren't dancing upon the keys of his computer, which was equipped with a modem to dictate the movement of family finances, whether from francs into yen, or gold into oil futures. He was a hearty man with long, thinning red hair, the broad sumo-wrestler face, but with freckles, and a gimpy leg from polio that necessitated the assistance of an ebony cane with a handle of ivory inlay. He had graduated from Harvard with an MBA in finance, but had succumbed to the pleasures of the flesh, only to awake in a shabby hotel room in Boston's DMZ in bed with a hooker dead from strangulation. The firm owned by Lorenzo Scorcese defended him *pro bono*, and when the jury announced a hung verdict, Metzenbaum walked. Straight into the arms of the family.

However, his presence at the table disconcerted the others. Earlier, in the rec room, Lorenzo had expressed the common concern in a whispered exchange with his older brother.

"You serious? Father would never invite the Wizard to a council. This is family."

"What did Pop always say, Lorenzo? He listened to a man with brains. You think Metzenbaum ain't got brains? Shit, he knows stuff you don't even know enough about to ask how it works. And me too. It don't hurt to listen, if the guy's got anything to say, is the way I figure it."

"The way you figure it," Lorenzo Scorcese had said, "or is it the way Mai Lee does?"

"Fuck you, ZoZo, and the horse you rode in on."

So Metzenbaum, all three hundred pounds of him, occupied the chair to the left of Angelo Scorcese, directly opposite Angelo's *consigliere*, Luigi Vacanza.

"Yeah," Vacanza reiterated, "the Don loves the races."

"Speakin' a love," said Rick Maggliocca, "what's doin' with Magda? Word on the street is you got an arrangement goin' for a wedding."

"Shuddup, awready," said Gino. "Luigi, lemme explain for the smart ass, okay? Coupla glasses a wine on top a what he's had today, know what I'm sayin'." And cranked his face at his younger brother. "What, I gotta spell it out? Apologize to the man."

"Whad I say? Huh? I mean fuckin' whad I say?"

Vacanza answered in a measured, solemn tone, "Don't gotta say nothin', Ricky. Word in the street is you are pretty enough to be a *faggella*. Who you gonna believe? Me, I don't make sport outta that stuff. If it's in the street, it started from the gutter."

The man known as the Killer lowered his face, conceding error. "No offense intended, Signor Vacanza. I meant only to wish your family happiness, to offer *complimenti*."

"Well, Luigi, much as we wish your Magda all the best, I gotta interrupt the love feast here," said Angelo Scorcese. "This is what it is. A coupla cute boys sold the Don a bill a goods. Sold him shares in racing dogs, registered greyhounds. Some old hippie he met at the track and this smooth-mouth jig. Trouble is the dogs are dead, and the Don's out fifty whacks, in cash. Now Pauli, he done right: he contracted outside people to collect on the misunderstanding, but the outsiders fucked up. And the cute boys are gone."

Metzenbaum, with the ebony cane propped alongside his chair, pushed stumpy fingers through his hair and chuckled.

"You got something to say?" inquired Angelo.

Metzenbaum had first to situate himself in the chair, squaring his butt so that he sat erect. "Just a thought: anybody who could con the Don, I don't care how goofy you say he is, the guy who gets over on your father is a guy I'd like to sit down with. I'd cultivate him, not try to waste him. Bottom line, I'd say Paul made an emotional call. This was business, not something that happened in the school yard."

Angelo Scorcese, who had in fact been responsible for the decision, listened with squinted eyes. Vacanza, the old war-horse, ceased shoveling food into his mouth, a certain sign that he had taken offense. Lorenzo applied his elbows to the table, palms up, a slim smile on his face, the gestures choreographed to suggest that his inclusion of Metzenbaum was Angelo's can of worms to deal with.

"Yeah," said Angelo. "Good point. So Pauli made a mistake. It happens. Anybody can be a armchair quarterback."

"Easiest job in the world," murmured Metzenbaum.

"Now that we're agreed," said Angelo Scorcese, "you got anything to contribute except the Monday-morning bullshit?"

"Simple. My guess is we've got sufficient contacts to determine if they've escaped Phoenix. If the evidence shows they haven't, then we advertise."

"Fuck you talkin' about?"

"Play their game. Get some other people down there

showing big money on the dogs. Flush the quail, Signore Scorcese, that's what it's all about."

Angelo Scorcese aimed his eyes at his brother at the far end of the table. Lorenzo's mouth turned down at the corners, and he delivered a flippant gesture with his hand, fingers flipping away from the palm, a visual, if reluctant, acquiescence. Without moving his eyes, Angelo Scorcese said, "Luigi?"

"It sounds like a plan," said Vacanza.

"All right, it's done," said Angelo Scorcese. "ZoZo, you arrange for the heavy hitters, handle the expenses. I want the cute boys and I want their money. Then I want 'em gone."

Metzenbaum sighed, then remarked almost petulantly, "It's not the way I'd vote."

Angelo Scorcese hiked both elbows up on the table and said, "That's okay, Wiz. You ain't bein' asked to vote."

Metzenbaum mopped up the last of his red sauce with a chunk of bread. "When you're right, you're right. So. I don't know about you, but I'm ready for those hearts your wife is famous for."

Chapter 20

Chub rode in the front seat with the driver, a shy, slender boy that Joe Scorcese believed wore ladies' perfume. The boy's name was Todd, and when he wasn't driving the limousine, he mixed drinks for Paul's guests and looked after Paul's needs. As a driver he was adequate, but Joe Scorcese would never trust him to do anything of a serious nature. Chub was a different story.

It was after six in the evening when the limo glided to a stop alongside the guard booth, there in theory to protect the residents from random intruders. Two armed guards, in eight-hour shifts, manned the booth twenty-four hours a day. There were hotlines to the Paradise Valley Patrol as well as the Phoenix PD. Joe Scorcese thought the whole operation pathetic, just window dressing, but the foreign consuls residing there ate it up. The limousine descended the private drive to wait once more, this time for a gap to open in the traffic on Tatum Boulevard. Almost two hours of daylight remained. Behind the tinted glass and breathing the efforts of the air conditioner, Joe Scorcese could feel the desert's remorseless presence—its intensity, its insistence. It was a force, and force was a thing always to respect. He thought about the one with the ponytail, always making the jokes, and the short black one that talked better than Lorenzo even. Paul had told him how they had responded to the offer of a settlement. It was the act of fools. Like the *munizza* that attacked him in the bakery.

From Tatum, the limousine accelerated west on Lincoln. Within minutes the white Mercedes was hurtling south on the Squaw Peak Parkway at a high, comfortable speed, not nearly the triple-digit pace it would have been accustomed to on the autobahn, but a speed considerably in excess of the posted limit. Joe Scorcese liked to arrive at least an hour before post time for the first race, which got underway at seven-thirty. He marveled at this chute of concrete and asphalt through the heart of Phoenix; you couldn't travel this effortlessly anywhere in the five boroughs of New York, even with a siren.

The dogs were a pleasant enough diversion, although he much preferred the running of the horses, the furious alliance of will and brute energy, but the horses did not run here in the summer. The heat was prohibitive: that was the traditional, sensible explanation given for the absence of equine sport, but Joe Scorcese had made inquiries. He suspected that mulish habits, or lack of imagination, had been dressed up as common sense. Why, he had wondered, could the horses not run at night, beneath lights, in the substantially cooler air? When he was prepared to move, he would entrust Paul with the project of lining up lobbyists, congressmen, whomever the family could convince or compromise in the media, to promote year-round racing for the horses. It was business waiting to be done.

When he was prepared to move . . . It would be soon. He stroked the fingers of his crippled hand, trying to generate some warmth. It was a futile effort. Since the onset of the disease, his right hand had become progressively cold and alien. And there was pain, or rather always the prospect of pain, enormous pain, if he did not protect the hand, guard it from even casual contact. It was a frustrating irritant, a humiliation imposed upon him by age. But it was as nothing next to the pain of betrayal.

At his instruction, Vacanza used an answering service to leave numbers where he could be reached; the Don and his former enforcer spoke several times a week, the Don contacting him during his visits to the track, the conversations terse, elliptical. Because Cato Dellacroce reported to Vacanza, Joe Scorcese had been kept abreast as well of Mai Lee's restlessness, her flirtation with Lorenzo, and her rendezvous with the stockbroker. The old man had deliberated carefully, reluctantly, exhausting every avenue of reason, until he knew in his bones that his own son, no doubt encouraged by his faithless wife, had engineered the attempt on his life. The two snakes deserved one another, he thought, the anger flashing through him, then gone, his thinking clear once more. Of paramount importance was the business, and integral to the business was family. Emotion was for women. There was no room for it in business.

Still, his Angelo, this Judas of a son, was the father of his grandchildren, and that had shaped his decision, his solemn promise to Vacanza on the day he was released from the hospital. Vacanza came alone that night to the two-story brick house in Middle Village wearing a clean white shirt and new suspenders and necktie with a precise knot in it, testimony to Magda's competent fingers. Lorenzo ushered him into the bedroom, where the Don rested, still taking his sustenance through tubes. The RN in attendance, a slight black woman with traces of gray in her curls, followed Lorenzo out of the room. Vacanza leaned over to kiss the Don's hand, but was waved away. So he sat in a straight chair beside the bed, his large hard hands on his thighs, his coarse hair looking as if it had been combed with his fingers, his face shadowy in the dimmed light, and his eyes bright with the dumb concern of a hound dog. The Don thanked him for coming. Then told him things. Then said: *Luigi, if it is as I suspect, I will ask of you a favor, in exchange for an alliance.* It was a promise he would honor.

He would make his move soon.

And take with him, as a man worthy of learning from Vacanza, the deadly cold, quiet one with the harelip, Chub. Joe Scorcese recognized abilities.

The limousine swooped down the exit ramp, glided through a green light, and hung a lazy left onto Washington. Within a minute Greyhound Park hove up beyond the right fender, its bright marquee bordered by blue lights. The window on the driver's side descended, and Todd pushed a pair of one-dollar bills, creased lengthwise, at the young Mexican sitting on a stool. The Mexican showed his teeth for an instant, a signal for them to proceed, and dropped the bills through a slot in an orange padlocked canister resting upon a sturdy tripod. In the brief interval of the transaction, the heat of the day, even at this late hour, penetrated the interior in a brash gust. As the window ascended, bringing relief, the limo eased forward and advanced toward the parking area, which was sparsely occupied due to the early hour, and also because it was a weeknight. The limo passed a bulky silver van advertising frankfurters, but not open for business. Joe Scorcese, from habit, noted the number of cars parked in the marked-off spaces. An average night. He guessed seventy-five to one hundred vehicles. Quadruple that by post time.

The limo drew up in front of the plate-glass doors of the entrance to the terrace. Wearing tangerine shorts and a lavender cotton shirt with lightning-shaped accents to match the shorts, Todd opened the curbside door for Joe Scorcese. Chub, dressed in a dark suit with dark shoes, escorted him through the heat and into the lobby, and removed his dark glasses, to scan the area, the stairs, the escalators ascending and descending.

Joe Scorcese, with his hands in the pockets of a maroon Arizona State University windbreaker, shuffled behind Chub to the ticket window and waited patiently for the harelip to convert ten dollars into two passes to the terrace. Among the people crowding the lobby, the Don behaved like a docile elder, slightly hunched in maroon sweatpants and white golf shirt, an ASU baseball cap on his faintly bobbing head, of no more notice to the patrons than any other feeble old man. Chub handed him a copper-colored token, about the size of a silver dollar, but lighter, which admitted him through the turnstile. Chub stood behind him on the escalator and followed him across the polished parquet to the bank of phones beyond the rest rooms.

Where the parquet ended, soothing carpet with a pattern of burgundy and forest green took over. From his jacket pocket Joe Scorcese laid a ten-dollar roll of quarters beside the far phone and eased his feet, in white socks, out of the leather huaraches his son Paul had bought for him. The shoes with rubber soles were comfortable enough, but of late he had begun to experience aching on the tops of his feet. Wriggling his toes relieved the pain some. Doing this in his stockinged feet, he nodded at Chub, who faded away to purchase a program and tip sheets.

He spent a dollar and a quarter for the phone-number information, deposited another quarter, dialed, listened, dropped more money down the slot, waited, and said, "It's me, old friend."

As you entered the terrace, there was a booth, a shallow arc of pale wood, to the right, behind which a young lady in a white blouse sold programs. Set farther back on the parquet floor was a wider booth, behind which another young lady in a white blouse sold tip sheets, and next to her hovered the terrace hostess, a nicely turned-out lady in a black dress, a beauty somewhat beyond her most photogenic years, but smooth and professional, her long and deeply red hair swept over her bare shoulders. Upon spying Joe Scorcese, she emerged to greet him with open arms, the light darting off her polished nails. In heels, she had a five-inch advantage in height, which suited the old man embracing her, his nostrils buried in her cleavage. She bent over to kiss him on the cheek.

"Your Mets are leading, Joey. Sam, your waiter, he just informed me. Gooden's throwing a shutout."

She backed away, and Joe Scorcese lifted her hand with his good left one and kissed it. Done with that, he brought his crippled hand around with a twenty-dollar bill in it, and said, *"Prego."*

"Oh, Joey," the hostess said, clutching him to her bosoms once more.

There were three bars to serve the terrace in addition to a proliferation of betting windows; there was even a hot buffet with a young man in a white apron and chef's cap standing over a slab of roast beef, carving rare slices upon request, the meat swimming in blood. Joe Scorcese stopped to watch the young man carve, admiring the man's flair. The doctors had cautioned him to stay away from the pasta and the cheese, and especially to avoid the red meat, and he had for the most part heeded the advice. Tonight maybe he would indulge himself. He was feeling lucky.

Clutching his forms in his bad hand, he glanced over his shoulder at Chub standing several strides away, a hand in his pants pocket, his eyes drifting over the crowd. Joe Scorcese motioned with his chin, and Chub approached. While Joe Scorcese paid for the meal, Chub commenced to fill the plate, knowing from experience what the old man liked and how much. As he came to the end of the smorgas-bord, he felt a poke in the kidneys and looked back.

"Tonight, Chub, I'ma have some meat."

"Your doctor," Chub said, although what he said sounded like *yo dahta.*

"You, mister meat cutter, I want the rarest you got."

"Your doctor!" Chub protested. *Yo dahta!*

The young man with the electric knife said, "Excuse me?"

"Slice it about a quarter inch, mister meat cutter. Don't worry about him. He's practicin' his English."

"Your doctor," said Chub, accusingly, following Joe Scorcese across the parquet.

Joe Scorcese turned his head a little to speak over his shoulder, as they wended their way through the crowd. "Chub, I like you. Let me worry what I eat. And keep you mouth shut. Pauli don't need to know everything. You understand I'm saying?"

Aisles of carpeted steps descended from the parquet level several landings to the glassed-in balcony. A central corridor was reserved for the most exclusive seating: these were tables with white linen tablecloths and upholstered chairs, with a television monitor on the table to watch re-runs, update odds, and follow the actual race on the track. A centermost table in front of the glass was reserved for Joe Scorcese, and another one, one level up directly overlooking the Don, was held for Chub. The waiter Sam, who had watched the old man descending, stood back as Chub situated him, setting down the plate, adjusting the chair, breaking open the linen napkin while Joe Scorcese raptly took in the activity on the television monitor, which had been tuned to the Mets game. When Chub had ascended to his table, Sam accosted his favorite patron. "Gooden sure is smokin' 'em tonight, isn't he? A carafe of the red, Mr. Scorcese?"

"No." The frail old man's twisted hand bobbed in the air above his plate. "Tonight, mister waiter man, you bring me a bottle of good red. Bring me a bottle of your best good red."

"I sure will, Mr. Scorcese. Feeling lucky tonight, huh?"

"I dunno. But I'm a go home soon. That is always a good sign, no?"

"You bet," said Sam, a slim and efficient and serious young man, with only fifteen hours to go before he graduated from ASU with a major in economics. He ascended the carpeted steps with the alacrity that had earned him the old man's favor, even as he was thinking, *bummer.*

Chub drank ice water, ate nothing, watched the old man slowly cut a piece of beef and snap it off the fork, his attention shifting from the television to the program, to the tip sheets, and back to the program. He laid down his knife and made notations in the program with a ballpoint pen. The waiter appeared, showed the old man a bottle, then deftly applied a corkscrew. He let a small amount of wine into a glass and stood waiting for the old man to taste it. The old man made him wait. Evidently something was happening on the television screen. Chub did not follow baseball—too boring. His idea of sport was to drive around late at night with a .22-caliber Colt automatic equipped with a suppressor and encounter a small animal, preferably domestic. Especially cats.

The old man had finished his meal and was enjoying his

wine when the dogs for the first race were led out and displayed. Chub was alert now. He watched the figure below carefully and caught the glance. He descended the steps quickly and took the folded paper with the numbers written on it and the hundred-dollar bill tucked inside it and climbed toward the nearest mutuel window. Curious to gauge the old man's mood, Chub unfolded the paper and looked at the numbers. What he saw was a boxed trifecta: ten-dollar bets on three greyhounds to finish in every possible combination of win, place, and show. Six bets in all. The old one was feeling hot, or else he was feeling the effect of the wine. Normally he wagered on the more conservative quinielas, where you picked the two dogs to win and place, in no particular order, as opposed to the trifecta, which required you to select the *exact* dog in the *exact* position it finished. So intent was Chub upon the Don's sheet of paper and its import that, upon gaining the parquet level of the terrace, he walked right into another patron, someone like himself with his mind on something other than where he was going. The man reeled from the collision, losing pencil and program, and stayed on his feet only by clutching Chub's triceps and hanging on. In a moment he had his feet under him and was apologizing.

Chub first checked his hip for his wallet and his hand for the paper with the money inside, and then glared at the man.

The man was backing up, trying to look apologetic. "Hey, I'm sorry. Could I just—would you mind, Sparky, if I picked up my stuff there?"

Chub said nothing, just brushed on by and got in line.

* * *

Just as Chub placed his boss's bets on the first race, not twenty yards away a man in jeans and a colorful shirt eased himself onto a bar stool next to a shorter man enjoying a draft beer. The man in the shirt wore a baseball cap with the logo of a football team, the San Diego Chargers, while the shorter man was dressed in a jogging costume, black sweats top and bottom, white Reeboks on his feet.

The shorter man said, "He's no dummy. You see the boy reach for his billfold?"

"Uh-huh. He's carrying. Under his left armpit. Long barrel, fat at the end."

"Silencer?"

"Be my guess."

"Man, this is some sort of craziness. You sure you know what you're doing?"

"Sparky."

Joe Scorcese stayed at the table until the tenth race, periodically checking on the Mets between races, and finished the fifth of red wine. It was a delicious Pinot noir, and it sat well with him. He had hit the trifecta in the first race, and that more than covered all of his spending for the night. He also popped for a winning quiniela in the fifth and eighth races, so he was walking out plenty ahead, in addition buoyed by Dwight Gooden pitching nine strong innings, allowing one run, to squash the Houston Astros. It was his lucky night, all right.

Chub eased the chair out behind him and silently slipped young Sam the waiter a twenty-dollar bill. Joe Scorcese always left after the tenth race, because he was tired and because he wanted to avoid the crowd. This part of the evening both men could have walked through in their sleep. Chub followed the old one up the maroon and deep green carpet and waited for him outside the men's room. This too was part of the routine. The old man took a strange pride in his regularity. Then down the escalator to the lobby where Todd was waiting for them, a thick paperback tucked under his arm.

Todd had spent the evening in a grandstand seat reading Dickens, occasionally pausing to watch individual patrons. He enjoyed this part of his day. He got up twice to whiz and once to purchase a hot dog and a Coke. He was halfway through *David Copperfield* and had come to the conclusion, from his surveys of the crowd, that Dickens would have been right at home here.

The three of them walked out onto the brightly lit sidewalk, into the breathless night air. They walked slowly, at the old man's pace, down the sidewalk toward the parking lot. In the beginning Todd offered repeatedly to have the limo waiting outside the entrance, but the old man waved his crooked hand at the idea. Joe Scorcese liked the walk. It worked off the effects of the meal and the wine, and he believed he slept better for it.

A few people had trickled out about the same time they had, but they were scattered now throughout the parking lot. Todd had parked the limousine, as he had been instructed to do, directly beneath a bank of lights. As they gained the rear of the Mercedes, Joe Scorcese noticed the silver van parked abreast of the limo, and wondered why he should have noticed it, until he recognized the lettering, but then it was too late. He heard the sound of movement and then a voice—low, very even and very certain of itself.

"Don't fucking move."

They had been lying beneath the limo and on cue had rolled out on either side with guns in their hands. They were on their feet now, visible to the Baker. The one who had spoken had cosmetically blackened his face and both hands; the shorter one, holding a gun on Todd, didn't need cosmetics. Both men were dressed in black costumes.

The one who had spoken said, "Keys."

On the far side of the limo the shorter one snapped his fingers and Todd dropped keys into his hand. The driver's door was opened, and the locks were released on all doors. The one who had spoken motioned for Chub first, and then the old man, to climb in back, and he followed them. It had taken less than fifteen seconds, the Baker judged, from the moment the man had spoken. Todd was there too with the shorter one. The men with guns sat on jump seats facing them. Todd was whimpering.

The one who had spoken said, "You, in the middle, put your arms around your friends," and when Chub did so, the man leaned forward to reach beneath his coat. He settled back, and Joe Scorcese could see that the man was holding a second gun. He heard a metallic sound that he assumed was the sound of the safety being released. "Let's keep on being smart here, okay? Son, you got nothing to cry about, just a little discomfort for a while. Lean over, put your arms between your legs and grab your ankles."

The short one pulled cord from his pockets and worked

quickly. From a pocket of his jacket he produced a roll of silver duct tape and wound it several times around Todd's head, covering the boy's mouth. Chub was ordered to assume the same humiliating pose—

He lunged instead, arms out and hollering.

For all of a split second.

Chub's gun made a sound like a polite cough, and Chub stopped hollering, his momentum not enough to carry him out of his seat, so that he collapsed there, face between his legs in a ghoulish parody of the position he'd been ordered to assume. His last breaths were audible, like someone shaking dice in a cup. The certainty of death filled the car when Chub's sphincter ceased to function.

With the Don bound and his mouth taped and additionally secured in a thin mattress with bungee cords, lying on the floor in the back of the van, Del Rebus climbed behind the wheel. Elvis Mahoney jumped onto the seat beside him, slammed the door and said, "Go, let's go. Jesus, I don't believe this."

The ignition cranked for agonizing seconds before the engine turned. Del revved the van several times before engaging the gears. "*Munizza*," he said, "now what do you suppose the old boy's trying to say?"

Chapter 21

The whole operation, from the purchase of the cuffs and leg irons at a shop on Northern to the black outfits and face paint, had been Del's inspiration. And the kidnapping had been flawless, executed swiftly and without arousing alarm, although there was the little matter of murder. Neither man on the two seats of the silver van was prepared to talk about that just yet.

The van lumbered east along Washington as far as Forty-fourth Street, then turned north. Besides driving the vehicle, Del Rebus worked a cloth in a cleansing cream and swiped at his face to remove the coloring. In the shotgun seat Elvis Mahoney had changed out of his dark sweats to the lime green shorts and white mesh tank top he had been wearing underneath. The van swung off Forty-fourth Street almost immediately, ambling down a poorly lit side street to its dead end, where it turned around and left behind a small bundle of burning black cotton, wispy remainders of a sweat suit.

They continued up Forty-fourth Street, careful to travel the posted speed limit. Elvis glanced at his watch: it was almost ten o'clock. Nobody behind them, nobody at all interested in the lumbering vehicle with the high center of gravity that caused it to sway on turns, like it did now, as Del swung into the mostly vacant parking lot of the mall at Thomas and Forty-fourth. And everything still going the way Del called it.

Except, Elvis Mahoney's mind blurted, *a fucking murder.*

They cruised the lot, surveying for any police presence, a squad car or motorcycle cop lurking to snag someone late through the light, or some poor schnook with a busted turn signal. Once Del was satisfied, they bore down on the northwest corner of the lot. The van pulled alongside Elvis's Charger. Del flipped off the van's headlights, but left the engine running. He swiveled to his right and moved, slightly stooped over, back into the van, out of the parking-lot light, to strip off the black sweats he was wearing. Elvis, in the meantime, slid back the van door and walked around the front of it to unlock the Charger and start the little hatchback. Then he leaned across the passenger seat to roll down the window, the knob slick in his hand, so that he almost lost his grip. The night was warm, even a little claustrophobic, but that didn't account, Elvis belatedly recognized, for the degree of perspiration. He wondered if Del was as pumped as he was at this moment. For two guys without any experience in this sort of endeavor, he thought they were handling it better than all right. Del was leaning out the open window of the van, and Elvis caught the black bundle, the sweats wrapped tightly around two guns. Del said, "You left your door open, Sparky. What, I got to do all the work?"

Pumped? Del Rebus sounded about as pumped as a guy in a hammock, a glass of lemonade in his hand.

He is one crazy son of a bitch, Elvis thought, easing into the left-turn lane on Forty-fourth, heading for a supermarket. Oh? So what's that make you?

A flamingo in Phoenix, he thought, and almost smiled.

Del Rebus continued north on Forty-fourth, crossing one of the multitude of canals that wound sinuously through the city and sustained it, waterways originally designed and dug by the Hohokam Indians to nurture a more graceful society. Or so he assumed, alone in that clarifying solitude in which a man finds himself, having killed close up.

Questions as he steered the van: Why'd the guy go so crazy? Why didn't he pistol-whip the guy when he moved? Why was pulling the trigger so easy, no hesitation?

These were issues, he decided, he would torture himself with later.

Right now, that's what he had to think about. And right now, he was just rounding the curve toward the intersection with Tatum Boulevard. He had thought about using the canal to dump Chub's gun; it was convenient and anonymous. It was also stupid. Too elaborate. The police were always fishing shit out of the canals. There was a place to ditch things that was even more anonymous and convenient: a commercial dumpster. Elvis was headed toward one (Del raised his wrist to look at his watch and saw that he was probably already there) behind a large supermarket, after which he'd hop onto the Squaw Peak and race back to the house off Doubletree.

Del wasn't surprised to see the Charger in the driveway already, the garage door open, the Charger parked behind the somewhat battered Oldsmobile, but what did surprise him was a fundamental miscalculation. The van was too tall to fit in the garage. It failed to clear by only a couple of inches, but it might as well have been two feet. Del uttered some four-letter words thinking about it. The weepy boy might have caught a glimpse of the van and had the presence of mind to hear its rocky ignition so soon after the abduction, and make something of it. It wouldn't be smart to leave the big lunking thing in the driveway. Better to put some distance between them.

Del shifted the van into reverse and gentled it down the driveway, maneuvered it swiftly around, and backed up the driveway toward a now-dark garage. He stuck his head out the window, squinting in the darkness until he saw Elvis illuminated by the red taillights. Elvis moved his hand to indicate he should continue a little farther, a little bit more, a little—there. Del switched off the lights and cut the engine.

The van doors were already open, and Elvis was unlocking the trunk of the Olds. Del's eyes had adjusted to the dark, and he could make out the shape of the old man trussed in the mattress. He grabbed the ankles and pulled.

For the second time that night he was amazed at how little the man weighed. He felt as if he were muscling a twelve-year-old. He cradled him in his arms and swung around, deposited him in the trunk of the Oldsmobile as gently as so awkward a task permitted. Behind the silver tape the small man spat sounds, neither intelligible nor loud. Del leaned over to shift the man around. "Better?" he said. "Sorry about the smell. The previous occupant couldn't hold his water."

In the Charger, Elvis raced the engine, signaling his impatience. Del eased the trunk shut, careful not to slam it: he did not want the old man to have a coronary. Not now, he didn't. Next week or next month, that would be fine. The little sack of shit would be doing the world a service.

They locked up the van and left it in the empty parking lot of Smitty's at the intersection of Shea and Tatum.

Fifteen minutes later Joe Scorcese was transported from the trunk of the Olds to the breakfast nook in the house, then released from the mattress, the tape solicitously pulled from his skin, his lips, although his arms and legs remained constrained. He was lifted into a chair, his eyes blinking rapidly, shocked by all the sudden illumination. The black fellow, the one he knew as Leslie Murdock, produced the ASU baseball cap that had fallen off his head while he was lying in the trunk, thinking things over. He set it on the table in front of him and went to the sink, ran cold water over a cloth, and came back with it. The cool dampness on his face felt good. *"Grazie,"* the old man whispered.

The other one, mister blue jeans, who had carried him from the trunk into the house, disappeared for a few moments, but leaned now over the table, wearing a different shirt and a strange grin. "My apologies for your discomfort," he said. "But in business dealings, caution is the watchword. And that's all this is, is business, Mr. Scorcese. A drink?"

"I have drunk enough tonight."

"Suit yourself. Sparky?" he said, walking past the refrigerator to a cabinet.

The black one was straddling a chair, back against his chest, sitting to the left of Joe Scorcese and pinching the bridge of his nose, his eyes closed. "Yeah, something. What're you?"

"Jack D on the rocks."

"Yeah. Okay. For me too. It's almost eleven."

"Two Jack Daniel's on ice," said mister blue jeans. "You sure we can't get you anything, Mr. Scorcese?"

"*Munizza,*" the old man muttered.

At eleven o'clock Del Rebus dialed Sport Time Lounge from a wall phone in the kitchen and asked for Paul Scorcese. The voice at the other end of the line said, "He's a busy man. Who is this, please?"

"I'm calling for his father. Believe me, Paul wants to talk to me."

"Hang on."

Frank Sinatra came on the line warbling "Moon River," and Del Rebus sucked up a lungful of smoke and reached for his drink, his second. At the table the old man seemed to be speaking to Elvis. That was good, open up the lines of communication. Easier for all concerned if the old man went along with the program. Now Frank segued into "My Way," a song Del should have appreciated but didn't—not when Presley did it, and not this Sinatra version either, which sounded like rapturous gloating. The singer'd never have enough arms for all the pats on the back he evidently believed he deserved. What a guy.

Paul Scorcese's voice mercifully cut the song short: "This is Paul."

"Your white Mercedes is still sitting in the Greyhound parking lot. Keys in the ignition. There's a lotta car thieves in this town."

"What about my father?"

"Be at this number noon tomorrow. We'll have us another real short talk."

Del Rebus put the phone down and reached for his glass. There. In about ten minutes Paul Scorcese would feel like he was in a world of shit. And he'd stay in it as long as Del maintained his edge, and everyone went along with the program.

Chapter 22

Since neither of them were apt to sleep much that night anyway, they stayed up talking, once the old man had been made comfortable, or at any rate as comfortable as he was going to be with one ankle cuffed to the frame of the bed they put him up in. The leg irons were stainless steel, brand new, bought earlier that afternoon at a place called the Spy Headquarters at a cost of $29.95 plus tax. This wasn't some toy for kinky sex; each cuff clacked shut with authority. An empty Corona bottle and a spoon were left on the night-stand for the old man to make some sound if he needed to visit the bathroom. The bedroom door would be left open. Or he could just call, but not too loud. Give them any grief, Del had explained patiently, and they'd bundle him into the mattress with his mouth taped, and he could sleep in a closet in his own excrement. The choice was up to him.

They picked up their drinks on the way through the kitchen and left the sliding glass door open and stretched out on recliners beneath the patio; they could see the shapes of ridges around them and the stars strung out across the sky. So quiet. This was the time of year of the so-called monsoons, when the prevailing winds swept up from the Gulf of Mexico, hauling some moisture and turbulence. They could feel stirrings in the air, which had the net effect of brushing the heat in different directions without mitigating it. The warmth, which could be corrosive in daylight, was more like a caress. The distinctive yip of a coyote, a little to the west, enriched the silence.

Elvis said, "You hear it?"

Del grunted, pushing his glass across his forehead, his eyes closed. He ached. And there was no pill for this ache.

"Feel this *whish* up the back my neck. Wild coyote middle of a fuckin' city. Now that's weird."

"Think that's strange, how about him? He's looking around wondering what the fuck's a city doing in the middle of his living room."

"Yeah, I suppose."

Del stood up. "Freshener?"

Elvis looked into his glass. "I'll pass."

Del Rebus went inside, pausing at the entrance to listen for any sounds from the old man's room. He came back out with more ice and much more bourbon in his glass.

"I tell you something. This is the best damn Jack I've ever tasted."

"Long as you stop while you can still taste it."

"What's this, another attack of the pissants?"

Elvis shook his head and waved an arm. "Forget it."

"Thanks. I'll goddamn try to." Del settled back in his recliner, picked absently at his eyebrow. "Jesus. Sometimes you're worse'n a wife."

"Del, you ever been married?"

"Fifteen years. To my hand."

"Yeah. Well, me neither. So let's not talk about stuff we don't know nothing about."

The two men sat staring out into the night, a few feet apart, the sound of ice cubes ringing off glass. The air that played with the tops of the eucalyptus and jacaranda trees, making them sway, almost writhe, was dropping lower, in the form of gusts. Moonlight spilling across the cool deck shivered on the surface of the pool.

"Might be in for some weather," Del observed.

"Meaning?"

"This time of year, without warning, winds start up and the sky turns this baby-shit brown, and maybe it just blows, or maybe the sky goes black and we get one hellacious squall. The ground here's cooked to the consistency of concrete, so what you get, in a matter of minutes, is flooding all over the Valley. It can become interesting. The summer monsoons. Keeps the road-construction industry fat and sassy and happy."

"So I've heard," said Elvis. "A guy owns a bar off Bell Road was explaining it to me."

Del made a sound that was the opposite of sniffing.

"Another little guy being flushed down the toilet. This fucking town."

Because he could taste only ice cubes, and he was a far way from feeling the bourbon, Elvis stood up. Also because he wanted to cut Del short, maybe dodge the bullet of his obsession.

"I'm buying myself another," he said. "Fix you one?"

"Appreciate it."

Del handing him the glass without looking up. Elvis forgiven for his attack of the pissants.

Other people were up late in Phoenix, unable to sleep.

Paul Scorcese, the moment he put down the phone, ignored his older brother's caveat by walking through the kitchen to the supply room, where some family soldiers were sitting around a white Formica-top table engaged in a friendly game of baseball. Treys and nines wild, turn up a four, it got you a free card down. A weenie game. The way the politicians continued to shy away from gambling, Paul Scorcese was beginning to regard the entire state as a land for weenies. No imagination. A nothing-happening place. He pointed at two of his people, snapped his fingers once, and they followed him through the kitchen and into his office.

He had changed into a black silk shirt tonight with black silk trousers and crepe-soled black slip-on shoes. He put on a white linen jacket with padded shoulders and thin lapels, and pushed the sleeves up to his elbows, looking at the two men he had invited in. They were made guys. The one with the acne scars on his cheeks, the undernourished look, they called him Mamba, after a snake, and Paul remembered him growing up in Queens, a kid with prominent cheekbones, long spidery arms, who hung out in Maspeth and had a real thing about jigs. Mamba had made his bones by taking out a black guy, some jig who was studying law at night school and got some taxi drivers all excited about their rights. The other one was Louis Lippi. Short, about Paul's height, but with shoulders and forearms powerful enough to operate a jackhammer (which he had done for three years) and still smoke a cigarette without shaking loose the ash. A square, efficient man from Ozone Park that everyone in the family except Paul called Lips, the obvious choice. Paul always addressed him by his birth name, Louis. A signal of respect for the man who would step into Chub's place, should the occasion arise.

Paul said, "Mamba, you got weight?"

"Same like Chub uses. Got a suppressor in my pocket."

They got into a pearl gray Mercedes 190, Paul Scorcese sitting alone in the back. Louis Lippi drove. Mamba, who had never done a job before in Paul's presence, fidgeted with the suppressor in his pocket, wondering what the job was, if he should screw on the silencer now, or what the fuck? Finally he dug a cigarette from a pack of them in his shirt pocket and leaned over to poke the dashboard lighter.

"Mamba," came the cold, quiet voice from the back, "no smoking. Not in the car."

They were there in less than five minutes. Mamba stepped out of the car to move the barricade, a chain slung between two metal poles plunged in bucket-shaped slabs of cement. Mamba struggled trying to roll one of the cement buckets across the entrance and Paul realized he had selected the wrong man for the job. Louis Lippi could have picked up both slabs and tossed them across Washington Avenue by now. The parking-lot illumination had been killed, but there was sufficient light from the sky to make out the limousine parked beneath a light pole. It was the only automobile visible.

At Paul's instruction they circled the limousine first, then Mamba was told to get out and keep his piece holstered.

The long, spidery man crept up on the stretch limo as if it were a slumbering beast. He tried peering through the smoked glass, an exercise in futility.

Inside the 190 Paul Scorcese moaned and jammed a finger on his window button, running the glass down. "Mamba," he said, "how 'bout, just open a door?"

"Yeah."

Then: "Holy fucking shit!" Leaning through the back door, Mamba said, "Chub? Chub?"

A minute later Paul Scorcese was reading the note left on the seat next to his dead bodyguard. The words hadn't been cut from magazines and pasted on the paper in order to baffle the authorities, because the writer had assumed (correctly) that people like the Scorceses would never permit the FBI to muck about in family business. The note, printed neatly with a ballpoint pen on a sheet of typing paper, good cotton bond, said this:

72 hours
10 mil cash
Or no Joe

* * *

Del said, "Any trouble dumping the guy's gun?"

"Piece of cake. Nobody back there that time of night."

"The dumb fuck."

Elvis didn't say anything.

"Whadda you suppose was his problem?"

"Not *was, is.* Man's problem is he's dead."

It wasn't a bad thing to say, puncturing some of the tension inside Del. It happened, Elvis seemed to be saying to him, nothing you can do about it now. Which was the truth. There would be nightmares, though, he was sure of that. You didn't look into a man's eyes, even in the subdued light of the limo, and kill him without remembering the look.

You'll be seeing that face a long time, buddy boy, he thought.

Elvis had pulled off his sneakers and socks and wriggled his toes, enjoying the sensation. He took a sip of his drink, his—he'd stopped counting. It was past midnight. "One thing you don't have to worry about," he said, "guy isn't going to turn up in any morgue. Not those people."

"True."

"No body, no one reported missing, so, if you follow me, *technically* nobody's been killed. One way to look at it."

Del Rebus cocked his head on the recliner to give Elvis one of his patented grins. "No wonder the old man thinks you're the cat's pajamas. You take bullshit, make it look like whipped cream. You do me better'n I can do myself."

Elvis shrugged.

Del sighed. "But you still can't tell a joke worth shit."

* * *

The moment they untied him and peeled the tape off his mouth, the kid, Todd, went goofy on them, hollering like a goddamn girl cheerleader. Paul, sitting on a jump seat facing the boy, told Mamba, who evidently had to be told to hold his pecker when he peed, to close the door, all the fucking racket, and then he slapped the boy hard several times in the face, drawing blood. The boy's cries dropped off, became nothing more than sobs and hiccups. Finally, in a trickly little voice, he begged them to move the corpse of Chub. Louis Lippi looked at Paul, who nodded, and Chub was wrestled onto the far corner of the seat, his arms still hanging, his head faintly bobbing above his lap. The stench wasn't overwhelming, but by the same token it wasn't anyone's idea of a breath of fresh air.

Paul Scorcese handed the boy his handkerchief and told him to clean up his face. He waited for the boy to minister to himself, saying nothing, looking directly at him, then asked the boy questions. He asked the questions in a soft voice, and when the boy answered, he nodded. When the boy had answered all the questions Paul wanted to ask, he patted the boy's knee, looked over at Louis Lippi, and climbed out of the limousine.

A couple minutes later Louis Lippi got out. He was flexing the fingers of his right hand, staring at them in the moonlight. He had done his job well, no noise.

Paul turned to Mamba, who was resting his behind on a fender. "You drive the limo to the house. Keep the windows rolled up, I don't want somebody in a car next to you wondering, hey, what's that smell," he said. "And Mamba? No smoking."

*   *   *

They were both mellow, no question about it. Because they had carried the ball by themselves on this one, the decision to split the ten million dollars down the middle, just the two of them, hadn't required a whole lot of sophisticated debate. It was quite simple: *their* asses were on the line. This was a totally different venture and they were the ones doing the work, and doing it without any textbook or manual of instruction.

Del mixed the drinks this time and brought them out to the patio and handed Elvis his.

"You check on him?"

"Sparky. I'm walking in a house, you ask me to check on him. Not once, twice. Before I even get through the fucking door. It sunk in, all right? I checked. Guy's snoring away like he just had a go with Miss America in the bridal suite of a Hilton, okay?"

And flopped down with his drink on the recliner.

Elvis said, after a while, "When this is over, you going to California, see Franny like you said?"

"Ah, Frances." Del held his glass in both hands. "I ever tell you how we met?"

"No, but she did."

"Really."

"Really."

"You know what the world looks like to a dog? Black and white and gray. Fifteen years, that's the world I lived in. The moment I saw her, bingo, there was all this . . . color. That's when I began to think about Phoenix. Score fast, score big, spend the rest of my life with that woman. That was the dream. But I think I fucked up, told her stuff that scared her."

"Told her what you went in for."

Del Rebus ran a finger alongside his nose, putting together how much he wanted to say. "No, she knew that already. Most of it. The husband, he hired a private dick to look into my business."

"Listen to Franny, man's a dick himself," said Elvis.

"Like my daddy used to say, he's his own best friend. Anyway, I told her what happened, my side of it."

"What *did* happen, Del?"

"C'mon, you know all about it. So tell me, what're you gonna do with close to five and three-quarter million dollars, cash?"

"Five point seven five," said Elvis. "Talk about that *whish* up the spine. Oowee! I can't even imagine. . . . Well, one thing maybe. Open a restaurant. People do like to eat."

"Next to getting laid, I can't think of anything I enjoy more."

"Hey." Elvis sat up, taking his feet off the recliner. "You said something about how you owned some restaurants once. I'm sitting here dreaming, and you've already done it. What sorta restaurants?"

So Del told him, although it sounded like someone else's accomplishment, not his own. It was strange. He had sold the ones he owned for pennies on the dollar in order to meet the attorneys' fees.

Elvis shook his head. "You think you got your shit together and wham, there's life, flipping you the bird."

Del was trying to remember a joke—any joke.

"How 'bout you, Del, what're you gonna do with all your money?"

He didn't hesitate. "Go to work on the flip side of my dream. Remember the silver-dollar dream? It was a pretty good one."

Louis Lippi drove Paul back to Sport Time, Paul sitting in front this time and saying nothing. When they pulled up to the entrance, Louis braked the 190 and Paul stepped out, then leaned back in: "You did good tonight, Louis. Park, but stay in a car. I won't be long."

Paul entered the lobby and glanced at the night hostess without interest. She had a lot of red hair piled on top of her head. Freckles on her boobs, which she was doing a good job of displaying for the love-handle fatty in the knit shirt, the navy blue SansaBelt trousers, asking about the expensive cigars. Tobacco, hell, the guy just wanted to see some tit.

Behind the bar Ruby glanced at his watch, his right eye swollen, but not shut, getting set to announce last call. Closing at midnight. A quiet little town, Paul thought, but he wouldn't be able to hide here forever. His father hadn't been subtle about his interest in Paul starting a family. All right then. How about a redhead with knockers? No, that wasn't what Joe wanted. He'd say, her, you keep her on a side if you want, but you don't marry her. No, what Joe wanted was marriage into a family of prominence. Some juiceless aristocrat like that bitch he'd seen with the old hippie in Sport Time that night when he had said to Ruby, *He's got con all over him.*

And then thought: Angelo!

Angelo was going to have a cow. Make that two cows. And rip Paul a new asshole while he was at it. First, letting the old man get conned. Then booting the ball trying to get back the money. Now the old man was snatched, his ace guy was vulture bait, and the hippie and the jig were holding them up for ten million dollars. And he was sweating bedding a woman? He'd bed a reptile from out of the swamps if it meant he didn't have to call Angelo with what he had to tell him.

He turned around halfway through the kitchen. Out in the bar he caught Ruby's attention. The boy moved down the bar toward him like someone without any more illusions. "Still feeling that kick in the tummy?"

"For the rest of my life I think."

"I want a bottle of Courvoisier and a snifter brought to the office. Have one of the waitresses bring it with a book of matches. No. What's the broad in the lobby's name?"

"Kit. You just hired her like last week."

"Have her bring it back. Have her bring two snifters. If I'm not there, tell her to wait. You understand?"

"Sure. Whatever."

Paul Scorcese went through the kitchen, leaned into the room where the soldiers were still playing cards and pointed at one of them. His name was Vincent Lament, the family name truncated at Ellis Island by an impatient functionary.

Paul and Vincent, with Paul's arm over his shoulders, strolled out the back of the kitchen past the dumpster to take in the night air. The tallest day of his life Vincent Lament never topped five two, but he was mean as a mongoose and had brains, or at least more of them than Mamba. Which wasn't saying much, since Paul believed Mamba belonged at the bottom of the food chain intelligencewise. But Chub had selected little Vincent to assist him in disposing of the dumb biker and told Paul later that he was a good man with a saw, didn't hesitate or flinch. When Paul explained the nature of the job, two more bodies to cut up and scatter across the desert, Vincent Lament looked straight into his eyes and said yes, he could do it, no problem. "It's just meat," he said, "is all it is."

Paul Scorcese felt suddenly light in the head, but managed to bid the little man good night.

Waiting for him in his office was the broad with the bottle and glasses and an expression on her face like she had to pee, but was afraid to ask for permission. Paul Scorcese, although he had been with some women, did not know what to make of them except to think them fundamentally dishonest and a pain in the ass. This one wasn't bad looking, not with the high-gloss looks of the lady with the old hippie, but nice eyes, almond-shaped and brown, and dark lashes, not the practically invisible ones most redheads have. Another thing: there was some color in her skin, a hint of tan, it wasn't that cheesy white.

"Oh," said Paul, by way of greeting, and strode past her to work the buttons on his sound system. Mozart filtered into the room.

Before he turned around, the girl said, "Ruby told me to wait, Mr. Scorcese. Should I leave now?"

"Kit, is it?"

"Why yes. You have . . . I mean . . . remembering my name like that."

"You're a pretty lady. That makes it easy," he said, closing his eyes as the music lifted him, even making his lies plausible. He breathed more easily, the attack of lightheadedness behind him. "You enjoy music, Kit?"

"It's Mozart, isn't it?"

He swung around.

"My mother, she taught piano. I can play a decent clarinet, but it isn't something I'm driven to do. Is this the 'Jupiter'?"

He crossed the room to where she was standing in the silly black bathing-suit costume that made the overweight straights go gaga. The bottle of Courvoisier and two glasses stood on the ebony desk, the light sloshing around in the crystal snifters. His face inches from hers, he said, "It's Mozart. And yes, it's the 'Jupiter.' You either know music or you've been reading my mail."

She smiled, lowering her face, accepting the compliment.

The impression was one of modesty and it stunned him, excited him too.

"It's an easy symphony to remember if you love Mozart and happen to play clarinet, only competently," she said, giving him the benefit of her eyes, something nice behind them. "He didn't write a single note for the clarinet."

"Please." He touched her elbow, but gently. "Sit down. If you would just sit with me for a while." She did, and he continued. "I'm having the cognac, will you join me?"

"I don't know, Mr. Scorcese."

"Paul."

He uncorked the bottle and dribbled a half inch of the

amber fluid into each goblet, and handed one to Kit. He asked her for the book of matches, which she had forgotten to leave on the desk, and when she produced it from her cleavage, with apologies, he said, "Now it's my turn to do a trick."

He struck a match and rotated her glass over the flame for a few seconds, then gave her the snifter and asked her to inhale.

"Breathing it is part of the pleasure," he said.

He sat down beside her and lit another match, rolled his own glass over the flame and touched her glass with his. They exchanged gazes over upturned crystal.

"These chairs," she said, "they're much more comfortable than they look." She rolled her bare shoulders, holding her glass with both hands, her voice full of gee whiz. She closed her eyes, seemed to inhale the music. She said in a soft voice, "The *Andante cantabile.*"

"Yes," said Paul Scorcese. It was past three in the morning in New York and bad as the news was, he wasn't about to spring it on Angelo in the middle of the night. He'd wait at least, what, four hours? Make that five, no six. That was the good news: he had six hours before Angelo tore him a new asshole. But it wasn't the only good news.

A woman like Kit existed.

Their hands touched, and after that it was just a matter of time.

Louis Lippi, still sitting behind the wheel of the 190, watched the sky go from black to gray to sepia, hearing birds off someplace, and lifted a cheek to let one go, an ace fart from the bottom of the barrel, holy murder, just as he caught sight of Paul Scorcese approaching in the rearview mirror. He thought about saying, *I was just thinking about Chub, I don't know why.* Let him know how much he enjoyed sitting in a car a whole fucking night.

Chapter 23

If he didn't wake with a grin—and he was willing to bet he did—Angelo Scorcese sure had one now, remembering last night. God. Mai Lee could be one ferocious lover when the spirit moved her. Normally what she did, she read stories to the young ones in French until eight o'clock, then brought them down to kiss Angelo, if he wasn't busy, and let the nanny put them to bed. Then sat by herself in the kitchen with a cup of mint tea writing down (printing actually, with a quick, precise hand) the next day's menu. That done, she worked the crossword in the newspaper and read a few chapters in a paperback, usually something by a woman writer with a name that sounded as if it had been manufactured in Hollywood. Sometimes she took the paperback upstairs with her and fell asleep reading it. But not last night. Last night, once she had finished the next day's menu, she had come into the den wearing perfume and fresh makeup and a soft, gauzy something that gave him glimpses of her breasts, hips, even the sweet shadow where her legs met. Said nothing, not interrupting his enjoyment of a dumb movie with Robert DeNiro in it, showing her smarts, because she knew how much he loved DeNiro. All the guy had to do was mug and Angelo Scorcese cracked up. She curled next to him, watched the rest of the movie, didn't laugh once, but squeezed his upper arm when he did and twice kissed him on the neck. Then took him upstairs and put some moves on him he had forgotten how good it could feel, the kind of craziness of desire they had shared in Saigon, going for the whole experience.

They had done it so much his foreskin bled and she whispered she might not be able to walk upright for a week. And finally fallen exhausted asleep he did not know when.

Now, sitting at the table in the kitchen where she wrote out the next day's meals, in sweats and nothing else, he slurped strong coffee and glanced through the paper, all the kids but the youngest off at the beach with Mai Lee. Therese was running water in the sink, jamming plates and utensils into the dishwasher. A radio was on, some station that played oldies but goodies, Neil Diamond singing something about a night-light or heart-light, maybe hot-wire, some damn thing. He was reading about the Mets, Gooden lobbing dynamite all night. Rate he was going he might win twenty-five games. Angelo Scorcese reached down inside his sweats, shook his member fondly.

A night like last night reminded him how wonderful girls could be; if anything, sharpened his appetite for them. Mai Lee inspired him to want a taste of all of them. Okay, rethinking that, not all. Certainly not something like Magda, Luigi Vacanza's brute of a daughter that Ricky said last night was going to be married. He wondered how much Lou was paying the poor stiff.

He had Therese bring him another cup of coffee. The weather guy on the radio was saying they were going to have another hot one, in the nineties, telling someone named Marcia that the Big Apple was going to be baked apple for the foreseeable future, ha-ha. Asshole. Where'd they find these guys?

The phone was ringing and Angelo waited for the machine to pick up, hearing Mai Lee's voice now with the little French sounds in it that drove his father crazy, asking whoever was calling to please leave a message after the beep . . . then hearing the voice of his brother Paul.

Paul didn't sound so good.

Angelo Scorcese snatched up the phone and they exchanged numbers and Angelo told him to hang on a minute. He looked out the front door to make sure somebody was sitting in the van. It was Cato's day to drive, and there he was, Jesus, singing in there like he was on some Vegas stage, using his fist for a microphone. Angelo picked up the phone and said to give him twenty minutes.

* * *

Not yet nine-thirty in the morning and the heat out here already weighed on you. Mai Lee had the right idea: hit the beach. Maybe he'd try it sometime. Better yet, arrange some time for the two of them to get away. How many years since they'd done that?

He was standing next to a phone booth on a fairly quiet corner just off Rockaway Boulevard near where it intersected with Sutphin. Fairly quiet, yeah, until a jumbo jet dropped down right over his head going into JFK, the noise so enormous it infuriated him, made him want to break things. Of all the phone booths in the borough, he had to be standing in the one smack beneath the final approach to JFK. This was going to be one fun conversation.

The phone rang at nine-thirty on the button.

Angelo picked up and said, "You're ten minutes late, fuckhead."

"You remember Louis Lippi?"

"The Lip, sure."

"He's my new driver. He farted, it smelled like he shit his pants. I had to wait for the car to air out."

"Explains it. Listen I was gonna call you anyway, we talked it over last night, about the two cute boys, and my idea is—new driver? I thought this guy you had, whatsiz name?"

"Chub."

"What?"

Another jet was descending toward JFK, sounding like it was going to take Angelo's head off. He told Paul to hang on and glared up at the silver underbelly of the plane.

"You were saying?"

"His name's Chub."

"Yeah, Chump. I thought he was an okay guy, you liked him. What happen a him?"

"That's part of the reason I'm calling," Paul Scorcese said, and told him about the events of the previous evening. Most of them anyway.

Angelo, listening, couldn't believe what he was hearing, turning the bill of his baseball cap forward, then backward, then forward again, stopping that to clutch his crotch, just not believing what he was hearing and at the same time knowing it was true. The hippie and the jig, they had big ones, he'd give them that. They had balls the size they probably had to rent a U-Haul. But he was thinking too, thinking hard and carefully.

He said, at last, "They think we keep our money in shoe boxes under the bed? Fucking seventy-two hours. From when?"

"Guy said he's calling me at noon, about four and a half hours. I'll pin him down."

"Do that. Feel him out, much as you can. Think it's serious, they'd do the old guy?"

"Didn't seem to have any trouble shooting Chub."

"Fucking lowlifes."

Another big jet was plowing the skies overhead and the brothers shouted at one another, with Angelo's share of the conversation consisting of: "Huh?"

"   . . .   "

"Speak up!"

"   . . .   "

"Fucking what?"

"   . . .   "

Then, "Jesus, Paul, you hear me now? I'm standing like five inches from JFK. Way it feels. Listen. I'll handle it. Touch bases when you hear from them."

"Can do," came the voice out of Phoenix.

"You okay, kid?"

"I keep waiting for you to rip me a new asshole."

"Pauli," said Angelo Scorcese. "Shit happens. Stay in touch."

"You got it. Mother?"

"Kid, what can I say?"

"Tell her I met a nice lady. Name of Kit. Would you tell her that for me?"

"Matter a fact I'm having lunch there. I'll tell her. But nothing about the old man. We'll take care of it, she won't know a thing."

"Wanna bet?"

Paul Scorcese heard the line go dead and stood there holding the phone outside Drug Emporium, staring out into the parking lot, smoothing an eyebrow with his middle finger.

And thought: That's all he said? Shit happens?

Limping from fatigue and the Jack, Del Rebus made his way into the bathroom in the darkness of early morning, relieved himself and flipped on a light, which was even more of a shock than the cold tile floor. He treated himself to a hot shower, a long one. He put on coffee, looked in on the twelve-year-old shape slumbering away in there, oblivious of the cuffed ankle, and went back to the bedroom to dress.

He sat in the breakfast nook, drinking his coffee black, eyes staring straight ahead at the softening night, profiles of the eucalyptus and jacaranda and beyond them the cliffs taking shape.

Fifteen minutes later he parked the banged-up Oldsmobile away from Assoud's van, climbed behind the wheel of the van and drove to an address in Glendale to pick up Assoud and his daughter, and from there to a wholesale center in south Phoenix for supplies. He spent the morning helping Assoud and the daughter run their business inside the zoo, enjoying himself actually, performing a service, a simple, honest exchange.

For his part, Assoud could only keep quiet and praise Allah for this crazy American that paid him a thousand dollars to borrow his van for a few days. On top of which he worked for no wages. Truly this was an amazing country, what could happen to a man here.

Shortly before noon Del said he had to be going. The daughter of Assoud gave him a moony look, having never met anyone who said and did so many strange things. Americans, she thought, laughed so much. Why?

Noon. He decided to drive all the way to Sky Harbor Airport, call from a public phone there. It had not been smart, he thought, however short the conversation, to have called from the house off Doubletree. Blame it on adrenaline. But from now on, any contact would be from a location totally anonymous.

Like this phone booth in Terminal 3. Some money had been spent erecting this place with the pricey shops and goofy sculpture, the mile-high ceilings. He felt pretty good, considering how little sleep he had had.

Rooting about in his wallet for the slip of paper with Sport Time's number on it, he came across the card Elvis had given him, the card belonging to Franny Lott's lawyer. A phone number on it and an address in San Francisco. The address told him Franny was paying for a high-power attorney, or the husband would be. There was incentive right there to want a reconciliation, the little prick. That night in Tahoe, even before the card playing got under way, he had started disliking the guy, David, listening to the tone of voice he used on his wife, not exactly snotty, but dismissive, obviously not even hearing what the lady had to say. Half the time not even looking at her when he spoke or she spoke. Del Rebus looked at her all right, whether she was speaking or not, and thought the guy was nuts. He behaved like a pampered only child. He was good-looking and smart, but down deep in there was the heart of a tyrant: held his breath to get his way as a kid, gave hard looks as an adult and froze you out. Thinking about the little prick now, he was almost sorry he dealt him the blackjack, let him off the hook for the checks. But throwing the hand, Franny had told him, moved her off the dime, gave her the courage to follow him out of the room and accost him, working the rings free from her fingers saying, "Del? Help me find the hostess so we can go someplace, you and I, and talk."

Frances.

He had said, "You have beautiful eyes."

"Thank you," she said. "You're the first one in a long time to notice they both work."

* * *

Paul Scorcese picked up on the first ring sitting in his chair in his office alone. It was a few minutes past noon. "Yeah?"

"Paul?"

"Yeah."

"You understand the situation pretty well, do you?"

"Seventy-two hours from when?"

"Technically, from 9:50 pm, yesterday. But what the hell, we'll be generous, give you a couple hours. Make it, to keep things simple, midnight. But Paul, I wouldn't wait to the last minute. Somebody's watch might run fast."

"How do I get in touch?"

"Oh, we'll be in touch."

"Somebody I spoke to said what, you think we keep it in shoe boxes? I think you might have a little problem there."

"Then somebody isn't thinking very smart."

And for the second time that day someone hung up on Paul Scorcese. He put down the phone and leaned forward to put his elbows on the desk, face in his hands, trying to sort things out on four hours of sleep. That was a mouthful of truth, what the guy on the phone said. It was no secret that Angelo did not lead the league in brains, although from everything he was hearing, since the attempt on their father's life, Angelo had held things together like a champ. But the old guy gets snatched, and all he says is that shit happens, *that* sounded like the Angelo he had grown up observing. Not exactly stupid, no, far from it; it was a failure or absence of imagination. He saw very clearly what he wanted to see, and that was his limitation.

Paul Scorcese called the house in Howard Beach, left

the number of the phone booth where he could be reached on the answering machine, gave Angelo an hour. He thought about dialing Kit's number, but didn't. She hadn't had much sleep either.

He found a waitress in the lounge and instructed her to knock on the office door, knock hard in forty minutes, until he answered. Then he went back to the office and put on Mozart, stretched out on his back on the carpet. He listened to *The Marriage of Figaro*—about a minute of it before he was asleep.

Mai Lee, with her entourage of bodyguards and children and children's friends, returned from the beach a little before five o'clock and found her husband in the kitchen with Therese and knew immediately that it was important to be alone with him. Something had him excited, and it wasn't the prospect of another night like the last one. This was different. He was drinking beer from a frosted mug, one hand unconsciously clutching his business, which he had a habit of doing whenever he was worked up over what he was thinking. The other thing: he seldom drank, except on special occasions.

He was standing there with his stupid baseball cap on backward leaning his shoulder against the refrigerator, the freezer half of it, and gesturing with the mug, telling Therese what a big hit the hearts and kidneys were.

In a white terry-cloth caftan Mai Lee came up to him, her skin still hot from the sun, the sweet scent of sun lotion in sharp contrast to the smells of garlic and onion. "*Mon ange*," she said, on tiptoe to kiss him on the cheek, "beer? I've never seen you drinking beer."

"Now you have," he said, and grinned. "Tastes goddamn good too, day like today."

"Oh?"

"So goddamn good I might have another."

And that was that. But he was still grinning, and that gave her confidence that whatever it was, she could get it out of him. She hadn't had a problem last night, had she? She knew all about the two wise guys cheating the old one out of fifty thousand and how they handled the guys Paul sent to collect. They sounded as if they knew what they were doing, but Angelo told her they were dead meat: the Wizard had a plan to suck them in.

But the plan could not have worked this quickly, in less than a day. So it was something else.

Something had happened about which he looked— proud? No, smug. Giving her this innocent look, but you could see it in his eyes, exactly as he'd looked that morning the crazy men tried to kill the old one. And her asking that morning if he had any idea who, with him sitting naked on the side of the bed, his big thing drooping but by no means soft, and him saying, *Who, me?*

She touched his arm with her fingertips, a light smile for him, and went upstairs to shower, to dress for dinner.

Del Rebus ran a finger along the side of his nose, watching Elvis chopping green peppers, mushrooms and onions. The old man sat at the table, his ankle cuffed to the chair, placidly chewing his omelet.

"Likes my cooking," said Elvis over his shoulder.

"Well, isn't that nice," Del said, still standing in the doorway. "You two have a pleasant morning?"

"We getting along just fine. I even learned some Italian." Pronouncing it Eyetalian. *"Munizza."*

"Oh yeah, that word."

"Means garbage. But I think he's changed his opinion of us."

"Good cooking'll do that."

"Yeah. He also made me a bet."

Del stood very still, alert. "Uh-huh."

Elvis put down the broad knife, rinsed and dried his hands, and walked over to where Del was standing. "He says we won't get shit," he said, "and I'm inclined to believe him."

Angelo Scorcese had to visit some people and did not get back to the house at Howard Beach until after midnight, but Mai Lee had waited up for him. It didn't surprise him. All through supper she had given him looks, led him with questions. Going up the stairs toward the light from the master bedroom, he weighed whether to tell her and thought, what the hell. She had waited this long.

One of his visits that night had been with the Wizard, who confirmed what he had suspected, that it would be a pain in the butt to put together ten million in cash quickly. The Scorceses weren't Colombian drug dealers. The family had investments, assets, dummy companies, a lumbering corporate structure. It would be a pain in the butt, but the Wizard stressed, it could be done. Angelo said it was something he wondered about is all.

Mai Lee lowered the paperback she was reading, a thick pink slab with the title in raised gold letters. There was an empty teacup and saucer on the nightstand next to her. She was wearing a long pearl-colored silk robe that showed off the coloring the sun had given her.

On his way to the bathroom to shave and brush his teeth, Angelo said, "Tell you, babe, that tan there, you could be in a commercial."

"It was a busy evening?"

"This and that," he said, "the usual shit."

When he came out of the bathroom, he was unbuttoning his shirt and swimming in fresh after-shave. "Those cute boys I told you about last night?"

"Yes?"

"They got cuter."

And as he undressed, tossing his clothes without looking where they fell or giving a shit, he explained the latest development and his simple scheme for using it to his advantage, dragging his feet over delivery of the money until the cute boys had no choice but to do Joe and run for their lives.

Lying beside him in the dark, running her fingers through the hair on his chest, Mai Lee Scorcese listened to him without interrupting. When he finished, she was still moving her fingers through the hair on his chest and saying nothing.

He said, "So. Is it perfect or what?"

"*Mon ange,*" she said, "if it isn't perfect, you're dead."

If he was grinning before, he wasn't now. And a great big good boner was going down for the count.

Chapter 24

A little before midnight Del Rebus drove to a Smith's, open twenty-four hours, with everything from groceries to movies to dry cleaning to banking, the intersection of Thunderbird and Fortieth Street. He put in a call to Sport Time and was transferred to Paul Scorcese.

"This is Paul."

"How we doing?"

"You."

"Me. Day one's about up, I thought, uh, how's the project coming?"

"Beats the shit outta me. Look, boyfriend, I have to tell

you something. I'm not running the show. That's coming from someplace else. But you hurt the old guy, I'm telling you this, I will find you. That's a promise. I will find you and you won't like it."

"Paul? Blow it out your ass. Whoever's running the show, tell them to be smart. Do it as a community service."

Del Rebus wandered into this spanking-clean supermarket with a shopping list from Elvis for shallots, broccoli, fresh mushrooms, and a nice piece of London broil. Elvis already had the garlic, the Oriental fluids and spices. The old mob guy, it turned out, liked his Chinese. Almost as passionate about enjoying the food as he was about despising his partly Vietnamese daughter-in-law, mimicking her accent. The little sack of shit could be a charmer if you didn't look beyond what he said.

Having acquired everything on the list, he wheeled the cart over to the liquor section, snatched up a bottle of Jack Daniels and looked at the price, knew he could do better at Walgreen's, but fuck it: he was on his way to being rich, regardless of the old man's opinion that the acting head of the family, Angelo, would queer the deal somehow.

Waiting in the checkout line, done with being amused by the headlines of the tabloids, he happened to glance up at the portrait of the store founder, mounted on a bulkhead. It was a painting done in the Rockwell mode, intended to suggest he was a friendly uncle brother buddy somebody next door kind of guy. Del thought he didn't look a whole lot like his father, which meant his father didn't look a whole lot like a shark at feeding time.

Del Rebus drove back to the house on Doubletree and

put away the groceries and poured himself a strong one, only a dash of water, wanting to back down the adrenaline. He had to be up early again to pick up Assoud and his daughter. She was a pretty but serious little thing, probably grow up to be an accountant. He put the glass down on the counter, half the drink gone, and refilled it.

Elvis was sitting in a recliner on the patio, but before joining him, Del ducked down the hallway to look in on the small shape in the darkness. The shape moved.

"You make your call, mister blue jeans?"

"What?"

"I got good ears. I heard you telling the colored boy."

Del Rebus grinned, leaning with his drink in the doorway, his eyes beginning to adjust. He could see the little man was lying on his back, but he could not see his face. "You don't miss much, do you?"

"You getting the money?"

"I don't have it yet, if that's what you mean. But I'll get it, don't you lose any sleep over it."

"Only way you getting money, like I told the colored boy, the only way is from me. From me you get one million, which I keep in my home, or you get nothing and have to kill me."

"You're one helluva poker player, Sparky."

"Lemme tell you something. Can I tell you something?"

"I'm right here."

"If a man tries to kill you, but he don't do it right, and you live, you think he stops thinking how to do it right? No, he don't stop. Except if he don't *need* to kill you, because he's got what he wants, and you are too weak to be a threat. Say if you are old and have trouble paying attention and maybe even drool sometimes and go and spend fifty thousand dollars cash on a deal, like my boy Pauli says, it might as well have a sign on it."

"Wait a minute." Del standing straight now. "Wait one fucking minute. What you're saying, this Angelo, your oldest son, *he* tried to take you off? And you bought into the dogs as part of your own con?"

"What I'm saying, mister blue jeans, you see me drool since I been here?"

An hour later sitting in a recliner, watching ragged clouds drift across the stars, Del Rebus had drunk just enough to speculate aloud that the situation they were in was one big cosmic joke. If the evil little sack of shit could be believed, they weren't calling the shots, the Scorceses were. Either way they went, they were tools, working for one Scorcese or the other.

If he could be believed: that was the sticky part.

"I know I believe him," said Elvis. "I look in the man's eyes, I believe him."

"Guy like that, Sparky, you don't look in his eyes, you watch your backside. Guy like that put anything in his eyes he wants."

"Shit, Del."

"I mean it."

"I say we take the money and run."

"I say we got two more days. Nothing happens, then we take the little guy's million. How's that?"

Elvis sighed, resigned to go along.

A coyote yipped off somewhere, a desolate sound.

"Some family," said Elvis, "guy tries to kill his own father."

Del Rebus kept his mouth shut tight.

Paul Scorcese, exhausted from the night before, slept alone and slept easily, slept right up to the instant his alarm rang, which he shut off to sleep some more.

His father, Joe Scorcese, slept less than a mile away with an ankle cuffed to a bed frame, snoring in there like a man accustomed to wearing leg irons.

Elvis Mahoney, after some shifting around, eased into unconsciousness dreaming about Heather Tamara Lee, who at some vague point in the dream shaded into Franny Lott, Franny Lott passing through the turnstiles, that one.

Del Rebus fell into a drunken black hole.

Almost three thousand miles away it was a different story. Lying on his back, his eyes wide open, Angelo Scorcese listened to the echo of Mai Lee's words, the echo prompting a response from him, another echo, another response, and so on. *If it isn't perfect, you're dead.* Goddamn smart-ass bitch. Trouble was, none of his responses struck him as altogether foolproof. After about an hour of this nonsense, Angelo rolled out of bed and found his bathrobe on a peg in the bathroom, pawed about on Mai Lee's nightstand for cigarettes and a lighter, and went downstairs to the den.

He was not a smoker. He lit the cigarette, took the smoke into his mouth, held it there, then expelled it from the corner of his mouth, sitting on the sectional in the den, staring at the blank fifty-two-inch screen, the big Mitsubishi a gift from Mikey, the Appliance Prince of Flatbush Avenue. From time to time, he stood up and walked to the kitchen, drank milk straight from the carton. In his enthusiasm for and confidence in his scheme, he had put away four beers, but now they gnawed at him. He had never much enjoyed or could tolerate alcohol, which had been cause for some un-subtle belittlement from his father, who joked about him as the Jew boy with wop brains.

Now he sat alone in the den of his three-hundred-thou-sand-dollar home in Queens watching the pink street lamps pale, sunlight creeping into the morning, and felt something approaching gratitude, although he would never admit it, for his wife. He had listened to her, and was still listening to her, and for that reason he began to think of himself as a Jew boy with Jew boys' brains. Didn't those guys always listen to their women?

It was light out. Therese would be barging in soon. He climbed the stairs, showered, shaved, and dressed in the bathroom so as not to disturb Mai Lee. Downstairs, he peered out the door to see who his driver was, spotted Va-canza's nephew, Bennie Focoso, behind the wheel of the van. He was a pistol, but at least he wouldn't be trying to match Frank Sinatra note for note if Angelo needed him.

He adjusted his baseball cap, jabbed buttons on the security system, and let himself out. They drove to Forest Hills, woke the Wizard, and invited him out for a ride; it was okay if he wore his pajamas and robe, his slippers, they just had to spend some quality time together.

Angelo instructed Bennie Focoso to take Continental

Avenue to Metropolitan, Metro across to St. John's. They'd walk in the cemetery, where they'd have privacy. Also, Angelo thought, it would put the Wizard in the right frame of mind, give him something to think about while he strolled in his pink-and-lavender-striped bathrobe, looking like an enormous Easter egg.

The cemetery was crisscrossed with paved lanes among the tombstones, and it was on one of these that Bennie Focoso followed them in the van. The Wizard's right shoulder dipped as he walked, his ebony cane punctuating their conversation. He broke a sweat within the first few steps.

When Angelo, leaving out the reason for the delay, explained the gravity of the situation, Metzenbaum stopped, used his sleeve on his forehead, then pointed with his cane at the cathedral in the heart of the cemetery. "You might want to pay it a visit," he said. "That's where they still believe in miracles."

"What're you saying?"

"Yesterday you asked me about a hypothetical seventy-two hours and I told you it'd be a bitch. Now we're down to forty-eight, and you're telling me it's for real."

Angelo held up his wrist to read his watch. "Closer to forty-five, Wiz. No, even less. It's gotta be on a plane and in Pauli's hands before that."

They were walking once more, Metzenbaum's cane going *cack . . . cack . . . cack* on the macadam. A brown car, a new Buick with two couples inside, old folks, rolled toward them and by, every head swiveling in astonishment at Metzenbaum's costume.

"I don't hear you," Angelo said, "but what I'd like you to think about is where you'd be without our family."

"I know that. Chrissakes, you think I don't know that?"

"You'd be in public housing, Wiz, with a butthole about the size of Cleveland."

"You paint a charming picture."

Cack . . . cack . . . cack.

Metzenbaum stopped. "Okay. This might work. You give me the names of three people, with passports, that we can trust. We got a bank in the Caymans and two more in Panama. Have them at my office as soon as possible. They'll have to wait awhile for me to move enough into them and get my confirmations, but better to have them there, ready to leave with my letters of introduction. They fly out, collect the money, fly directly to Phoenix, Paul should have it all tomorrow afternoon, early evening at the latest. It should work."

"Wiz," Angelo Scorcese said, "look around, see what could befall you if it don't."

Chapter 25

Del Rebus parked the Olds like yesterday, across the lot from the van, and sat smoking a cigarette in the dim light. There was another car in the lot, but it was empty. Nothing unusual going on that he could see. He got out, locked the Olds and walked to the van. Twenty-five minutes later Assoud and his daughter were aboard, start of another merry morning. Del thought he'd get that little girl to grin if it killed him.

* * *

It was a video store on Nineteenth Avenue, a little after eleven in the morning, a mom and pop by the size of it. Phoenix detective Horatio "Buddy" Johnson parked directly in front of the store in his white unmarked Chevrolet. He could see someone inside behind a counter, a short guy on the telephone. Locking up the Chevrolet, Detective Johnson cast a glance at the sky, a solid haze up there, almost a pantyhose-tan color. The heat, around 110, was bad enough, but the humidity, that was the real bitch, there was no escaping it. The curse of living here. Out in it, his fingers, his face, his whole body in fact, felt bloated, unwieldy. Part of the feeling, of course, was a consequence of sitting alone in a motel room on Thomas with a six-pack of Pabst and a pint of Romanov vodka: last night's grim celebration of a second marriage going down in flames.

He shucked the silver wrapper and added another stick of grape-flavored gum to the wad he already had in there.

Air-conditioning. An electronic monitor mounted on the door emitted a singsong sound as the door closed behind him. The guy on the phone smiled apologetically. A couple of arcade games stood just to the left of the entrance. Row upon row of squat A-shaped wooden cabinets displayed empty movie boxes, the movies themselves in black cases behind the counter. A large alcove at the rear was also equipped with shelving, more movie boxes there. The carpet was a medium gray and the walls were a lighter shade of it. A cool, soothing color. Moving around, waiting for the guy to get off the phone, Detective Johnson decided this was a slick little operation. Guy was probably rolling in it. And what was this back here, just past the big-screen television, little room with saloon doors on it. The detective nudged open one of the doors, hearing the guy hang up the phone, and saw shelves with more movie boxes, the boxes crawling with pictures of beautiful bare naked ladies. Yes.

He aligned the doors and approached the long white counter, the little guy behind it smiling. "Help you?"

There were boxes of candy bars and microwave popcorn on the counter, and Detective Johnson snatched up a Nestlé Crunch, peeled off its wrapper. "Detective Johnson," he said, removing the gum from his mouth and placing it carefully on the peeled wrapper lying on the counter. "You reported some unreturned rental property. You the owner?"

And that was the end of the guy's smile. "Yeah, I'm the owner," he said. "I reported it about ten days ago."

The way it worked, when the department received a call on something like this, the nearest available uniformed officer was sent to the store to obtain a description of the unreturned property along with whatever information the store had on the perpetrator. The uniform wrote up a report, called in to get a case number for it, turned it in at the end of the day for assignment. The theft of videotapes and machines did not qualify as a high priority crime. It was something a detective could look into when he had a moment, stopping by the victimized store more as a courtesy than anything else, although it was frightening how screwed up some of the reports were. Real rumdums out there riding around in their blue suits. The little guy looked like he'd seen his share of them.

"Just a minute," he said, and moved along the counter, opened a drawer, and came back with the customer's signed receipt, a white card with information on the customer who never returned the merchandise, and a smaller white card that the reporting officer had given him, with the case number scratched in the corner. The guy dropped everything on the counter in front of him and backed up against the shelves where the movies were kept and folded his arms on his chest. Yeah, the guy'd been through it before, showing it in his pissy little stare. Well, fuck him.

Detective Johnson fished wire-rimmed glasses from a pocket inside his suit coat along with the report taken by the uniform, got the glasses on his face, unfolded the paper and resumed munching on the chocolate.

The little guy took a phone call, a short one, probably from his wife, because he said, "Detective's here. You know, those two movies and the machine . . . yeah, isn't it . . . next time they call sucking up for a donation . . . that's right . . . when hell freezes . . ."

The guy got off the phone and they spent some minutes going over the report, which, true to form, contained errors both of commission and omission. The guy, whose name was Pat Peck, lightened up as they went along, although he slipped in a few jabs about the city itself, everyone in his pocket from the county assessor to the charities to all the advertisers with their inflated promises and more inflated bills. Johnson humored him, even sympathized a little, or as much as a man can whose own life wasn't exactly a picture postcard, because a question had occurred to him.

"So Pat, I see you got you a room back there, them movies do good for you?" This wasn't the question.

Pat Peck seemed as eager to talk about something other

than the scumbag who had ripped him off as Detective Johnson was. "Save my ass. All due respect, shady is the only
business to be in in this town."

"No shit."

"No shit."

"That the stuff you see on cable, or hard core?"

"Hard."

"I seen one—it was what, month or two ago?—stag
party for a guy on the force. There was this blond, had 'em
out to here. I mean she's lying on her back, planes had to
change elevation."

"She have a tattoo on her shoulder?"

"Yeah!" He slapped his hand on the counter just as his
beeper went off. He hoisted the hem of his coat to read the
beeper attached to his belt. "You gotta phone I can use?"

Pat Peck motioned him to the far end of the counter
and hoisted up a white touch-tone.

The party at the other end picked up on the first ring.
"Dingle here. This Buddy?"

Dingle was a motorcycle cop, a drinking companion
from way back when. They bowled on the same team.

"It's me, John. Whacha got?"

"I'm corner of Shea and Tatum, calling from a Smitty's.
In the parking lot's an Oldsmobile, license number DGB
one-oh-eight, you said you were interested in a couple days
ago."

"Sweet jumping Jesus."

"Yeah, thought you'd like it. Happened to pull over a
heavy pedal, and I'm writing him up, practically parked right
next to the sonuvabitch. God's on the good guys' side for a

change. It's at, lemme see, the west edge of the parking lot. Next to that big white-and-green church it looks like out of *Star Wars.*"

"Gimme fifteen minutes, John, I'll use the siren." And he hung up the phone, moved along the counter to liberate his gum. "Where were we? Oh, yeah, the tattoo. In this movie I'm tellin' you about, gal got both heels in backuver head. Gotta be double, triple-jointed to do that. You got'ny of her?"

"Few," said Pat Peck. "You want me to make a copy of the signed invoice? That's the usual procedure."

"Yeah, do her," said Detective Johnson. And now the question: "Hey, what's it take to become a member here?"

The sky was approaching the color of smut when Del Rebus parked the van in the Smitty's lot. He had skipped the noon call to Paul, not wanting to appear anxious or predictable. Give him some time to think about things. The sky told him there'd be some rain big-time, real soon, so he strode with purpose toward the Oldsmobile, get home, grab some sleep before picking up Assoud and his daughter. The serious one, that he'd finally gotten a laugh out of, by squirting himself in the face with a container of mustard. Oldest shtick in the world.

Doing finger snaps against his palm, Three Stooges fashion, Del came abreast of the Olds, unlocked and opened the door, got in and winced from the heat of the leather. Before shutting the door he turned the key and ran down the front windows—

"Sir? You own this vehicle?"

—and over his left shoulder saw the man approaching around the rear fender of the car next to his, the man with light hair, broken nose, going to fat inside a sad, drab suit that only a cop would wear in public, so he turned the key—

"Turn off that engine! I'm a Phoenix—"

—and yanked the gearshift into reverse, mashed the accelerator, and saw that little bit of disbelief in the cop's eyes. A mistake. Then saw him pivot, try to bolt, too late, the door catching him square on his fat ass. Watched him whirl away from the door with not quite the polish of Ginger Rogers being released by Fred Astaire, nice shoes though. When he next saw him, the cop was folded in a fetal position, eyes closed and not saying much, his badge still clutched in his hand.

Seeing what appeared to be two store employees charging toward him, Del shifted into drive, cut the wheel hard and accelerated. A glance in the mirror showed him the cop on his knees, shaking his head slowly from side to side. His nose was bleeding. Del got out of there.

He drove straight for the house on Doubletree, trying to block out his fury, his frustration too, because it was clear to him that his run here was ending. Too many signs pointing to it: shooting the man in the limo, getting foxed by the old sack of shit, and this, the cop. The dumbass, what did he think, he flashed a badge and that made him king shit? Guy, once he gets back on his feet, should run, not walk, to the nearest shrink, have his head examined.

But the real sign, the one that hammered it home?

It was a petty miscalculation. Of two inches. In order to park the van in the garage. Two inches, and he wouldn't have been made in a public parking lot. It must have been the beefy biker, the one he'd made crawl beneath the Buick, who gave the cops a description, maybe even the license plate. Son of a bitch. Two effing inches.

It was comical. It was on the order of a twenty-five-cent seal grounding a sophisticated, gazillion-dollar space launch. Del Rebus almost wept from a sense of outrage and bafflement.

This town. Just when he thought he had it beaten—its power, the insidious poison of failure—it dropped a two-inch banana peel in his path. Another of the world's oldest shticks. To let him know he wasn't going to win what was never in the cards to begin with: the harsh pleasure of revenge.

Chapter 26

The recipe called for flank steak, but that wasn't a cut readily available in Phoenix, at least anywhere Elvis had shopped. London broil had proved to be a more than adequate substitute. First trimming away all the fat, he sliced it into thin strips against the grain, talking intermittently to the old man cuffed to a chair, who was reading *The Republic* in the breakfast nook, one bent finger moving down the column. When the old man came across something that interested him, he read it aloud, and Elvis and he discussed it. Sometimes the old man closed his eyes listening to Elvis.

"The beef," Elvis was telling him now, "I like to marinate

it five, six hours. Mostly the cookbooks are mum on the length of time, but I like to give it a good soak. It's like sauces, the more time you give them, the better they are. Patience leads you to the heart of the flavor."

The old man's eyes snapped open, his finger moving across the newsprint without purpose, lost, quivering like a seismic recorder. "I loss my place," he grumbled.

"Again?" said Elvis Mahoney, coming over. "Good thing you weren't the man in charge of the map for Lewis and Clark. They'd still be stumbling around somewhere in St. Louis. Here. Mets game. They brought their bats last night and whomped on Houston. Now if you'll excuse me, I got to mix the marinade."

"Whadda you use?"

Elvis knelt, searched a moment beneath the island, pulled out a large stainless-steel bowl. "Basic mix," he said. "Black soy sauce, cornstarch and sugar. That's it."

"My daughter-in-law, she don't even cook."

"The Vietnamese lady?" Elvis asked, fairly certain, but not positive.

"She talk with this accent, it make a decent man sick. Zees and zat. Like she was born onna throne. Like cooking for her husband and family is beneath her. Cooking is a act of love. On toppa that she puts bad ideas in her husband's head. I know. Because otherwise, Angelo, he don't have no ideas."

"Kind of an easygoing guy," said Elvis diplomatically.

"A man with brains, like you, I'm a listen. Angelo, you don't listen, you tell. What he thinks with is his schlong and his stomach, that's all. Like all stupid people, you tell him something the right way, he thinks it's his idea, mister big shot. Ah," he said, waving the crabbed hand, "I am talking too much. The vice of an old man."

Having measured the ingredients of the marinade and dumped them into the bowl, Elvis used a soup spoon in a brisk fashion, rotating the bowl until he had whipped up a thick black sauce. Into it he plunged the slim strips of London broil, worked the meat so that every slice was moist with marinade. Then he washed his hands in the sink, dried them, and placed the stainless-steel bowl in the refrigerator.

"So you want to own a restaurant," the old man said.

"It's one of the things I dream about, yeah."

"Elvis is really your name?"

"From day one. My father sold him a car once. Never got over it."

"Elvis, lemme tell you something. This son a mine, Angelo, he ain't gonna pay. Truth. Now what I wanna know: is this mister blue jeans so stupid he would kill me? Because he does, there won't be a safe place for either you in this world. And you know who will hunt hardest? Sure you do. Do us both a favor: encourage him to see the wiseness of my offer. That, or kill him yourself."

Elvis brushed his hands on his jeans, not to dry them but as something to do while he weighed what the old man was saying. He took up a chair opposite the old man.

"Mr. Scorcese, I tell you something," he said. "The man's been there for me. I owe him. I owe him a lot. I couldn't kill him if you were Jesus Christ Himself saying to. Same token, I won't let him mess with you. You gonna have to trust me on that, but the way I see it, I'm trusting you for about the same thing. Has to do with having a future."

It was then that they heard the garage door activated,

rising, heard the murmur of the engine of the Oldsmobile, the door descending.

Elvis pushed back the chair to stand up, turned, and shortly saw Del Rebus emerging from the rec room in one of his flowery shirts, a tight, thin smile in his face and something in his eyes that Elvis recognized having seen once before. It was his first day in Lompoc, actually his first few minutes in the yard, after Del had saved his ass. Lester made his threat and Del just watched him, a finger brushing alongside his nose, *there*, a decision was made, no looking back. The next day the incorrigibly stupid Lester was a dead man, his face charred like a burnt bun. Now, however, Del was reaching into the refrigerator for a cold Corona, cracking it open with his teeth, spitting the bent cap on the countertop. Lifting the bottle, toasting them. His lips curled up at the corners. "Why Sparky," he said, "this old gentleman telling you ghost stories? You look like you pooped your shorts."

Elvis watched him tip the bottle to his lips, suck down about half the contents before he took it away, pinch the residue from the corners of his mouth. "Matter of fact," Elvis said then, "we were talking about how *not* to become ghosts. Two of us more or less agreed it wouldn't be a smart career move."

"Is that so?" Del finished the bottle and walked around the butcher-block island to reach into the refrigerator for another bottle of beer. He came over to the table and pulled out a chair to Joe Scorcese's right, turned it and straddled it. He nodded at them both, Elvis first, then the old man. "We rehashing last night's proposal, or's there something new on the table?"

The old man folded his bad hand over his good one and looked directly into Del's eyes. "Nothing new. But it's sure and it's there and it don't stay on the table much longer."

"Oh?" said Del. "You that tired of living?"

"Del—"

"It's okay," said the old man, waving at Elvis with the crabbed hand, but his eyes on Del. "Are you, mister blue jeans?"

"What?"

"That tired of living. Because as I explain to Elvis here, my son Angelo, who will not pay a penny to save my life, he will put a price on your head—you and Elvis—you will be dead men. I don't give you a week."

Del Rebus exhaled a faint whistle. "It's something to think about," he said.

Elvis could feel a smile breaking out not only on his face, but all through his body, an enormous rush of relief. At last, the man had seen the light, bowing to the sweet persuasion of caution. Hot damn!

Del saying now, "You may have something. The question is, how quick can you deliver?"

The sky was black with intervals of venomous green, when lightning wired the air with jagged, bone-colored strands of naked energy, the green sinking back to black. Del Rebus watched the raindrops explode on the surface of the pool, trying to orchestrate things in his mind. His original plan, to make the exchange in the parking lot of the zoo, looked as if it were being vetoed by the monsoon. The weather was

pushing him to improvise. Okay. He did not object to playing this on the edge. What the hell, it was no different from
Nam, or surviving in the yard, you went with your instincts
and kept a tight sphincter.

"All I gotta do is make two phone calls," Joe Scorcese
said. "Like I do every night I go to the races."

Elvis said, helping himself to a Corona and coming back
to the table, sitting, pulling on an earlobe, "What the fuck,
let him call from here. We're gone by tomorrow, Del."

Del Rebus stroked the side of his nose with a forefinger.
He glanced at his wristwatch. It was a little past one o'clock.
"You can have it here tonight, the mil in cash?"

Joe Scorcese permitted himself a wink. "You betcha."

The man might be small and shrunken, crippled a little
bit, but he was alive, didn't miss a trick. "You're quite the
little charmer, aren't you?" remarked Del. "Bet young Joe
never had to worry about sleeping alone."

"I done okay."

"Listen at him," said Elvis. "Okay, my ass. Del, he told
me some stories. The man has done things. Was balling—
listen to this—man was balling the same chick as President
Kennedy was."

"Oh?"

The little man shrugged. "Is no big deal. Practically any
girl back then you was fiddling had been fiddled by that one.
He love a fuck, Johnnie did. He was a machine."

"My daddy," said Del, "a die-hard Democrat, thought
he was the second coming of FDR."

The old man's face pinched up and he waved his
bad hand. "That one, I spit on his grave. It all started with
him. Government this, government that. Inna pockets—

yours, his, everyone. You, mister blue jeans, you say I'm a bad man?"

"Not to your face, I wouldn't."

"I hold you up every year, take a chunka your money? No, I don't, but government does. Every year it's more and more, because they spending more to take care a you. That's what they say. If a man robs you, do the police that you are paying for catch him? Maybe. There's some good coppers. So what? The judges that you are paying for will let him go, most a the time, and if they put him away, do you get back your money? Or say he rapes and murders your wife: you get to put him against a wall and shoot him? You get anything like justice? That's what you paying for. Me, you come to me, you get justice."

Del looked at Elvis and Elvis at Del, neither man doubting for an instant the sincerity of that last sentiment.

Elvis spoke first. "I hear that, Mr. S. Look what they do to honest folks, the IRS. Honest folks pay in all year, money taken from their paychecks called withholding? End of the year, if they paid in too much, and a lot do, they get a refund from the government, no interest on that money government got to play with for a year, uh-uh. But this is the cute part, Del: that money they could have had last year, spend how they want, no problem, that they were *enfuckingtitled* to, this year it's treated as taxable income."

"Huh," said Del, and turned toward Joe Scorcese. "Some ways it's hard to tell who the real criminals are."

"No, it isn't," said the old man. "The real ones, they tell you they taking care a you. Sign this, sign that. Me, you don't sign nothin'. All I give is my word."

"And a million dollars," said Elvis to Del, "tax free."

* * *

"Whadda you saying?" said the man in the phone booth in Forest Hills wearing the Mets cap backwards, the black T-shirt and double-pleated army green cotton trousers, the black ankle-high boots with steel toes.

"I'm saying I didn't hear from them at noon. That's all there is to it. You keep calling like this, I won't be in the office when they do call. So what I'm saying, wait to hear from me, okay?"

"Just fucking make it clear the money'll be there. Just do that."

"Ange, consider it done. Soon as they call."

"The whole ten million."

"I got ears."

"Fucking lowlifes. Makes you wonder what the world's coming to."

Del Rebus worked on the scenario, from time to time looking outside to curse the monsoon, as part and parcel of the bum luck this town dealt a man. Why, what derangement of the senses had led him here, to this place that was a sucking wound in his memory? He must have been nuts. No, not nuts, in love. Pumped, all the juices flowing, a world beater. Nuts.

What he worked out, while not without risk, satisfied him: it was swift and it was neat. Elaborate plans include more opportunities to muck up. Simple was best: quick in, quick out.

He explained it to the old man. The delivery guy, what

was his name? Okay, Vacanza. First of all, it was important that Del have a physical description and some idea of what the man would be wearing. This Vacanza is going to fly Northwest, which brings him into Terminal 3. They would phone LaGuardia in New York to make the reservation. Vacanza deplanes in Phoenix, he takes the escalator down to the carrousel area, to the Hertz desk. There will be an envelope there with his name on it. Inside it would be a phone number to call for further instructions. This much he told the old man. Then he warned him: anyone other than Vacanza shows, or if Vacanza isn't alone, or if Del spots anyone suspicious in the terminal, that's all she wrote. No deal.

The little man looked into his eyes and said, "I make the promise to Elvis, I keep it. You keep your end, I keep mine."

When they had cuffed the Don to his bedpost, Elvis and Del sat in the breakfast nook, speaking in hushed voices.

Del said: "I don't trust the little bastard, but that doesn't mean we can't do it."

Elvis said: "Thing worries me. Once Vacanza's got his instructions, the plane info, he calls Paul. The place could be crawling with their people."

"Probably will be."

"So after he picks up the number at the Hertz, how do we get him away from the terminal? Guy doesn't exactly know his way around Phoenix."

Del: "We hit him before he goes to the Hertz."

Elvis: "In the public fucking terminal you tell me most certainly will be Scorcese people around?"

Del: "I'm going to meet him as he comes up the ramp past the scanners. Just a few words, let him know where to go. He'll be scanned in New York, so no way he's carrying.

That's our edge. Now what I need to do is call for a taxi to take me to the airport, work out a few kinks, rent a car, find somebody on a tight budget. Few other chores. So if you could take care of the reservation for Vacanza, I'd appreciate it. Get that done, then let Joe make his phone calls, standing right there, of course."

Elvis: "No. I thought I sit out in the rec room, watch Phil or Oprah, one a them."

The rain had abated and the sky was softening, easing into a misty gray. The cab arrived for Del within twenty minutes.

Using an 800 number, Elvis nailed down a six forty-five flight out of La Guardia for Vacanza, which with the time variance gave the man almost three hours to put things together and be on the plane.

Then Elvis uncuffed the old man, helping him from bed with a hand behind his shoulder. "Show time," he said.

They stood in front of the wall phone in the kitchen, and the old man dialed the answering service, wrote down numbers on a pad Elvis proffered.

The first number dialed, the one for Vacanza's Market on Metropolitan, Magda picked up, said no problem, her father was in his office, please hang on, Padrino.

The old man said to Elvis, "We inna luck."

"Old friend?" he said into the phone, and commenced to speak in a language not English. It caught Elvis off guard, so it was several seconds before he snatched the phone away, covered the mouthpiece with his hand. "Joe? The fuck you think you doing?"

The old man turned his hands, palms up, and locked

gazes. "He is an old man, Elvis. His English is not so good. I use the language so he understand completely. Otherwise, he might be confused, make a mistake, and mister blue jeans panic, I could be a dead man."

"Just keep it in English. Take your time. We can afford it."

The Don completed the instructions in English with a few translations, after asking permission, and hung up, gave Elvis an accurate description of Vacanza.

"So," said the old man, "what you wanna chain me to now?"

"Up to you," said Elvis. "I guess anywhere but the mailbox or diving board."

"What is it you fixing tonight, beef with oyster sauce?"

"Yeah, well. A kind of improvisation on that."

"Hey. You ever do anything with kidneys and hearts?"

Chapter 27

There are two ramps in Terminal 3 on opposite sides of the escalators. The north ramp, servicing Gates 15 through 26, was the one up which Vacanza would arrive. As you faced the ramp, to the left there was a five-foot-square basin filled with bromeliads and a slender tree with ash gray bark and waxy leaves. Del Rebus sat on a side of the basin, smoking a Gauloise. At the entrance of the ramp stood the equipment and uniformed personnel to scan all carry-on luggage, purses included, while the would-be traveler was compelled to step through a metal detector before retrieving his or her baggage. As the parade of passengers traipsed past, Del was reminded of Franny's remark in Sport Time regarding the infestation of bola ties. A guy in a khaki shirt and pants with a circular insignia on his left short sleeve pushed a cart around loaded with cleaning ingredients and implements, a bright orange vacuum mounted on the front. When he stopped to empty the ashtrays in the grouping of seats next to the basin of bromeliads, Del read the name Steve stitched in crimson thread on the top of his breast pocket.

From where he rested his butt, Del had walked off the distance three times to the men's room, approximately eighty steps, less than a minute of easy walking across the dull brown carpet with the pseudo-Aztec pattern worked into it. Inside the men's room, directly to the back, two shower rooms commanded fifty cents in coin for the luxury of showering behind a locked door. Del put his quarters in and liked what he saw.

These weren't five-star accommodations, but suitable for what he had in mind. Maybe five feet deep, floor and walls covered in yellow tile, around the sink too, the toilet perched opposite the shower stall to the right. In the room he was in, the stall door stuck, had left a black mark on the tiled sill. As long as he had paid his fifty cents, he took a leak in there.

He walked the area some more, counting his steps from spot to spot, working on his timing, until he thought he had the floor plan memorized. Returning to the basin off the ramp with the bromeliads and tree, he studied the seating, the angles from the restaurants and bars, the shops and ice cream parlor, all the avenues of vulnerability. There were many. If the deception worked as far as the men's room, he was certain he was home free. But for a number of slowly ticking seconds he would have to be damn good.

He loved it; for a mad moment he did. Then the dread filtered in. He gazed at the fluted pillars that ascended to the ceiling, the surface of them pitted, suggesting ludicrously a notion of antiquity. Also in his field of vision was a gravity-defying sculpture that reigned twenty feet high opposite the ramp, composed of severed parts painted chromium and red. As the chromium base rose, it narrowed, and at its apex, the red segments hovered like broken chunks of the Russian sickle. Humongous canvases attached to the bulkheads depicting so-called Southwestern art (emphasis on pastels) only added to the conflict of styles. It was a mirror of the city itself: a confusion of identity. Maybe the whole place was a mirage. And his father's defeat and his shame . . . only bad dreams? Pretty to think so.

He glimpsed the gentleman in khaki shuffling past a gift shop named By George, and stood up, put on a show of unlimbering. Del made his way along an aisle parallel to the one taken by Steve the janitor. It was brightly lit and flanked by retail shops. Both aisles led to a bank of glass doors accessing onto the parking garage. Del circled the art gallery that faced the doors, glanced into an empty arcade, and accosted Steve about midway up the aisle, caught him in the act of emptying an ashtray.

"There you are," he said, sounding perfectly tickled at having found him.

Steve was about Del's size, an inch shorter and flabby, but close enough. His hair was medium brown and he wore glasses with round brown plastic rims. The expression on his face mixed surprise with an eagerness to please. "Yes?" he said.

"Steve, isn't it?"

"Yes, it sure is."

Del seized his hand and shook it, slapped his shoulder with the other hand. "Stu told me to look you up."

"Stu?"

"New special assistant to the head of Human Resources. People that determine promotions."

"Oh."

"Steve, here's the thing. An old buddy coming to town for a reunion, he's arriving this evening around eight forty-five. Now we'd like to play a little practical joke on the guy and Stu says you're the guy can help us. I'll take care of the uniform, but I need your cart for one hour starting eight-thirty. During that time you can enjoy a smoke in the garage or play some Double Dragon in the arcade there or go down, I don't know, flirt with one of the hostesses at the rental-car desks, whatever's your pleasure. And for your trouble, my friends and I will pay you five hundred dollars, cash. How's that grab you?"

The young man's eyes threatened to dislodge his glasses. "Fucking A!" he said.

They exchanged high fives.

"Steve, you ever hear the one, how a Mexican knows he's hungry?"

Del Rebus rode the escalator down to the ground floor, where the baggage carrousels were located, and approached the Hertz service desk. A bright young lady in a severe costume greeted him with a smile, her dark hair pulled back to bare her ears, her long nails a shade of white that suggested she'd dipped them in liquid paper. She said her name was Karen and how could she help him. A smile shaped his lips, hovered there, to let her know the question deserved—indeed, had provoked—additional thinking. He wound up renting a four-door Chevrolet, black, with full power and tinted windows. He and Karen joked about the funereal color. He paid for it on his credit card, told Karen a salacious anecdote while they waited for approval on the card, collected the Chevrolet, drove it and parked it on level two, close to the plate-glass doors beyond the art gallery.

He took the escalator a second time. Went to Avis, goofed with an attractive attendant there in the process of renting a nimble Chrysler LeBaron, all white, then sped east to a costume shop in Tempe. Stopped at a Smith's for hair dye and continued north through the rain to the house on Doubletree.

Crossed the sautillo tile, saw the wok on the burner, Elvis chopping vegetables, the old man tucked back in the breakfast nook, the cozy little king of the kitchen, prince of plates, duke of fork.

Cradling his plastic sack, Del pinched rainwater from his forehead and greeted the old man with a smile. "Few more hours, Joe, you'll be a free man. How's that sound?"

The little man with the dark, raisinlike skin and dead eyes didn't seem to give a shit one way or another. He said, "I love a kitchen. The smells. It is the heart of a house."

"We tradin' recipes," said Elvis, chopping away.

"Shit," said Del, depositing his package on a chair in the nook. "Assoud and his daughter."

"What about 'em?"

"They need a ride home."

Elvis laid down the thick stainless-steel knife and rinsed his hands in the sink and dried them. "Del? Let him lay out for a taxi. Amount you gave him he can afford it. Tomorrow you show up in the van, same old same old, tell him what you want."

Del bowed to this logic reluctantly. "It's just, he's some little guy trying to get by."

"Ain't we all?" said Elvis.

Luigi Vacanza watched the two carry-on bags trundle past the black flaps into the darkness for the scanner to examine the contents, make sure he wasn't smuggling guns or explosives. He walked through the metal detector at LaGuardia Airport in Queens, New York, without raising any alarm, found the pair of carryons at the end of the conveyer belt, slung the bags over his shoulders and strode without haste along the ramp. There was a bar before he reached his gate, the point of embarkation. It was loud in there, revelers loosening up for their flights, and the light was comfortably dusky. Vacanza found a stool on the far side of the horseshoe-shaped bar, one with no one sitting beside him. He settled the bags on the floor between his legs and studied his watch. He had forty-five minutes to kill.

He was wearing a double-breasted brown suit that pinched him under the shoulders and in the crotch, something of a surprise, since he moved around in it easily last Christmas, when he had purchased it. But it was the finest suit he owned (also the only one without stains or cigar burns), and it was important to look presentable to the Don. His brown wing tips shimmered with polish and his tie, which he dared not adjust, gripped his throat in a savage, but perfect knot, thanks to Magda. It was for her, he told himself, that he was enduring this agony and humiliation.

Finished flirting with two stewardesses, the bartender aimed a forefinger, thumb cocked, and gunned them down by way of farewell, then ambled up the bar grinning smugly at his cleverness. He wore a white shirt and what appeared to be a length of black ribbon tied to his throat like shoelaces and a plaid vest in which red was the predominant color. He reminded Vacanza somewhat of his nephew Bennie Focoso, the hotblood, the way he carried himself, the cocky stride. He put both hands on his side of the bar and leaned on them, and said, "Whacha pleasure, pal?"

"Gimme a double vodka martini, dry. Olive, none a that faggy lemon-peel garbage. You handle that?"

The bartender's eyes went narrow. "I can handle it," he said.

When he brought the cocktail, and had placed it on a napkin, he leaned forward, much farther than before. "Mr. Vacanza?"

Vacanza tasted the martini and admitted yes, that's who he was.

The bartender said, "Someone left a little something for you. I guess a kinda going-away gift."

* * *

Elvis held the pale brown bordering on blond ponytail tinged with gray between his index and middle fingers and intruded the scissors, squeezed, and said, "Gone." He lifted the shock of severed hair for Del to see in the bathroom mirror, then dropped it into the wastebasket. Bending forward, Del filled his cupped hands with water from the tap and drenched his head, then sat down with his bare feet in the tub. Elvis combed out the wet hair and clipped him neat, then toweled his hair dry. With a towel wrapped around his neck, Del applied the dye, Elvis assisting on his nape, both men adamant in their admiration at how women managed this by themselves. Twenty minutes later Del climbed into the shower and emerged with a head of short chestnut hair. In another ten minutes he was dressed in a khaki uniform with a round badge on his left sleeve, glasses with round brown frames and plastic lenses, cloddish black shoes on his feet. Beneath his nose he glued a bushy mustache that closely matched the color of his hair.

Elvis phoned Northwest to confirm the arrival time of Flight 107 out of LaGuardia. It was right on schedule.

Wearing dark glasses with electrical tape attached inside the lenses, Joe Scorcese sat serenely in the Chrysler with his hands shackled, the chain between the cuffs running behind his bucket seat, so that his wrists were secured a little behind and below his hips. Elvis drove and Del sat alone in the backseat reviewing his game plan. Once Del was dropped off, Elvis would circulate among the terminals until the guy in the brown double-breasted suit appeared on the south side of the terminal, on the sidewalk next to the Northwest counter; at that point Elvis would pull up to the curb, uncuff the old bird and push him out, circle half the terminal to enter covered parking. Del, as soon as he saw the white Chrysler, would back out so that Elvis could park, and the two would depart in a black car, nothing like the one Joe Scorcese or this Vacanza might remember.

It was going to fly. It *had* to. There was a maroon-and-gold tote bag on the seat next to Del and in it was one of the .45s Elvis had confiscated from the moron bikers that had confronted him in the desert. And lodged beneath Elvis's seat was the .357. If the scheme fell apart, didn't fly, at least each of them had a parachute, sort of. Del's throat felt as dry as his palms felt moist.

It was eight-twenty when they drew up to Terminal 3 and Elvis braked back in the taxi zone, away from the hubbub. Del squeezed his shoulder getting out of the car, then leaned in through his window. "Sparky?"

Elvis glanced in his rearview mirror, then stared straight ahead. "You take care in there," he said.

"Something I wanted to say, about Frances."

"Shit, Del."

"I'm not blind. Two buds in love with the same lady, it's okay. It happens. Something goes wrong, well . . ."

"You gotta bad feeling about this?"

"No. Just nerves."

"You scared?"

"Shitless, if you want to know the truth. But it goes with the territory. Adios, Elvis."

Elvis watched him pass in front of the hood hauling the maroon-and-gold tote bag and melt into the melee. Elvis, he thought, not Sparky. Not adios, Sparky.

* * *

The cart was a pain in the butt to push, because the front wheels had a tendency to lock, causing the cart to crab constantly to the left. But as the minutes progressed, Del's confidence increased. For one thing, his uniform and the duties he performed granted him a measure of camouflage, a sense of blending into the brown carpet. Another thing: no sign of anyone taking a keen interest in the north ramp. The screen displaying arrival and departure times continued to list eight forty-five as the arrival hour for Northwest Flight 107, in which case the plane was touching down right at this moment. Perfect. Del was working his way around the south ramp area and would be in position to have an unobstructed view down the north ramp in about ten minutes, time for the plane to taxi to the gate and begin offloading its passengers. The moment he spotted Vacanza, he'd remove the thirty-gallon trash bag he was filling with cigarette debris and replace it with another, the one that had his tote bag inside it, the .45 inside it, and unzip the tote bag.

Then, for the space of a minute he'd be walking behind the man, his heart in a complete free fall.

Vacanza, riding in first class, had slept for most of the flight, and when he awoke, an hour out of Phoenix, he requested a vodka martini and told the stewardess to keep them coming. He drank four of them and felt right with the world by the time the pilot announced their descent into Phoenix. Gathering his two carryons—they were black-and-white-checked with wide black straps—he was among the first passengers to deplane. He found a men's room and a clean stall and locked himself in there. From one of the bags he removed the rectangular package, the "gift" he had received from the bartender in LaGuardia, which he had asked his nephew Bennie Focoso to arrange. It was what the cowboys in the organization would call a pussy gun, but it did the job. It was a .22-caliber revolver with a two-inch barrel, fit inside a large hollowed-out paperback. Ideal for close-up work and the concussion sounded like an innocuous snap, no more resonance than a firecracker. Vacanza liked it. He tore up the wrapping and flushed it down the toilet. He dropped the disemboweled paperback down a chute beneath the paper towel dispenser and stepped up to the mirror, dragging the bags, to inspect the knot of his tie. His Magda would approve.

Vacanza hauled the bags along the ramp, in no particular hurry, since nothing was going to happen until he picked up the phone number from Hertz. Then it would become time to act. He understood that from the first words the Padrino had uttered on the phone, before switching to English: *Bring a friend to use onna cocksucker!*

He trudged up the ramp, his cramped clothing dragging on him like a harness. He saw pillars and something red and silver that instinctively reminded him of artsy-fartsy Manhattan, what Angelo's wife Mai Lee would ooh and aah over. A goddamn joke.

The guy with the fluffy pink duster turned away from the basin with the tall tree in it and said, "Mr. Vacanza? Try the men's room over to the left. Your left."

Surprised him. Guy had nice moves, big balls.

Vacanza spotted the sign for the men's on an angle to his left, past a gift shop. He started that way as the guy worked his way around the ashtrays, then didn't see him until he had been in the men's for a good minute. The guy in khaki entered with a brown plastic sack draped over his shoulder and nodded toward the back. Vacanza watched him insert two quarters into a slot, engage the mechanism and open the door. He flexed his wrist, indicating Vacanza should enter, and he did.

The two men stood face-to-face, of equal height if not weight. The guy said, "Let's do it. Show me the money."

Vacanza set one bag on the sink, the other on the toilet seat. The guy settled the brown plastic bag next to the door to the shower stall and stuck his hand into the bag, brought out the big Colt.

"You fire that," observed Vacanza, "won't be a cop in this city won't hear it. Put it away. I bring money, not guns."

"I hope so," the guy said. "But humor me, will you?" His hand moved over Vacanza's torso. "Okay," he said, and stepped back.

Vacanza manipulated the straps on the bag that rested on the sink, lifted the flap to expose the tight bundles of hundred-dollar bills, then turned to the bag on the toilet seat.

Vacanza said, "Where I find the man?"

"Joe?" He laid the Colt on the edge of the sink to look inside the bag.

"Yeah. You see I bring the money."

The guy with his hand in the bag lifting and looking at the packets of one-hundred-dollar bills glanced sideways. "I see money," he said, "but I don't know I'm in a position to say it's a mil. If you'd give me a moment here, handsome."

"Where's a man?" Vacanza said.

Satisfied that there was something close to a half million in there, Del dragged the black plastic sack over and scooped the contents of the checked bag into it. Vacanza reached for the black-and-white-checked bag on the toilet, lifting it, and said, "Here's the rest. But you tell me where I find the man first."

"Relax." He was holding the plastic sack and looking into it, shaking it a little to redistribute the weight. "You go down, wait next to the Northwest desk outdoors, the south side. A white Chrysler will pull up. Joe's inside. A well-fed Joe, by the way."

Vacanza dug a hand into the bag of banded hundreds.

Del Rebus saw the gun, not soon enough, and now it would never be soon enough, the barrel less than a foot from his face. Welcome home, he thought, experiencing rage at his own helplessness, his foolish confidence, even as he felt the grin creep into his face like an old and comfortable habit.

"What?" said Vacanza, his tiny eyes growing tinier. "You think is something funny?"

"I dunno. You ever hear the one—"

His hands came up fast with the strength of his desperation going for the gun, and then the room echoed with sound and Del was sitting on the floor in the corner of the small, tight room coughing blood, his legs straight out in front of him for some reason jerking uncontrollably. There was a shadow over him, Vacanza leaning down to take the plastic sack with a half-million dollars, then the shadow went away, but the light was filmy, shivery, objects blurred and wobbled. The Colt on the edge of the sink trembled, bright as mercury, shiny as the dream he chased—the elusive, silvery, doomed dream. He couldn't speak from the coughing and bubbling in his mouth and wondered if he'd pissed himself, or would that come later. One more indignity. He tried to move his hand to find out, but couldn't. The light was softening, settling, almost the color of early morning such as the one when he had stood on the patio pointing a gun at the North Star, as if it were possible to strike back for the loss of Franny Lott. Payback, walking out a winner—what jokes. That belief he shared with his father that intelligence and endeavor would carry the day, another joke, both of them ultimately naive about the true forces involved. Sparky! Shit, not him too. He couldn't bear to drag down Elvis. . . . A tomato red Caddy convertible, imagine that, all leather right off the showroom floor and his father at the wheel with a Gauloise, just the one with the martini, the epitome. . . . He couldn't move his hand to his crotch and that annoyed him, but he was relieved—no, elated—that Franny Lott was gone, free from the mess he had made of things. At least he hadn't fucked up in front of

Chapter 28

It was nine-fifteen, according to the disc jockey on the radio, when Joe Scorcese, riding blind behind the taped dark glasses, asked peevishly after his baseball cap, the maroon one he'd been wearing the night they snatched him.

Elvis ignored him, staring through the rain-stung windshield, the wipers swatting a melancholy cadence. The rain, far from mitigating the desert heat, if anything intensified it, gave it body, palpability. Even with the air conditioner operating at its peak, the air inside the car crawled over the skin with an oozing quality, as if the desert were some vast infection lanced by the piercing rain. From time to time, Elvis took a hand from the wheel and scraped the palm in the material of his shorts. Approaching Terminal 3 once again, he maneuvered to the right through the horde of automobiles, in order to cruise past the terminal looking for a large man in a double-breasted brown suit. Easing into the three lanes of terminal traffic, slowing down, Elvis said, "Sorry, Mr. Scorcese. You were saying?"

"Your friend in a blue jeans."

"What about him?"

"It is his fault I loss my hat."

"I'll buy you a new one, mail it to Sport Time. We'll buy you two of them."

"I never like that one. He is not a reasonable man, shoot Chub like that, threaten me. That was foolish. He tells too many jokes, like he think life is not serious."

Crawling along, concentrating, Elvis half listened to the old man's words, responding perfunctorily, "Oh, I think he takes it serious enough." While Elvis scanned the sidewalk, he watched obsessively for the police wearing their pale blue fishnet vests crisscrossed in neon yellow, the word *operations* struck in black fore and aft in a band of yellow. And then he spotted the man in the brown double-breasted suit next to the Northwest counter, no question about it, the man with two bags slung from his shoulders, and Elvis tugged the steering wheel to the right, braked ten feet beyond the reception counter. He fitted the key to the cuffs, the left first, then the right, and removed the taped glasses from the old man's face. He leaned across his lap to fling open the door, and there was the big guy in the brown suit, the rain blotching it fast, and there was the barrel of a gun aimed right at his forehead.

"It's you lucky day," said Joe Scorcese, "now you working for me. Unless you got something better you think you gonna be doing."

They caught a red-eye flight—Joe, Vacanza, and Elvis—on America West that would bring them into LaGuardia a little before eight in the morning. In the seat next to Elvis, Joe slept most of the way with his mouth open, emitting rattles and gurgles periodically, but never waking. Evidently, nothing—not leg irons, not murder—interfered with the man's sleep. Joe told him, of course, matter-of-factly, like someone detailing the ingredients of a recipe. "It is no loss," he had concluded, tapping him on the leg before exiting the Chrysler. "Believe me, you better off. I am a good judge of usefulness."

Joe had told him also he would not see one penny of the million dollars, but something else might be arranged if his work was satisfactory.

Elvis Mahoney slept very little. The light in first class was kept discreetly dimmed, and the two stewardesses, moving up and down the aisle, performed their duties with surreptitious grace, as if ministering to an exclusive ward of patients, who just happened to be hurtling thirty-five thousand feet through heaven. Elvis grieved silently for a friend, not even curious or apprehensive about what Joe Scorcese meant by work.

Remembering Del, who had been a teacher to him, and when you got down to it, a savior of sorts too.

* * *

Bennie Focoso was his driver for the second day in a row, and what a pleasure that was, not riding around with a schlub that listened to dinosaur music featuring trombones and saxophones and the deep-chested thumping of bass viols. Angelo Scorcese felt more comfortable with straight-ahead rock 'n' roll, say anything by the Stones, the Kinks, Creedence, definitely Hendrix (but when did you hear him anymore?), Neil Young and Crazy Horse, some of the stuff Elvis Costello was doing, and even the so-called country-western licks from the likes of Randy Travis and that guy with the big hat, Garth something. Willie Nelson was an ace. Just give him a beat or a hook to hang on to, and Angelo was sold.

He had spoken to the Wiz a little after four o'clock and was reassured to learn all of the money had arrived in Phoenix, was in Paul's hands even as they spoke. He instructed Bennie Focoso to drive him to his residence in Howard Beach, for a family meal, because he had been spending too much time away from home, tending to the various and sizable egos within the Don's empire, and this (the time away) was a certain prescription for regret. Family mattered more than anything. He actually said this. Then he said, "Brooks!"

At the wheel Bennie Focoso turned his head ever so slightly, a gesture schematically similar to adjusting the tuner on a radio when static intrudes. He had a long narrow face, almost gaunt, from which projected a nose shaped like a dinghy's rudder, creating the impression that it steered his face, and where it generally steered him was into other people's faces, other people's business. But to Angelo Scorcese's non sequitur, his only response was, "Huh?"

"Garth Brooks," said Angelo Scorcese, "the singer."

"I don't know any fuckin' Garth Brooks the singer. An' fuck's that got to do with anything anyway?"

Angelo Scorcese looked at the skinny kid who always arrived five minutes behind his nose and explained patiently, "I been trying to remember the guy's name is all. He's this young hotshot, country-western singer I heard a few songs by. Over to the Wiz's I think it was. He's big into that."

"Country?"

"Loretta Lynn, the Judds, Porter Wagoner, Dolly Parton. Chrise, her tits get much bigger, you won't be able to see that pretty little face. Keith Whitley, that drank himself into the grave. Those people."

"Buncha rednecks."

"Well," said Angelo Scorcese, tipping his head to one side, as if weighing Bennie Focoso's opinion, "they can sing a song, though."

"Least they keep the jigs in their place. Say that for 'em."

"Don't tell Charlie Pride that."

Bennie Focoso rolled down the window to yell at a driver in a lane to his left, concluding his remarks by jamming a middle finger at the hot, humid heavens. "No offense, Angelo, okay?" he said, pumping the knob to drive the window back up. "But you talk shit like that, you give people the impression you gettin' soft. Next thing we know, you'll be kissing that snake Sharpton on the cheek, sending checks to the N double-ACP."

"Bennie, I tell you," Angelo Scorcese said, lifting his ball cap to push a hand through his thick hair, staring through the windshield at the traffic on Woodhaven Boulevard, "people could have the wrong impression. I hope you ain't one of 'em."

"Not me. But I just thought I let you know."

"That's a habit of yours," said Angelo Scorcese, "you might want to curb. Hey, turn on a radio. Let's hear some boogie-down music, long as we're going to be crawling in this shit for a while. Cato, every time I get inna van, I gotta change the station. He listens to music made by guys in bow ties."

After some fiddling around, a station was found that met Angelo Scorcese's approval. They moved along Woodhaven at something resembling a border-checkpoint pace. In the heat the van's air-conditioning suffered from Bennie Focoso's habit of rolling down the window to express his opinions of other citizens' driving, and as a consequence both men sweated in their seats right along with the Jamaicans, Haitians, and Orientals in their vintage seventies Chevrolets, Buicks, and Ford Victorias, great vehicular boats with every window rolled down and at least a half-dozen occupants, and all of them coursing along the boulevard according to their own secret genetic rules of the road. The impulse to curse these aliens right along with his driver arose in Angelo's breast, but it was washed away in the relief of knowing that with the ten million dollars he had covered his ass. He had done the right thing, everybody would see that. In all his blathering about the importance of family, Angelo Scorcese was rehearsing what he intended to tell Mai Lee, a convoluted exercise in gratitude. And thinking of this in the heat and frustration of the pokey traffic, Angelo Scorcese developed a physical ache for his wife.

So that when the van finally rolled up the drive of the house in Howard Beach, Angelo emerged from it with ideas, especially focused upon Mai Lee fresh from the shore, her skin still harboring the sun's heat, the perfume of lotions about her. Jesus, there would never be anyone like that dink bitch.

He opened the black Spanish-style screen door and the steel one behind it with the peephole, and immediately turned to the panel on the wall to the left, punched in a series of numbers to prevent the alarm from ringing. The house was cool and the light was soothing, as if the hall were lit by a perpetual dawn, and the smells from the kitchen, such smells. Upstairs he could hear the nanny, Gretta, singing to his youngest, whose skin was too sensitive for the long days Mai Lee liked to spend shifting between the sand and water, as if in a restless quest, not for escape, but relief, some temporary satiation. Ah, Gretta. Now there was some active cooze. He moved up the hall, drawn by the aromas emanating from the kitchen, comparing himself favorably to those dudes in the Bible who traded in shekels and myrrh and kept a few ladies on the side, right there in the same tent. Think about it, was the only way to go. Strode into the kitchen, but instead of Therese, there was a goddamn jigaboo stirring sauce in a pan, turning from the oven to address the onions and cloves of garlic, lifting a cleaver from the counter.

"Yo bro'," said Angelo Scorcese, "shouldn't you be outside stealing hubcaps?"

Elvis Mahoney stared across the kitchen at the creature with the baseball cap on backward, a single eyebrow, shadowy jaw, the general air of violence only barely restrained, and said, "Angelo, isn't it? I believe they're expecting you in the dining room, dinner for two."

Luigi Vacanza, from the inside, parted the doors and stepped into the hall behind Angelo Scorcese to say, "Welcome home, Angelo. Your father wishes to spend a small amount of time with you, have a meal together. In here."

There was a motel on Grand Avenue that did a brisk business in afternoon liasons, primarily lovers looking over their shoulders, although sometimes a husband and wife would enter hoping to add a new dimension to their marriage, and once in a while kids too, suffering from hot pants and no convenient place to get out of them. The motel made no bones about its appeal, advertising in the sports sections of the major dailies, stressing its water beds, mirrored ceilings, VCRs in every room, and a large rental library, the nature of the movies available left to the imagination, of which little was needed.

It was a little before the dinner hour when the anonymous caller phoned 911 and blurted the name of the motel, the room number, and the single word, *"Morte,"* which the dispatcher, of Polish-Estonian extraction, presumed to be the name of a man.

Lieutenant D. James Cox, monitoring reports on his scanner, knew better, and even though technically they were off duty, he ordered Fitzsimmons to stand on the pedal and rolled down the window to attach the gumball to the roof of their sedan.

In the lobby bending over the check-in desk was a young patrolman, his chin in the palm of his left hand, his hat lying on the desk beside his elbow. He had a pad out and was writing in it when the clerk—a slight, balding, very agitated individual, whose wrists trembled inside his once white shirtsleeves—broke off his querulous litany to say, "Gentlemen, may I help you?"

Lieutenant Cox raised his right hand, the detective's shield flopping down, and introduced himself and his partner. The patrolman, a lanky, bright-eyed boy by the name of George Spanopolis, identified the clerk: "This here's Jimmy Swell, Lieutenant. He's got this song he likes to sing over and over. Go ahead, Jimmy."

Jimmy Swell, every atom of him quivering and vibrating, tried to compose himself by fitting a cigarette between his lips and lighting it. While he worked at it, Lieutenant D. James Cox fed himself a wafer of dried plum and glanced around the lobby. The ownership had not exactly squandered a fortune. The area comprised no more than two hundred square feet, floored in a pattern of red and white rubber tiles of a quality and shade that strongly suggested they were purchased at a factory closeout. The plaster walls were painted a shade of white even mustier than the tiling, although by happy coincidence they matched quite nicely with Jimmy Swell's shirt cuffs. The reception desk was just a chunk of something covered in white Formica that hadn't received much attention recently, bleary with ink smudges and fingerprints, coffee-cup stains and cigarette burns. In a small alcove behind and to the right of Jimmy Swell, there were displayed boxes with brightly colored covers of semiclad ladies, their poses and dress suggestive of another world, the demimonde, a place away from society, like a vacation, where the libido could be itself. There were no chairs, pictures, plants, or even ashtrays in the lobby—not a single amenity, in short. It had the crabbed air of an institution. Lieutenant Cox pulled on his bottom lip as it rode over his upper and snapped it. It was in a sense a tribute to passion that it could survive passing through portals such as this. He adjusted the pale gray homburg on his head and tried to forget about anticipation, desire, excitement.

He slipped another disc of dried plum into his mouth and said to the patrolman, "Spanopolis. You one of the Greek's kids, that's got the diner down on Queens Boulevard, in Elmhurst."

"Yes, sir."

"Son of a gun. So what's up, you getta look at the room?"

"My partner's standing outside of it, name of Cruz. Jimmy here," and Spanopolis turned around to look at the clerk, who was not so much standing there as shimmering, like an object on the verge of vanishing, "go ahead, Jimmy, sing the Lieutenant here your song, how there's nobody in the room."

Jimmy Swell removed the cigarette from his mouth with his left hand, passed it to his right hand, and had another tug on it before his right hand took it away. "Well," he said, his fluty voice full of exasperation, "as I've been trying to explain to this *person*, there is no one registered to that room number. I have all the keys right here. As far as I'm concerned, this is just a form of harassment, police hanging around to upset our clientele. I must inform you, Lieutenant, I have contacted our attorneys. So until you can show me a subpoena."

Lieutenant Cox put his hand up, showing the clerk the pink-and-white map of his palm, and said, "Spano my friend,

Wall, if you would give Mr. Swell and myself a few moments of privacy, I would appreciate it."

When his partner and the patrolman were gone, Lieutenant Cox spent a few moments arranging his hat and then, standing at a respectful distance from the reservation counter, lifted a panel of his pale gray suit away from his shoulder, so that the black-checked grip of his new nine-millimeter semiautomatic was visible. "Jimmy," he said, "it seems to me you can open the door for the law, be a conscientious citizen, maybe pick up some friendly publicity, or I blow away the lock, accidentally, and your employers can bring litigation against the city of New York. I don't give a fuck what your attorneys tell you, going to court is what they get paid for. I don't think it's what you're being paid for, is it? Think about it."

The door to room 1021 faced south onto the parking lot, and as a consequence its valentine-heart hue had been reduced to something closer to the color of a young girl's lipstick on a faded envelope. Ivy climbed the red brick around the door, dusky green in the late afternoon and somehow reassuring too, as if beyond the threshold life went on, more or less, as usual. Instructing Spanopolis and Cruz to remain outside, let no one through, Lieutenant Cox fitted the key to the lock in the doorknob, and he and Fitzsimmons entered.

Light filtered through the venetian blinds, but given the hour, its stretch into the room extended to a few slashes of illumination in the carpet, falling short of the bed. Still, it was sufficient, once their eyes had adjusted, to show them the clothed shapes on the bed, a man and a woman side by side on their backs, eyes open. It was clear even in the dim light, even in death, that the woman was possessed of remarkable beauty.

Breathing through their mouths, detectives Cox and Fitzsimmons pulled on tight, translucent rubber gloves. Cox stepped over to the light switch, flipped it on, and poked his head out the door. Spanopolis, resting his fanny on the fender of a sapphire Jaguar, snapped to attention. "Officer, you want to contact the coroner's office? They'll need to bring two body bags. Call homicide, have them assign someone pronto. Where's Cruz?"

"Taking a leak."

"Christ. Soon as he comes back, okay?"

"You got it."

Cox closed the door, muttering to himself, and approached the bed, where Fitzsimmons gingerly lifted the woman's hand and let it drop. She was dressed for the beach in a long robe with pastel stripes in it, a bathing suit beneath it, leather sandals.

"Pretty warm bodies," said Fitzsimmons, "both of 'em. Very little lividity."

The man wore a suit and black Italian shoes and there was no question how he had died, one pop in the left temple. Cause of the woman's death was a little less certain, since most of the front of her robe was soaked in blood.

"If we find a weapon," said Fitzsimmons, "it looks like murder-suicide. Otherwise, looks like somebody's pissed-off husband or wife surprised 'em."

"Not here they didn't," said Cox, bending over, resting one knee on the carpet beside the bed. He pinched a lapel of the woman's robe to open it and said, "Lookit the guy. There's hardly any blood on the bed."

Fitzsimmons stood at the foot of the bed making notes in a spiral pad, itching for a cigarette. Goddamn Cox, dragging them into this; by the time they waited for the coroner, he could kiss his night good-bye. So much for the new Clint Eastwood.

Cox said, "Oh my God," in a tone of voice that struck at Fitzsimmons's innards.

He looked. He looked beneath the lifted robe. He saw it wasn't anything like the movies. "Fucking animals!" he blurted, stumbling for the door, for the feel of the hot, gritty air in his face.

Both patrolmen backed away when they saw the young detective stagger out, Stanopolis going so far as to rest his hand on the grip of his service revolver.

"Pop!" said Angelo, his arms spread as he entered the formal dining room, "You look great, terrific. Just terrific. Don't he look terrific, Lou?"

The Don sat in a chair on the far side of the table facing the entry. His hair was smoothly combed and parted down the middle, so that two swaths of it hung magisterially above his temples. He was wearing a clean dark suit and white shirt, starched and pressed as only his wife could do it. His eyes lifted at the approach of his oldest son, but there was a solemn light in them, a fixed and even savage expression of sorrow outlasted, left behind. There was a dark, scraped quality about his features, like something carved for a voodoo ceremony, a thing of pure menace. He raised his hand of ruined fingers and made a faint, palsied gesture. "Siddown, my son. There, where you see the plate, the glass of wine.

Luigi, tell the colored boy we ready to eat, whenever he's ready."

The fruit vendor, still wearing the brown suit that pinched unmercifully, nodded and slipped silently from the room, closing the doors behind him.

"Pop."

"In a minute. Gimme a minute."

The Don's eyes roamed the walls, taking in the sunlit colors of the Caribbean, the stark and sometimes nightmarish figures depicted on linoleum board and canvas. Then his gaze came back to Angelo and he shook his head. He leaned forward and with his left hand lifted his glass of wine. "Have some wine with me, my son. It will make our conversation easier."

"Sure. Happy to." Angelo rose from his chair to lean over the table, to touch his father's glass with his.

"Grazie," said the Don. "Salute."

"To your health, Pop. Jesus. I can't believe it. Couple hours ago I hear the money's out there, in Phoenix, and here you are. I mean, how . . . ?"

The Don shrugged. "Things happen fast. And now I am here in the home of my son."

"But—"

"You have not tasted the wine. It is excellent. Look at the vintage. The year of your birth, 1950."

Angelo did not sip, but gulped a full half of his glass.

The doors to the hall parted and Luigi Vacanza led Elvis Mahoney into the dining room, Elvis wheeling a cart with a platter of kidneys and hearts simmering in a red sauce, a crystal bowl of pasta on the side, a loaf of warmed bread too.

"We don't have time for courses," the Don explained, "so I thought, how 'bout your favorite. Is okay?"

"Of course. What's not to be okay?"

The Don's eyes moved. "Elvis, this my son. He has an appetite I think you the man can satisfy. Serve him first, please. An old man needs hope more than food."

Vacanza sat in a chair at the end of the table, the one normally reserved for Mai Lee, although he backed it away, making it clear he was not partaking in the meal. He worked patiently with a file, digging at a dark substance under his fingernails.

Elvis apportioned the servings, parked the cart with the platter behind and to the left of the Don, and bowed from the waist, nothing ostentatious, said, "Coffee when you ready, Mr. S."

He closed the doors behind him.

"Elvis?" said Angelo Scorcese.

"Yes," said his father.

"Jesus. Ain't nothing sacred?"

"Eat, my son. While it's hot."

"Yeah. Hey, this ain't bad. Therese could take a lesson."

"The colored boy has a feel for it. I like him. He's gotta brain. He has a dream, own his own restaurant. Maybe we do something for him. Do you think you could pass the bread?"

"Pop, you want to help a fuckin' nigger—"

"This a table. Watch you language."

"All I'm saying, we ain't the N double-ACP, least the last I looked. Chrise, you start putting jigs on the payroll, guys like Bennie Focoso start getting funny ideas. Bad enough having the family name behind one jigaboo."

The Don raised his index finger, finished chewing, and with his eyes on Angelo, said, "Luigi. More wine here, please." And waited for the large fruit vendor to fill the two glasses and resume his seat at the foot of the table. Then said, "Listen to me: Mr. Lord run his business good. Never no trouble. Always show the respect. Bennie Focoso, I don't care he gets funny ideas. His uncle, my good friend Luigi, he will tell him different. So Bennie Focoso is not my worry. But you, my son, with your funny ideas that I know are not your own, you are my worry."

The Don lifted his glass to sip the deep red wine watching his son react to his words, forking up the pasta, the diced hearts and kidneys, mopping up the sauce with a chunk of bread, all the while keeping his eyes on his plate.

Swallowing, Angelo said, "Afraid you lost me there, Pop. What funny ideas?"

The Don put down his fork, touched his lips primly with a napkin, then glanced down the table at Vacanza, who looked up, then resumed digging at the dark substance beneath his fingernails with an air of obsessive determination. The Don reached for his glass of wine, sipped from it, his eyes on his son. "On toppa everything," he said, "you insult my intelligence. You make me ashamed of my blood in front of my old friend here. The only reason I do not kill you— now, instantly—is that I cannot permit the family to be humiliated before the world."

Thrusting back his chair, Angelo was about to rise when the sight of the small revolver in Vacanza's outstretched hand discouraged him.

"Siddown," said the Don, his voice softening. "That's better. Now listen to me: that, what you arranged for me in the bakery, it must never leave this room. Only we three will ever know of this shame you have brought to me." The Don closed his eyes and his right hand rose, shook visibly; a tear inched from the corner of one eye and the Don's head moved slowly from side to side. The tear crawled over the sharp creases of skin with a molten quality, as if it were less the product of sorrow than the issue of some unyielding substance temporarily transformed, a distillate of stricken belief, of pride gravely injured. In the light of the room it gleamed against the old man's skin, a smooth and silvery thing. He did nothing to arrest it, only moving his head slowly from side to side. Then he said, "That is the first condition. Do you accept?"

Angelo Scorcese, a lout in many ways, nevertheless recognized that his father held an unassailable position, and even dimly perceived that he was being treated with astonishing mercy. "I—yes, I accept. Pop—"

"Do not interrupt. I don't wanna hear no explanations or excuses. I don't wanna hear nothin' outta you except what I expect to hear. Second. You takin' over things in Phoenix for the family."

"That fuckin' cow town? Pop, I gotta home here, friends, my whole life I lived here."

The Don lifted his glass and took a sip, held the glass beneath his chin. "That ain't what I expect to hear."

"I thought that was Pauli's deal."

"Pauli's movin' up, Angelo. Gotta girl he likes good, his mother tells me. I think it's time he gets married, take over the Las Vegas business for the family. So how do you answer me, on the second condition?"

"Like I gotta choice. Sure, Pop."

"Good. Now one more thing: the kids, my grand-children, they gonna need a mother, at least the young ones."

Angelo Scorcese lifted his baseball cap to shove his fingers through his hair. For the first time in his life the world assumed a murky, viscous quality, a condition in which the old certainties were spurious, and this first brush with horror left a taste in his mouth like smoke. "They gotta mother," he insisted, though the words came out as a gasp of disbelief.

"You been getting too many bad ideas, my son. First, the bakery, then this business with the money, to save your own father. I spoke to a Wizard. You wait a whole day, before you decide maybe your father's life is worth ten million dollars. Those a kind a bad ideas you been getting. Well, you ain't getting 'em no more."

The taste of smoke almost overwhelmed Angelo Scorcese. "What're we talkin' about here? Pop, the fuck we sayin'?"

"After a decent interval, what I'm saying is you will have as your wife Magda Vacanza. Is all arranged."

Angelo Scorcese slumped over the table, his right arm sweeping the glass of wine away, a rosy blur, splintering on the marble floor in a chimelike explosion. "Mai Lee," he cried, "what about Mai Lee?"

The Don took a sip of wine and said, "You have had the pleasure of her one last time. It was her heart you ate."

At a gesture from the Don, Vacanza stopped digging beneath his fingernails and rose to refresh his old friend's glass with wine. They watched the shaking figure, lying in his own sickness, their faces hard as totems.

Chapter 29

There was snow in the air, the weightless flakes tumbling down out of a sky the color of smoke and melting upon impact. Stepping out of the small Mercedes he leased, Elvis Mahoney turned up the collar of his blue cashmere coat and stuck his tongue out to catch a flake, tickled by the effect of the chill thing, having since the age of ten lived his days and nights in Los Angeles. He did not think about acid rain or any of the other foul chemicals in the atmosphere, but simply took what was there, a new taste, in this city that was forever foisting surprises. He was in the early, uncritical stage of a love affair with New York. He knew it, admitted it.

There were no bad memories to haunt him here, no dead friends.

He rapped with his key ring on the rear door of the restaurant he managed in Queens, a coded arrangement of taps that told anyone in the kitchen who was knocking. It was ten o'clock in the morning, beginning of a fourteen-hour day. He liked the hours. He liked going home to his condominium in Forest Hills for the most part too exhausted to brood about the past. Lady friends helped. He was doing all right, paid a decent salary, as well as being awarded points by the Don, a percentage of the skim. Say nothing of the money made in Phoenix.

Let into the restaurant that faced onto a service road off Queens Boulevard, formerly known as Arpeggio's, Elvis Mahoney moved around the kitchen chatting easily with the staff as he inspected the seafood, the fruits and vegetables purchased fresh that morning between the hours of four and five. Toward the chefs that he had inherited from Arpeggio's, he showed the greatest deference, directing them with nudges as opposed to confrontation, and as a consequence a very real camaraderie had developed within the confines of the kitchen. The waiters, who had been retained, were only reluctantly coming around, offended in the first place by the idea of submitting to a man of color; secondly, by the revolution in decor—the expanded bar area for the large-screen television, the recessed lighting, the heavy red curtains removed to admit light, the new deep green carpet, pale wood furniture, forest of plants in brass floor tubs and wicker troughs, the jungle murals on the walls in place of the black velvet nudes; but what had really irked the holdovers was the shift from music made by crooners of the fifties to the rockers, rappers, screamers and groaners, spawn of the nasality and blues permitted on the air during the sixties. No longer a restaurant, this was a grill and sports bar that featured some of the most succulent entrées in Queens.

As the take from tips increased, the waiters discovered, individually, songs that they enjoyed, some with melodies they could whistle. So, things were coming along. The host, Mario, who had occupied his station through three eras of ownership, had developed the habit of catching Elvis Mahoney by the elbow periodically to whisper, "You doin' a helluva job, Mr. Mahoney. Helluva job."

Paper bunting hung in festive loops above the bar, strands of red and green intertwined in celebration of the approaching Christmas, and the bar itself was trimmed with silver garlands. Behind it Ziggy was occupied checking the pressure on the beer kegs, but stopped as Elvis approached, and went along the bar, reached down to bring up a pot of coffee, poured a cup. Ziggy was the son of Bennie Focoso's older sister and he opened, willing to work four hours a day off the books, before he went off looking for trouble. Elvis had tried to tell him what would become of that tight little ass of his if he landed in the bin, which he most surely was going to, given his inclinations. Ziggy, like most twenty-one-year-olds, believed himself immune to the laws of probability, treating Elvis's admonition to a shrug.

Elvis tasted the coffee and smiled. "Why Ziggy, I think you're gettin' the hang of it."

"About fuckin' time," said the boy. "Uh, you ain't gonna like this."

Elvis put down his cup and looked alert. "What's that?"

"There's a new health inspector, came by a while ago. A real dick," he concluded, and spat on the floor.

Elvis closed his eyes for a second. "Zig, not on the floor, not anywhere in the restaurant, okay?"

"Yeah. Fucking sleaze. You wanna punch his fuckin' lights out just lookin' at him."

Elvis peeled off the cashmere coat and folded it over his arm. "All right. How much the guy trying to squeeze us for?"

And so the day had begun in earnest.

Elvis Mahoney generally left the grill around midnight, leaving two Scorcese people in charge to close at four and count the money. It was now nearly eleven-thirty when Mario opened the door to his office, admitting voices and laughter from the bar.

Mario closed the door and came over to the desk Elvis was sitting behind and leaned over, winking. "Is a lady on the phone for you. Says it's long distance."

"Mario, what are you whispering for?"

"Is a lady, long distance. Voice like music. On hold."

"Thank you," Elvis whispered back.

Mario winked and left.

Elvis picked up the phone. "Yes?"

"Elvo? Did I hear that man correctly?"

Elvis grinned. "Yeah, you heard him right. I'd about given up hearing from you. I think I left a message with your attorney, what, two, three months ago. Just, you know, see how you were doing."

"We were out of the country, darling, that's why. Only just returned yesterday."

"We?"

"David and I. We're trying to work through . . . the past. And he's been sweet, Elvo, he really has. Quit his job creating computer games to consult with the Brazilian government, set up programs to devise strategies with regard to the rain forests, soil depletion, that sort of thing. It's where we've been all these months."

His eyes had begun to smart, much as they did when he spent an evening in a room full of smokers, and he poked at them ineffectually. "Brazil," he said, to be saying something. He thought he could hear music and loud voices in the background.

"Much of it in-country too, Elvo. Not like the zoo. Real nature with real threats. And here I thought being with Del had begun to get too hairy. I got to know real fear, on a day-to-day basis, and you know what?"

"What's that?"

"I can be a tough cookie."

"I bet you can."

"I don't have much time right now, Elvo. We're hosting a cocktail party for I think about a hundred of our dearest friends. Are you okay?"

"Me? Hey, I'm hanging in there."

"Phoenix. It was a little crazy, you know that? I never felt like I knew what was going on. Really going on."

"Seems none of us did, chile."

"How's Del?"

Just like that. Elvis ceased to fight it and let the tears roll as he explained to her what he had read in the papers upon returning to Phoenix to clear out his and Del's personal effects, among which he discovered the names and addresses of their two silent partners, to whom he mailed their rightful shares.

In the silence that followed Elvis could hear the sounds of celebration. Then Franny Lott said, in a voice that had done some crying, "He loved to see people laugh."

"Didn't he though?" Elvis felt better. "You know what he'd really love, Franny?"

"The look on that Mexican boy's face when Del told the one about the drunks and the light bulb . . . What? What would Del love?"

"The phony ID we used. That's what they found on Del, and that's the way he was buried. As Mr. Irwin Field. Talk about a joke. So at least technically, Del's immortal. Christ, he's probably telling someone a lousy joke even as we speak."

Franny Lott said, "They weren't all lousy."

And shortly thereafter they hung up without any more to say or explain. Elvis Mahoney eased himself into the blue cashmere coat, bound his throat with a white silk scarf, and made his way through the patrons at the bar, some of whom knew him by name and tried to buy him a drink. He begged off, pleading fatigue, and went out into the night. A more serious snowfall than the one of this morning had transformed the city, laid down a breathtaking disguise of freshness and innocence. The pink neon sign above the bar and grill shone in the snow like a young white girl's blush, if young white girls ever blushed anymore. Well, what business was it of his, one way or the other? The worst that could be said of Franny Lott was the same that could be said of him:

they were survivors. He turned around, trying to recall the punch line to the one about the drunks and the light bulb, and gazed at the sign. The pink neon had been shaped to spell the word: FLAMINGOS.

Del Rebus had been right. Elvis couldn't remember a joke to save his soul.